A Sensual Affair With A Billionaire

Darla Tverdohleb

Ukiyoto Publishing

All global publishing rights are held by

Ukiyoto Publishing

Published in 2022

Content Copyright © Darla Tverdohleb

ISBN 9789360160319

All rights reserved.
No part of this publication may be reproduced, transmitted, or stored in a retrieval system, in any form by any means, electronic, mechanical, photocopying, recording or otherwise, without the prior permission of the publisher.

The moral rights of the author have been asserted.

This is a work of fiction. Names, characters, businesses, places, events, locales, and incidents are either the products of the author's imagination or used in a fictitious manner. Any resemblance to actual persons, living or dead, or actual events is purely coincidental.

This book is sold subject to the condition that it shall not by way of trade or otherwise, be lent, resold, hired out or otherwise circulated, without the publisher's prior consent, in any form of binding or cover other than that in which it is published.

www.ukiyoto.com

To My Twin Flame

Contents

What's Wrong With Me?	1
Doamne Fereşte!	5
The Black Church	11
How To Pick A Stunning Guy	16
Over Fat Frog	20
The Baby Contract	24
Closed Deal	29
Moye Solntse	33
Let The Romping Begin	37
Deflowering	41
Perfect For Him	45
First Dinner Together	48
Thoughtfulness	52
He's Back	57
Kisses And Ice Cream	61
Hard, Medium, Or Gentle?	64
Against The Hard Trunk	68
Keepsake	72
Lunch Date	76
Forced Shopping	80
Withdrawal	84
Just To Be Clear	88
Hot Moans	92
Surprise?	97
About Maksimillian	101
Value	105
Bonding?	109
Deets	113

Raining Bullets	117
Phone Sex	122
Thinking Of Him	127
Touched By Her	131
Lube It!	135
What If…?	140
Preggy Topic	144
By Her Side	148
Hot Seat	152
Walking Away	156
A Chance	160
Traumatic	166
Forgiveness?	170
The Next Step	173
Bringing Home A Man	177
A Break	182
Pregnant	186
Confirmation	190
His Arrival	194
Her Plan To Keep The Baby?	198
Moldova	203
Why She Ran Away	207
Make It Work	211
The Birthing	215
Domovoy	220
The One	224
Days Of Wine And Roses	229
About the Author	*233*

What's Wrong With Me?

Maksimillian

I adeptly rolled the condom on my hard staff while the woman I was with in this luxurious room watched me. She was already naked and so excited to get this thing going between us. Ever since we were at the birthday party—a mutual friend's—in one of the multi-function halls in this same five-star hotel, Anichka had already started flirting with me. It was the first time we met, but it didn't matter, since I'm used to one-night stands and no-strings-attached relationships—if I could count it as one. I always made it clear in the first place to avoid any complications and consequences later. It was not only because of unwanted pregnancies but the disease I might catch. After all, health is wealth—not to mention that I already have wealth as one of the owners of Frolov-Usmanov Inc.

Yes, I am one of the Russian billionaires and still a bachelor at the age of thirty. I own most of the company, that is, since my cousin Rurik Frolov co-owns it. The company stretched its arms in different industries, such as steel, real estate, telecom, investments, and dating apps. The latter was truly amazing, giving us billions of profits every year. Well, it may not good investing in people's emotions and criminals maybe used them, but it wasn't that bad. Some did find their *soulmates* by technology nowadays.

Now, Anichka bit her lip, as her dark green eyes surveyed my lean, well-built body and especially my big and long staff. She looked happy to see it from the way she smiled widely at me. Well, every girl did whenever they see my proud boner.

I pushed Anichka down the king-size bed, which was covered by white sheets. The lampshade in the far right corner was our only illumination, and the heavy curtains were drawn at the ceiling-to-floor glass window, which was to my left.

I touched the soft wet flesh at the center of her thighs and ran my fingers up and down her slit. She moaned and writhed beneath me. I rubbed her swollen bundle of nerves that I knew every girl would love to be touched there, making her wetter. Her legs opened wider, and her back arched, obviously wanting more.

"Ahhh…" she moaned again and again. "Stick it inside right now, Maks!" she said in a begging tone.

"I'll stick it in in my own time, got it?" I uttered and held her hands above her head. I always loved the missionary position as I could see the woman's face, especially her eyes when she begged me to take her. And by this, I could lord over her body as much as I wanted to. There were also times that I would love to do it rough. Many, in fact, loved it rough, and that was enjoyable for me. For both.

Anichka breathed hard and fast, too much excitement building in her luscious body. She had huge breasts and pink tips. Her curly blonde hair was scattered on the white pillow. She did look amazing. Nonetheless, she was merely one of those women I wanted to take just once. I knew that by the time we were done here, I would feel nothing.

I propelled my hard cock inside her warm and wet canal, and she moaned louder.

"Ahh! Ahh!" Her voice softly reverberated in the room. "Yes! Yes!" Her green eyes were smokey with lust, and I watched her breasts move forward as she thrust them closer to me.

I sucked one puckered tip as I rammed her body, hearing her endless moans. Her legs wrapped around my waist and urged me to go in deeper. And I did. Her mewls became louder and prolonged, and I pushed deeper into her. I loved the way her feminine walls getting tighter and tighter as she was nearing her climax.

I slammed into her as forcefully and as deeper as I could. Then, I let go of her taut peak to watch her face. Her eyes were now close and her mouth open, while she felt my huge manhood filling her tightly.

She screamed when she reached her climax, but I didn't stop driving in and out of her body until I released. Our bodies were damp with sweat, and I removed myself from atop her. I rolled to her right side, and she turned to me with a wide smile plastered on her pretty face.

"You were great, Maks!" she complimented me, panting.

'Of course, I am,' I thought, and I softly chuckled—but didn't say anything. My breathing was getting back to normal, and so was hers.

I got up to go to the bathroom, dumped the rubber in the toilet and flushed it. I stepped under the shower, leaning my hands against the wet tiled walls while the warm water rushed down my body, relaxing it. And yet, my mind was in chaos.

I had always liked the one-night stands and the pleasure these gave me, but they always left me empty afterwards.

'What's wrong with me?' I pondered. *'What am I supposed to do with my life?'*

***

Zenovia

"W-what did you say?" My brows knitted as I stared at Antonia, my best friend who was thirty and was actually five years older than me.

That Friday afternoon, I took half of the day off from work as a hotel receptionist, and I was at her private clinic to consult her of my physical discomfort. It had been days since I felt a pain whenever I remove my bowels and even when I urinate. I also had this pelvic pain whenever I had my monthly cycle, worse than before. Since she was an OB-GYN and my best friend—thank God for that—I could open up to her easily.

"I'm suspecting it's endometriosis, Zen," she announced with a frowning face. "Do you know what it is?" She pushed a strand of her fake short red hair behind her ear while looking at me intently. Her dark brown eyes seemed to assess my reaction since earlier.

"Y-yes. I heard about it. But h-how do we know for sure?" I swallowed the hard lump in my throat. I did check for my symptoms on the net and saw some articles about it.

"Well, there's this called rectovaginal exam as a physical exam to know if there are nodules behind your uterus and along the ligaments that attach to your pelvic wall. But there may be no nodules that can be felt. It's not always the nodules that can verify it."

"Then let's do it!" I said to her.

Her face was torn into laughter and pity. Her lips curved and then became a line in a split second. "Zenovia Cuza, seriously! Did you hear what I said? The physical exam means I have to insert a finger in your ass and one finger in your vagina!"

"So?" I was almost desperate, scowling at her. I didn't know why she was hesitating to do it when I needed to know what was really happening to my body! "Why are you telling me this and not just do it?"

Now she barked in laughter. "Do you want me to take your virginity by my finger right here in my clinic, huh?"

And my jaw slackened.

Doamne Fereşte!

Zenovia

Thinking of my best friend taking my virginity right here in her clinic did not only gross me out but also more than that. I did have mixed feelings given my unknown state at the moment.

'Doamne fereşte!' (God forbid!) I never thought I could get something troublesome like this. I never ever thought I'd be in this situation in the first place, although I did know that at one point in my life, I could catch or contract something and that I may be hospitalized or see a doctor. And never had I thought I'd need my best friend like this, either.

"And to let you know, this physical exam can cause you unusual pain or discomfort," Antonia further explained to me. "It's not conclusive and can't be relied upon to truly establish the diagnosis of endometriosis. I can be wrong, Zen. But… we can instead use ultrasound to rule out other pelvic diseases, and perhaps, we may find out the presence of endometriosis in your vaginal and bladder areas. But then again, unfortunately, we need to be more accurate to diagnose it."

'So why are you telling me all this and not just go straight to the point?'

I took a deep breath, trying to normalize my heartbeat, and did not blurt out what I had in my mind. I knew she was just explaining to me things, but I was getting edgy. And actually, I was on the verge of panicking and breaking down right now.

"Okay. Okay. So, what then?" My thoughts were reeling at the same time. I was really afraid of what might happen to me in the future. Besides Antonia and my parents that I didn't speak with much, I was all alone in life. I had no siblings to talk to or to vent my anger on either.

"For an accurate diagnosis, I have to directly inspect the inside of your pelvis and abdomen and thus need a tissue for biopsy of the implants, as it's necessary. Meaning to say, I need you to be at the hospital, since we need either laparotomy or laparoscopy."

I took a deep breath once again and closed my eyes for a second or two, then I looked at my friend. "What are these… -tomy and -copy you're saying?" I queried, didn't get what those medical terms were. I guess that slipped from my mind when I was reading some articles or that I may not altogether have met these words before.

"Laparotomy involves opening the abdomen by using a huge incision."

"What?" My eyes bulged, and I looked at my stomach. Of course, it wasn't directly since I had my shirt and jeans on, as I was sitting on the visitor's chair in front of my friend's desk, while she sat behind it in her grey swivel chair. "You're going to open me up?"

"Well, if we must, so that we'll know for sure…"

"No, no, no, no! I don't want to be sliced open!" I protested in panic. I wasn't afraid of blood, but I was afraid of wounds. Did it make sense? Of course not! I was that weird!

"As for the laparoscopy, it is the most frequent surgical procedure that most usual employees used for the diagnosis of endometriosis. Laparoscopy is just a minor surgical procedure that is performed under general anesthesia—"

"*Doamne fereşte!*" I cut her off and crossed myself. As a Catholic, it wasn't really my habit compared to Antonia, who was an Orthodox and would cross herself thrice, but at this point… God! I thought this was just getting worse and worse. I wanted to get out of here, for the first time. Before, whenever I visited my friend at her clinic, I was always happy to just chat with her, especially when she isn't busy. She had a specific time for her private clinic, and the rest was at a Iaşi hospital.

Iaşi is a university city in Romania and is somewhere northeast of Bucharest, more than a five-hour car drive.

"But there are some cases where a patient is just under local anesthesia," Antonia added, trying her best to educate me. "This is most commonly performed as an outpatient procedure, so you don't need to stay in the facility overnight. To tell you more, so that you have an idea, laparoscopy is carried out by first puffing up the abdominal cavity with carbon dioxide by a small incision in the navel."

I instinctively palmed my navel area as she spoke, and I grimaced while thinking about what she said. I thought this was really graphic, imagining that I'd be on that surgery table and my friend was doing it to me.

"There's a thin, tubular viewing instrument, which is called the laparoscope, that is then inserted into, let's say, your blown up abdominal cavity. That way, I can inspect your abdomen and pelvis. Through this, endometrial implants can be directly seen, if you have, that is," she said with a gesture of her hand in between sentences.

I visibly gulped twice while she gave me a measuring look. I may be amazed at her professionalism, but I knew she was telling me all this like a friend, filling me in with those little details, so that I would understand what I was about to get myself into and be prepared in the near future.

I had no words, although my mind was in a riot right now. What if this was really endometriosis? What then?

"I can schedule you immediately, within next week, once we're done with the ultrasound today, if you want," Antonia spoke again, bringing me back to the present.

My eyes wavered.

'Today,' I thought miserably. That was indeed immediate. This was going all too fast! I didn't like it. I felt nervous.

"Hey, hey, Zen!" Antonia flicked her fingers in front of my face when I zoned out again. "Hey, don't worry, okay? Having this endometriosis is not the end of your world!"

"What? How can you even say that? You should know what it is! You know what this entails, Antonia," I told her bitterly. "Now, tell me honestly, so I can at least fully prepare myself."

"We're not even sure if it's endometriosis yet, Zen."

"I know, Antonia. But what if you're right? What's going to happen to me, honestly?" My voice croaked.

***

Maksimillian

Days passed by quickly. After that encounter with Anichka, I buried myself at work. I was happier when I kept myself busy and not think about life at all.

My parents died in a helicopter crash when I was eighteen, the reason why I had to work at the company at such a young age. I was even the first to step in the family business, ahead of my cousin Rurik who was two years older than me. He joined the company and started to work his fat ass off at the age of twenty-three. My uncle, my late father's younger brother-in-law and was Rurik's late father who died a few years back, was the one who taught me everything about businesses and people around *us*. He taught me the importance of legalities and everything in between, but I did man up on my own.

"So, why did you call me to meet you here? You missed me, *moy kuzen* (my cousin)?" Rurik smirked as he sat down on the stool at our favourite bar in downtown Moscow one weekend night. It was summer, late June, so it was warm for us.

We both wore white shirts and dark jeans. His had a round neck, with his stomach slightly bulging in the middle because of his chubbiness. The edge was tucked in, making him look ancient. As for me, I wore a V-neck shirt, and it was untucked. He wore loafers, while I wore sneakers.

I put the tall glass of my Black Russian cocktail down the bar, while the stocky bartender in his thirties eyed us once in a while as he served other customers. He already knew us, since we were patrons here—not just because we were rich.

There were quite a number of people at the bar, mostly men. Some women were with their guys, but they didn't drink hard liquors to keep their femininity. As far as I knew since I became aware of drinks and other adult stuff—and it had nothing to do with being sexist at all if I'd say this, as I'm not—Russian women don't drink vodka. It was considered unladylike.

The liquor scent wafted in the air. Russians *do* drink a lot. It is one of the reasons why there are numerous traffic accidents and deaths, mostly men, in the country. The cars would just collide with another vehicle or swerve off road and crash even in the middle of the day.

"No, why would I miss someone who's an eyesore?" I returned while he ordered a drink for himself, his favourite whisky.

Rurik guffawed. "Wait 'til you see Mother back from her Greek vacation," he said.

"Is it already two months since she was there?" I asked and downed all the remaining content of my cocktail.

"Yes, but she's not through with her vacation. I think she's still going somewhere when she arrives back home," he said and drank his whisky, half of its content. He gritted his teeth as he savoured his drink and swallowed. He eyed me with furrowed thick brows. "Tell me, Maksimillian Usmanov, what the hell's wrong with you, huh?"

I took a deep breath and signaled to the bartender that I needed another glass of my cocktail. Then, my sea-green eyes regarded my kind cousin with seriousness.

"Honestly, I don't know what I would do with my life. You and I have it all in terms of money and everything, Rurik, but I can't see and feel the joy in all of this. Now, tell me if I don't have a problem with this. Is it even normal? I don't sense my purpose except when I work."

And this all happened just last week. My talk with Rurik proved to be fascinating because he did lend his ears to my whining, if I could call it that. Fucking pathetic, really. I wasn't easy to break down just like that, and I wasn't the type to complain about the mishaps in my life, but my cousin could always sense if I had a problem, even how little it is. He was that perceptive.

And now, I found myself in Braşov, Romania, inside The Black Church because my aunt dragged me onto this vacation.

I was listening to the organ playing and was secretly recording it on my phone even though taking videos or other sorts of recording was not allowed. But just because! I thought the music was heavenly.

When I surveyed the other people seated on the long benches facing the front that had the organ playing, where the altar was located as well, my eyes suddenly caught a glimpse of the black-haired woman across the aisle. She was openly staring at me with those slightly big grey eyes of hers… and everything seemed to fade away right then…

The Black Church

Zenovia

It was confirmed. I did have endometriosis, and the cause was unknown. How could I be so unfortunate with my life?

"What's the worst that can happen to me, Antonia?" I asked her on the phone when I was out of the hospital and was at my own apartment. It was already night, and I did not even have to stay overnight at the hospital as an outpatient. I had to leave work for a couple of days, though. I wasn't feeling good or keen to go to work anyway.

My stomach area felt numb from the procedure. The small incision in my navel was still fresh, but the pain was nothing I couldn't handle. Anyway, I had the pain reliever for it.

"Well, one of the symptoms of it is infertility actually, but we detected it earlier, and it's mild endometriosis you have. You're still healthy when it comes to fertility, as we already examined that. But it could reach to that point of infertility if you don't take medication. The good news is you can still have the baby you desire. Yay!" she said, trying to cheer me up.

Yes, I did want to have a child, and I needed not have to be married for that. I could just have the child on my own without the father, if only I could arrange it that way.

I sighed heavily and sat on the sofa in my living area. My apartment had a bedroom, a kitchen with a dining area, and also a living room. It was not really big, but it was comfortable and spacious enough for someone who lived here alone. My unit was on the fifth floor of an eight-storey building, so it was nice to look out of the window during the night and see the lights from the other buildings and the streetlights, as well as the passing vehicles and the different lively colours of neon lights of some nearby establishments.

I gathered my knees, ignoring the little pain in my navel when my thighs pressed against my abdomen. My sight went through the glass window, since my curtains were out of the way.

"How can I even have a baby when I don't have a man?" I scowled, my lips protruding, and I grimaced afterwards.

"Right. I forgot you're slightly a misandrist. But I don't get you. You still want a baby," she said. "For that, you do need a man, Zen!"

And yes, we circled back to that.

"I can't afford the in vitro fertilization. It's way off my pay grade!" I told her and sighed again.

"Well, I can help you with the IVF if you want," she offered as though she was just going to give me a piece of cake.

"You do know my stand on your being so generous to me, don't you?" I returned gently.

"Well then, you do it in the normal way." I could just imagine her eyes grow bigger to point it out.

"Right. It's more enjoyable," I sarcastically returned, thinking of my parents that were divorced.

My mother was a Physics professor at a university in Iași, while my father was an engineer who remarried and had a sixteen-year-old son. Right, I did have a half-brother but whom I couldn't vent my anger on if I wanted to. How could I forget that detail? We were not close, although he wanted to. In fact, he would always leave me messages in my social media inbox, asking how I am and when we could see each other in Bucharest, since they were living there now. They moved from Iași a couple years back. And yet, I never answered his messages. If I did, it was just to say "I have no time."

Reminding me that I was "slightly" a misandrist was maybe mildly put by Antonia. She did know I hate men generally, though I did want to have a baby. And, of course, I'd need a man for that.

"Uh! About that. I think I forgot to tell you that with endometriosis, you might feel pain during and after sex, Zen. Sorry to tell you this late."

"Right!" My voice went higher. I did remember about it in an article I read on the net.

Just a great life I have! How could I even enjoy making a baby if this was the case?'

"But don't worry, I'll tell you some tips on sex positions you can try, so that if and when you found the right man you want to have a baby with ASAP, you can do it without or less pain."

My mouth opened. We were best friends, but I hated to talk intimate things with her. It just so happened she was an OB-GYN that I had to consult my problem with. But everything was really mortifying. Although Antonia was not the one who would put on the brakes when it comes to intimacy topics because she openly discusses hers with me, I didn't mind because it wasn't mine. Nonetheless, she did know that I *am* still a virgin, as she knew too well I never had a relationship, intimate or not, with a man. Unlike her, who did have five boyfriends so far, if I did count them right. Now, she was hunting for men. In fact, she wanted me to go on vacation with her just so we could concentrate on finding a man for me! And, of course, for her as well on the sideline.

Looking back, our friendship started when she and her family moved from Piatra Neamţ to Iaşi when I was ten, and we became neighbors. Their house was bigger than ours, since they were well off. However, no one liked to speak with her, as she always dominated the conversation. It was only I who endured it, that's why she was so taken with me. From then on, she claimed that she was my lifetime best friend, and she'd take care of me no matter what. But I did know better. I was the sister she never had. She always wanted to have one, but her mum couldn't get pregnant anymore because of her heart problem.

"Maybe I'll get back to you on that. I have to hang up now. You know, I still have to call *Mămică*," I said to Antonia.

"Okay, my best regards to your mum, Zen! I'll drop by to see you tomorrow and see how you're doing, all right? Bye!"

After I hung up, I did call my mum. I asked how she is and stuff like that. When she asked me how I am, I wasn't brave enough to tell her. I didn't know how she would react if she learned I wasn't really well.

"Have you started dating?" she asked, without teasing in her tone. She was curious, and God knew she was dying to know if I'd settle down soon.

I rolled my eyes. "I didn't call you to discuss my love life, *Mămică*!" I was irritated.

"But we can," she insisted. "Why don't you date? You're already almost thirty!"

I blew my face in vexation, trying hard not to shout at her. "That's still five years from now. Don't exaggerate for heaven's sakes! *Mămică*, I won't date ever, all right? Just accept it. I'll never get married just like you did and then break up afterwards! I can't let my child, if I have one, suffer the same fate as I did. Men are dicks, *Mămică*! You should know that better than I do! Look what *Tati* did to you. He cheated on you, and then, what? He divorced you and he's now living happily with his little family, leaving us in a miserable state!"

I heard my mother sigh. "If your father did it to me, it doesn't mean your man will do the same thing, Zenovia. Just give yourself a chance, will you?"

And I hung up, feeling so annoyed with her. I did feel remorse that I hung up on her. It was so rude of me, so I just texted her to say sorry.

***

A month later, I was in *Biserica Neagră* (Black Church). It turned out that I was alone in this vacation, which Antonia and I planned, but she was the one who paid for it all. It was indeed unfortunate, as she had an emergency at the hospital just before we were supposed to leave, and no one could attend to it because her fellow OB-GYN got sick and couldn't work.

Antonia told me she would be here maybe in a couple of days to join me. I knew she badly wanted to have this vacation with me, as it had been long since we had our last one—maybe three years ago. Even though I'd lived in Romania all my life, I'd never been to Braşov (a city in south eastern Transylvania); so was Antonia. It was why we picked this place to have a summer vacation for two weeks. There were many places we could visit and have fun.

Now, as I listened to the organ played by one of the priests, I looked up at the interior balcony of the church. It was empty, but there were about a hundred or so guests in the church, seated on the long benches.

I swept my eyes around me, taking in all the beautiful details of the Gothic-style monument of Romania. During the Great Turkish War in 1689, the church was partially ruined and burned when the Habsburg forces invaded. The church was then repaired with the help of Danzig masons, and the vaults were completed in Baroque style.

The sound of the organ echoed in the church; it was mellow and beautiful with a gothic vibe, but it was good to listen to it. Then, I saw *him*... opposite to where I was seated. I was at the farthest side of the bench on the left side facing the altar, while he was exactly across the aisle. Without the aisle, we could've sat side by side.

I had no idea, but my heart skipped a couple of beats, before it did again, only to hammer my chest hard. I could feel my blood warming up and travelling fast in my entire system. His eyes were the most beautiful green I'd ever seen—thanks to the lights I saw them well.

"You need to get laid, Zen! Let's search for someone who can make you that baby you so want in Braşov!" I suddenly recalled Antonia's words while we planned our vacation. These words rang in my head, as though she was just right here in the church.

The music's vibe seemed to turn into a more romantic one for some reason. I had no idea if it was just my imagination or not. But then, the gorgeous man held my eyes like he held me physically that even if I wanted to look away, I couldn't.

And my breath became ragged.

How To Pick A Stunning Guy

Zenovia

I never admired such a man before. Obviously, this was the first. He had short brown hair in a classic scissor cut. In my guesstimate, if he stood up, he would be a six-foot guy. Even in a simple blue V-neck shirt and a pair of black jeans, sported with black-and-white loafers, he looked like a model right out of the magazine and came to life. His nose was straight and long that seemed to be perfectly sculpted, it was almost impossible! His eyebrows were a bit thick and were almost the same shade as his hair. And then, my sinful eyes dropped lower, to his peach-looking lips. Never had I ogled a man before, and it was the lips to top it off!

My throat suddenly went dry, as he still held my gaze. Or rather, stared at me.

I did forget where we were for a long moment. I had no idea how long I stared at him like that—like a schoolgirl gawping at her ultimate crush. Now that was both mortifying and pathetic. But then, there was a nagging feeling that urged me to speak to him.

As soon as the organ stopped, and the show was brought to its finale, I stood up but hesitated when a lively older lady held his arm, as though to get his attention. She leaned in closer to tell him something.

Căcat! (Crap!) I thought he was all alone, but it turned out he was with an older woman. Was she his Sugar Mummy? Because I couldn't say she was his mother, since there were no similarities between them. She was really so elegant and beautiful for a woman her age, which I guessed was in her fifties. She looked really rich, judging by the jewelries she wore and the nice dress she had on. She was slim and tanned with dark blonde hair. There was a jolly vibe in her as she smiled at him, walked ahead of him, and disappeared with the crowd that slowly strolled out of the church.

And then, I saw him standing there, still staring at me.

'Should I just go approach him and pretend to say something and see what he'll say afterwards?' I asked myself. *'Maybe I should, right? I am the one who needs a child. And for that to happen, I need a sperm donor who's all too willing to give up the child to me! He must just be the right one, since he has a Sugar Mummy, and he will most probably just think we're going to have an affair that will not bind him to me. I guess this is a good plan! Maybe even great.'*

Ah, *Doamne*! Where had my morality gone?

Nonetheless, I drew a deep breath and smiled at him.

'All right! Let's do this! I'm going to do this. I can do it, can't I?' I tried to think positively. With all the negative things that have happened in my life, I should be positive even for once!

Not to brag, Antonia always said I had a stunning smile. If I gave it to a man, she was sure the man would melt. Well, it was being tested right now.

Still, I thought this was a bad idea and a bad plan, but I couldn't just go on with my life all alone. I wanted to have someone that I could hold and call my own. And that was a baby!

'Okay, keep smiling, Zenovia. It's for the sake of having a baby!' I told myself, not leaving my eyes from the stranger's handsome face. I had no idea if he was Romanian or not. But most probably not. So, I figured I should talk to him in English.

"Hi!" I greeted him almost too enthusiastically for my liking, while my heart pumped really hard against my rib cage.

He beamed back at me, with that mysterious kind of smile. Or was it a confused one because I was talking to him? Now I had no idea!

"Hey," he drawled.

Oh, *căcat!* His voice was low, deep, and so sexy! I had to look around us to check if we were not yet in a room, since he used such a bedroom voice. Now what did I know about bedroom voices?

Doamne!

But then, when I heard his voice, there was this kind of subtle electricity that travelled from him and went straight to my abdomen and down my core. My femininity throbbed for some reason. It was odd.

His stunning sea-green eyes assessed me more, as I got closer to him. I noticed his lashes were long and really nice to gawk at. Also, he smelled… yummy and addictive. It was musky and purely masculine, and my brain recorded all of him at this very moment.

"You… were not supposed to record anything," I whispered to him conspiratorially.

He chuckled softly, which showed his even white teeth. Oh, *Doamne*! The sound of it made my heart dance for some reason. This was really odd. No one had ever made me feel something like this. But *căcat!* My opening line was so lame! I'd just realised it. But then again, I wasn't an expert in approaching guys, since I'd never done it before. It was always the other way around, but then, I always snubbed them.

"Can I invite you somewhere for some refreshments?" he asked instead, eyes darting outside. Maybe he was looking at the weather outside or he was anticipating for his Sugar Mummy to come back and that he didn't want her to see us talking. Maybe his Sugar Mummy was territorial or something, and he didn't want trouble inside The Black Church. That would be epic or a scandal at that, if I must say!

Now, I did get his accent. Russian. My heart made a cartwheel because of it. This was even better! He wasn't Romanian, and it would be easy for me to keep the child if he would agree to my proposal, which I'd tell him later. Moreover, I guessed my smile did wonders, just like Antonia assured me many times before. He was still staring at me, like he wouldn't want to look at another being or object ever but me.

So, I gave him another stunning smile of mine that showed my little dimple in the lower left corner of my lips. "Won't your beautiful companion mind if we do?" I subtly mined for more information about him.

He chuckled again. "That was my Aunt Marisha, my late father's younger sister, if you want to know. My name's Maksimillian Usmanov, by the way," he said, extending his right hand.

Doamne! He was so polite.

I looked at his strong-looking hand. His forearm was well-muscled, and so was his arm. His shirt wasn't large or small, but it did fit him nicely, showing off his great physique. I could tell even without seeing that he had washboard abs to die for!

I had no idea how it came to mind, but there was something about him that made me guess and feel good that I guessed right… or something along those lines.

Without thinking, my hand just moved to clasp his warm one. My smaller hand seemed to get lost in his, and he gave it a gentle squeeze while he looked at me in the eye.

"It's nice to meet you, Maksimillian. I'm Zenovia Cuza. You can call me Zen if you want," I gently replied to him with a toothpaste endorser-type of smile.

"Oh, you have no idea what I want to call you!" he muttered in a teasing tone, still holding my hand, as if he didn't want to let it go.

I didn't know, but his words and his gesture made the butterflies flutter in my stomach.

'Could he really be the one?' I wondered once again.

Over Fat Frog

Maksimillian

When Zenovia smiled at me, the whole Black Church seemed to brighten up. It occurred to me that she could be an angel with that sexy smile, which showed off her little dimple. At that moment, my mind was blank, except that I was like in a trance… that it was only her that I saw and no other.

As she walked over to me, the slight sway of her round hips was noticeable. Her slender body in a white floral sleeveless sundress moved in an alluring way that I'd never seen in a woman before. It was not even done consciously. It was purely natural. I'd know when a woman tries to seduce me at the first approach, but she appeared being herself.

When she was right in front of me, I could gauge she stood five feet and four inches in her flat open-toe shoes. She raised her chin to look up at me, and her eyes looked seductive when she raised them up to me. Her creamy skin up close was something my hand was itching to touch. She had a smooth oval face, with natural red lips, as I hadn't seen any sign of lipstick, curly lashes that no mascara touched, and her past shoulder-length hair that was jet black was striking and silky that I wanted to grab it and play with it.

My heart missed a beat, and I almost gasped. Her scent was soft floral that I'd never smelled before. It seemed exotic.

Secretly, my two bodyguards followed us out when I invited her to have refreshments. It was amusing actually to hear from her about the prohibited things to do in the church and that she had mistaken my aunt for a special *companion*. I did have an idea what she meant by it. I believed she was just trying to be cautious, to see that she wouldn't get into trouble of some sorts.

I noticed that she had no idea who I was, even though I told her my whole name. Or did she just pretend she knew nothing about me? I knew that my name and my cousin's come out of the news in Europe once in a while, especially recently because of the new dating app we just launched a few months ago. We already had three of them released for the last four years—when my cousin suggested it to me. So far, the dating apps we rolled out were a huge success.

Walking through some wide and narrow alleys, Zenovia and I agreed to enter an Irish pub. There, the atmosphere was quite intimate, because of the dimness. There were only a few people at the time, which was pretty good for us. My bodyguards took a table some meters away from us. They ordered their own drinks, and I ordered mine, a Fat Frog.

"I'll just have a fresh orange juice," Zenovia told the young blonde waitress, who took the order. "Thank you."

"Not into cocktails?" I asked with a quirked eyebrow as my eyes roved her beautiful face.

"At daytime, no. I try to stay away from alcoholic beverages."

"Why? Romanians do love to drink, too, right?"

"Ah-hmm," she agreed, smiling toothlessly. Still, her dimple showed off. "I have zero tolerance in alcohol," she admitted shyly. Then, her smile faded as she averted her eyes and added, "My father loves *palinka*, while my two late grandfathers loved *țuică*."

I could sense there was tension in her voice when she mentioned her father. Right at that moment, I wanted to know all about her, but she didn't seem too keen to open up more than that. It was like a passing comment, so I just left it as that. And right now, there was nothing I wanted to do but to kiss her. The urge was just too great, unlike what I'd experienced before. Never had I gotten this desire as I had for her right now. But I tried to hold it back.

We talked some things about Brașov, where she would visit next or where I would like to go with my aunt, how long she would stay here, and if I had plans in going back home soon. I did tell her it depends on my aunt or my mood.

The way Zenovia talked just kept me getting more and more interested in her. She wasn't like other women who really loved to talk about themselves or ask me questions about my work or anything about money, how many mansions or cars I got and anything along those lines. Was it because she had no idea who I am? Or was it because she just took it for granted if she knew me? Not to brag or anything, my name made it to Wikipedia, so all the basic info about me was present there. But still, she could've had asked just like others who would want to know a person at their first meeting and in the process of getting to know each other. I believed that was the most normal thing to do or to talk about.

But then again, Zenovia wasn't like any ordinary women I met. That was for sure.

She met my eyes once again, and to keep myself from reaching for her as the desire in me intensified, I asked, "You want something from me, don't you?"

She laughed. It was both throaty and girly. Her face brightened, and at the same time, it turned rosy. She looked at me with sexy but quizzical grey orbs, slightly furrowing her beautifully arched eyebrows.

"How did you know?" She whispered her question.

I chuckled. "Every woman who comes near me wants something, but I can tell your reason is different from theirs. So, what? Have I guessed it right so far?"

"What if you did guess it right?" She had this look that challenged me, and of course, it intrigued me even more.

"Tell me what it is, Zenovia." My voice became hoarse, and it was so low that came out as a whisper. I loved her name on my lips, rolling off my tongue. Not to mention, I wanted my tongue to roll somewhere else, preferably all over her body.

Before she could reply, the waitress was back with our drinks. As soon as the latter left our table, Zenovia started to drink her refreshment while looking at me.

I smiled a little and drank half of the content of the light green liquid in my tall glass. It was cool, potent, and so sweet. I loved how the taste was left in my mouth.

"Can we have a sexual affair until I get pregnant?" Her voice was so low that I thought I must've heard her wrong.

I gently swallowed while the lines formed on the space between my brows. "W-what? What did you say?" I breathed. My heart violently pounded my rib cage. It was something that no one had ever caused yet. But her. And yet, no one had asked me such a thing before.

"Will you be my partner until I have your baby?" she rephrased. Her eyes held mine.

Good Lord! She must be so serious! There were no curvy lips that I saw at this moment, but instead, it was like she was pleading with her beautiful grey eyes. There was something in her entreating gaze that made my throat dry, and it poked my heart.

Oh, I was so lost! And before I could even stop myself, I leaned forward and caught her chin with my fingers. "Oh, fucking yes!" Then, I crushed my mouth to hers.

The Baby Contract

Maksimillian

Zenovia's lips and tongue were so delicious and sweet, setting aside the orange juice taste. It was intoxicating. Her lips were so soft and addictive; I couldn't stop myself from deepening the kiss and pushing my tongue inside her mouth, which made her moan a little.

Fuck! That sound was so good in my ears. Add to that, her kissing me back was already driving my hard staff insane, jerking inside my pants.

"Let's get out of here," I whispered to her when I broke off the kiss.

Her eyes slowly opened, and she looked dazed. It amused me to see her smokey grey orbs gazing at me with so much desire. I knew she wanted more. I could feel it straight to my boner!

"W-where are we going?" She managed to ask, blinking, as though waking up from a trance.

I was still holding her chin, and my mouth was so close to hers. I could feel and smell her warm intoxicating breath. "Is your hotel close by?"

She cleared her throat. "Yes."

I immediately stood up and took my wallet from my jeans back pocket, then summoned the waitress to our table. I left the five hundred Romanian bill, told the waitress to keep the change and grabbed Zenovia's hand.

"Let's go," I urged her.

I discreetly signaled my bodyguards with just a look, and they stood up slowly to follow us.

"I just used a cab," she informed me, slightly embarrassed.

I wondered why though and smiled at her. "It's no problem. I rented a car, so you can just tell me the address, and we'll enter it in the GPS." I winked at her.

My bodyguards would just follow me, and one already called my aunt that I would bail on her, so she should just have to entertain herself around here while I am busy with a girl. Anyways, she must have foreseen this when I agreed to have a vacation with her. She didn't expect much that we'd explore together at all times. She understood my moods about this whole vacation thing. Besides, I knew she was also doing the same, while a couple of Russian bodyguards inconspicuously tailed her, as per my instruction.

Back in The Black Church, she told me there was a man she wanted to talk to. But that actually followed when she saw Zenovia staring at me and told me about it, as if I wasn't having an eye contact with the Romanian girl.

Now Zenovia gave me a small smile. The car was parked near The Black Church, so we had to retrace our steps.

As soon as we arrived in front of her hotel, which only had three stories and was situated on an elevated part of the city, she held my forearm. In the rearview mirror, I saw my bodyguards in another vehicle, unostentatiously parking not far away. They would just wait for me here, outside the hotel while I'd go in with Zenovia.

"Wait," she said before I could get out of the car and open the door for her. I had no idea, but I showed my gentleman side to her, which was rarely displayed even with the women in my family. But well, I only had Aunt Marisha as my family.

"What is it?" Despite the drive, I still had my boner. *Chert poberi!* (Damn it!) I couldn't wait to fuck her already.

"I-I need you to sign something first before we do this."

My jaw hung open, as I stared at her in disbelief. I was even speechless.

"It's for both our interests, I promise," she quickly added. "Besides, I can show you all my medical papers to assure you that I don't have any disease that might contract you."

Wow! This was unbelievable! Incredible even. I hadn't expected this coming. At all. See what I mean that she wasn't ordinary? I just knew it from the start.

So, there I was glancing at the scanned documents saved on her cell phone; her lavender-polished finger was fast to swipe every single one of them and enough for me to read them, since they were translated in English. I could say she was prepared to have this affair with anyone. And it so happened she had eyes on me to be the father of the baby she wanted.

Apparently, I hadn't thought much about the baby she talked about. All that registered in my brain was that we would have an affair for a period of time, which only God knows until when—until she got pregnant. Most probably, only God knew if this was going to last for only a month. Well, more or less.

The condition just hit me now. The baby. I must have been under a spell or something, but then, when I looked at Zenovia again after checking all those authentic-looking documents, I didn't doubt her at all. I could see the sincerity in her eyes.

"I have here the contract that you must sign before we do the act," she added.

I couldn't suppress a chuckle. This was an affair, not a business deal. But then, she was so serious about it that I couldn't help but go along. I found myself nodding to her in agreement, which made her eyes dance in satisfaction. Ah, *chert poberi!* I would even give away my company just to see her happy.

'Now, where did it come from?' I wondered.

In just an hour of being with her, I must have lost my mind. Logically, it wasn't good. But then, everything about her screamed illogical, and I was acting spontaneously. Or was it something from deep inside me that propelled me to do it, which was supposed to be out of my own set of norm?

"You're really serious about this, aren't you?" I said.

She nodded. There it was again, her pleading eyes. And something else. Desperation? But why?

"Why?" I had to know. After all, I was going to be the father of her baby. I wanted to know what I was into.

"I want a baby, but I don't want to be married. I don't want to be bound with someone," was her reply. "To top it off and most importantly, I need this baby ASAP!"

I stared at her for a long moment, and then, I glanced at the agreement she already prepared, which said:

Agreement for Having a Baby

This agreement is made on ____ day of July, (year) in (city), Romania between CUZA, Zenovia (address), who's known as Party A from here onwards,

and (man's name and address), who's known as Party B henceforth.

This agreement shall perform and fulfill the following:

1. Sexual Affair

    a. Party B agrees that he will have a secret affair and agreement with Party A.

    b. Party B must protect Party A's reputation during and after the affair. In return, Party A will do the same.

    c. Party B will not engage in other sexual activities of any form with a third party until this agreement has expired. The same goes for Party B.

    d. Party B will agree with everything Party A says with regards to sexual positions and the like. Party A may consider Party B's suggestions if it doesn't harm or hurt her.

    e. Forced sexual engagement is a no-no. If this is breached, the responsible party shall face the legal consequences.

2. The Baby

    a. Party B agrees that Party A will have the sole and legal custody of the baby.

    b. Party A will not ask a single cent from Party B from pregnancy onwards.

    c. Party B will not appear in front of Party A or the baby when it is born, meaning that he will relinquish his parenthood as soon as Party A has conceived.

3.   Termination

a. This agreement can be terminated when either Party A or Party B wants to, or

b. This agreement is terminated when Party A is clinically confirmed pregnant.

c. No financial liability is included in this agreement or affair from the beginning to end and its aftermath.

The signatures in this agreement are legally binding in both parties' countries.

Party A (signature and date)   Party B (signature and date)

I saw she already signed hers with a date. Then, my eyes lifted to meet Zenovia's. Should I agree to all this?

Closed Deal

Zenovia

My heart was beating so fast. As I watched Maksimillian's face while he was considering the agreement I presented to him, I was ready to hear his refusal.

What decent man had the right mind and heart to relinquish his parenthood? To think that he could very well support the baby and take it away from me, if worst come to that, it was already alarming on my part. As I could guess, he was someone who had lots of money. Not because I saw the thick wad of money in his wallet, but by the way he moved and spoke to me. He was a really decent man.

However, I had no one that I had set my eyes on to be the potential partner in making a baby but him. Even though he might be a threat. I hoped not, if he signed the agreement.

It may be early to say, as I just got here since yesterday afternoon, but he was the first that caught my attention. Plus, he showed me that he was a gentleman so far. He paid for our drinks, and he was someone who listened when I spoke. It was rare for a man to stay quiet if he was egotistical and arrogant.

'Add to the list that he's a good kisser,' my mind piped in.

I almost scoffed but was attentive enough to him. How could I even think he was a good kisser when I had no one to compare it with, and it was my first time to be kissed? But his male taste mixed with the Fat Frog cocktail was so good.

The way he moved his soft lips against mine was stunning that my mind stopped to work at that moment. I could not think of anything else but him. I did not even consider where we were. And the way he thrust his tongue into my mouth to explore it and tease my own tongue, it made me feel breathless and had the resident butterflies flutter in chaos in my abdomen. It was the first time I felt something like that. It must be true from what I heard that a person would feel something like this with the right one.

So, the right person must be Maksimillian. I just hoped he would sign the agreement as I handed him the stylus now.

"Why do you want to have a baby ASAP?" he suddenly asked out of curiosity, obviously. His hands rested at his sides while he regarded me with those sexy sea-green eyes that could chase away my logical mind.

I knew I had to be prepared with everything just in case, that was why the documents were all ready. He must have thought I lost a screw or something. But then, his eyes did not seem to judge me as such. So, to me, that was… I don't know… a relief of some sort?

My eyes wavered, with his gaze probing mine. His question caught me off guard. Should I be honest with him? Maybe I should, since he had the right to know and so that he would know why I'm doing this.

I swallowed hard and blinked a couple times. "I have a problem with my reproductive system. If I don't do this as soon as possible and my condition worsens, there's the possibility that I'd become infertile and cannot bear a child in the future." I knew I shouldn't feel so rushed or pressured, but I had no choice. I did want to have a child of my own, a child that I'd raise with all the love I could give, teach her or him good things, and show my child how beautiful the world is no matter how ugly the system is.

'Oh, Doamne! Even just one child, that's all I ask of you. Please, please. Let me have it with Maksimillian.'

I was startled when he gently touched my cheek. I wasn't even aware that tears raced down my face. My vision became blurry, but I could very well see the pity in his eyes. No, I didn't want pity from him. I want his sperms! At least one of them, so that I could have the baby I so badly wanted.

When he finished drying my cheeks with his tapered fingers that gently followed the trails of my tears, he took the stylus and signed on my cell phone screen. It was not my plan to make him go along and sign this agreement through pity, with me crying in front of him, but it was for understanding and his will to create life with a stranger like me.

I knew it was a crazy idea that Antonia had when she suggested this thing, but I knew it was for my own interest if I didn't want a steady man in my life. A man who could probably or eventually hurt me like my father did to my mum. I needed to play it safe. I needed to guard my heart. I was already hurt when my dad left us for another woman and started a family with her. And I certainly didn't want another man to walk away from my life, unless it was my choice. And here it was. This was my choice. I wouldn't be hurt by this. It was only an affair with the main goal, which was already clear from the start. What could go wrong?

"So, are we going to have this notarized?" he asked while signing.

I nodded. From what I knew, I had to make this legal, so that everything was set in stone per se.

I studied his side view features as he signed. It was brief, but there was only one conclusion I gathered. He was such an attractive man. I must be so lucky I found him. I could almost picture out our baby.

"I'm wondering if I can visit your home when your vacation is over, and you're not pregnant yet by the time," he slowly drawled, as he gave back the stylus. His eyes caressed my now tear-free face.

I smiled at him, wondering at the same time if he was truly an honourable man. Surely, he wasn't a perfect man. He must have flaws like all the others on Earth. But then, who cared at the moment?

'I know I don't.'

The important thing was that he had signed and that he showed me his driver's license and took a picture of it himself before he gave my phone back.

He looked at me with renewed interest. "Fuck it! You're just so beautiful, and I can't let this opportunity pass me by, Zenovia. I know you must think I'm crazy for agreeing with you on this matter, but I can't think of anything else on how I can have you."

"W-what did you say?"

Instead of answering me, he held me by the nape and caressed it, sending tingles all over my body. My breath hitched, and my femininity throbbed without any warning. Or was it because of anticipation?

"You heard me, Zenovia. I want you ever since I saw you at The Black Church."

My lips parted because of that revelation.

"Now, will you show me your room?" he asked with a mesmerizing smile that melted my inhibitions and logical thoughts.

'Are we really going to do it now?' I suddenly panicked.

'If not now, when would you want to start, Zenovia?' the other part of my brain pointed out. *'Remember that you still have a hymen to break.'*

Ah, for God's sakes! This thought didn't help at all. I was already nervous, feeling my hand go cold and damp and my heart beating so wildly in my chest.

Moye Solntse

Zenovia

Oh, *Doamne!* There was no turning back. Maksimillian already signed the agreement, so my being panicky now must be settled. While he got off the car, I recalled that I must take a pain reliever, as per my OB-GYN's advice. I must take it before I'd engage myself intimately, to prevent pain.

I fumbled in my small shoulder bag and took the pill before he could open the door for me. He may have seen what I did or not, but he didn't comment. Maybe he didn't see it and thus hadn't questioned me what I just swallowed. It might raise concern on his part and would think twice despite the fact that he already signed the document. It was easy to destroy it anyway, if he'd just take my phone away and break it. And then, everything would be null and void.

Well, his being an honourable man still had to be put to test. I just hoped I dragged a good enough man in my hotel. Even more so, I prayed I hadn't dragged a psycho. It would be terrible and scary! It might end tragically for me for all I knew.

'*Doamne fereşte! What am I doing?*'

My heart was beating fast as we walked into the hotel lobby. It was not so large but spacious enough. The smell was fresh and clean, very welcoming. There were pendant lighting fixtures that were aesthetic with their modern design, spiralling and glimmering crystals. The walls were beige and had a pink stargazer lily painted on the wall behind the reception desk that was chest high. The desk was made of shiny wood in brown colour, and packets of leaflets as well as brochures were on it.

The dark-haired receptionist in her thirties smiled at us, but Maksimillian did not even glance at her. He was just focused on where we'd go next, and I showed him to the lift, going to the left side of the hallway. Going to the right was the hotel restaurant, kitchen, and souvenir areas.

There were no other people there except for us. I could practically hear my heart pounding hard. When the lift closed, I pushed the last floor's button. Then, Maksimillian suddenly caught me by the waist and pressed my body against his. I gasped as I hadn't expected this action from him. My hands automatically touched his muscled chest, while my back arched.

My throat went dry, so I gulped while meeting his lust-filled sea-green gaze. I could feel the hard bulge that was proof of his desire for me. The heat emitted from his body seemed to flare up mine, while his scent already wrapped around me like a thin blanket, promising me something that was going to happen in the next few minutes or so. Plus, the throbbing I felt deep in my core intensified.

"Zenovia," he whispered, before bending his head and claiming my soft red lips.

I loved the sound of my name rolling out of his tongue. I felt sexy and desirable for some reason.

I took in a sharp breath the moment his lips contacted with mine.

"*Moye solntse* (My sunshine)!" he whispered. He then continued to brush his lips against mine. I did not know what that phrase meant though, but I did not care right now.

I felt his hands knead my flesh while he ground his hips against mine. We both groaned softly at the brushing of our bodies despite the clothes we wore. At that moment, I never felt like shedding my clothing off instantly. I had the instinct to feel his warm skin against mine. The feeling was too strong that I could not almost believe it. Never had I felt this with anyone before.

Was there something wrong with me? Was this a psychological effect or something because I so desired to have a baby? But I had no time to even analyse anything, let alone everything—as the feeling he made me feel overwhelmed me, reigning in my system and thoughts.

He pushed his tongue into my mouth to tease and challenge mine for a duel. I met it hesitantly, and I heard him take in a sharp inhalation and moan. I must have done it right. I did not know, but I thought my heart danced because of it. I began to feel braver and bolder. I moved my lips and tongue against his.

'Doamne! Why do I like kissing him?'

His hands started to go down to grasp my hips and knead them. Hot liquid fire began to flow out of my femininity, making it throb even more and wanting it to be filled. For some reason, I felt this way. It was odd if I'd analyse it. But maybe it was just because he was one attractive guy that I felt attracted to for the first time in my life.

The lift dinged and opened. Both of us were already starting to pant, and our lips were forced to part.

"Where's your room?" he asked huskily, lips hovering over mine.

"312," I answered.

"Give me the keycard," he ordered gently.

Without any hesitation, I fished the black-coloured thin card from my purse and gave it to him. I gasped when he carried me in his arms after taking the keycard. My hands wound around his neck, like it was the most natural thing in the world. I could feel his strong shoulders, and the excitement in my system went higher.

My one hundred-eight pounds weight must have been like nothing to him at this point. My slender frame was obviously an advantage for him that he could just easily pick me up like that and carry me into my room.

He closed the door with his foot. From the closed doorway, to the left, his smokey eyes automatically landed to one specific furniture. It was where a queen size bed was located. The furniture was covered by white-and-green stripe bedsheet, with a white cover that matched the pillow cases.

Although the sun was setting, the light streamed in from the gap of the velvet green curtains that I had drawn myself before I left earlier. The room was a bit warmer than normal, but the scent was fresh like lemon.

Maksimillian crossed the red-carpeted floor, muffling the sound of his steps, laid me down the soft bed carefully, and took the remote control for the air conditioning overhead to turn it on and set it to twenty-two degrees. He put it back on the bedside table. Then, he took my shoulder bag to place it next to the remote control before taking off his shoes, joining me in the bed on all fours and kissing my lips.

I hadn't even asked myself if I was already prepared for this. It was instantaneous and spontaneous, as though it was only natural for me to do *it*. My hands searched for the skin under his shirt, wanting to feel it. He groaned when my palms made contact with his warm and taut stomach. Just as I thought, his abs was incredible.

I looked up at him when he stopped kissing me, grey eyes questioning him silently.

'Is he going to back out now or what?'

Let The Romping Begin

Zenovia

In this very close proximity, Maksimillian's iris looked wonderful—like a combination of light green around his pupils and a kind of blue in the outer layer next to the colour green.

My breathing, just like his, was not normal.

"Are you sure about what you asked of me, Zenovia?" he queried in a hoarse tone. His eyes travelled all over my face. Then, I felt his fingers gently push a few strands of black hair off my face.

I slowly blinked, watching his handsome face thoroughly. His straight, long nose was prominent that it made him look so manly and attractive. His peach lips were slightly parted, and I craved to taste and feel them against my own, as I knew how good they'd taste. They were truly… moreish.

"Yes!" I answered in a whisper. "I am sure. I've never been too sure in my life. This is what I want. I want a child with you, Maksimillian."

He swallowed and closed his eyes to kiss me once again.

And there I was, thinking he'd stop and call this whole crazy thing off. I couldn't be so relieved in my entire life but at this moment. I knew that this whole situation wasn't normal, and what I really did for him to be on board this was out of the norm. Perhaps. But desperation could lead people to do impossible things in normal circumstances. And I was really desperate to have a baby soon! Before my infertility period comes, and it'd be already too late.

My condition was chronic, as I'd been informed. Although there may be chances that it could be inhibited, still, I did not want to risk this chance I had. It may be just a small window, but I hoped I could still do it before my condition could get worse or before I'd opt for therapy, which could involve my infertility. Either way, as I understood and if I'd really be unfortunate, I'd lose the ability to deliver a life into this world.

'But just one... at least one. Oh, Doamne! I don't want to be alone. Please let me have this baby...' I silently prayed while I kissed Maksimillian back. My lips moved against his slowly, while my eyes burned with tears that would spill any second.

He started to take my clothes off until I was naked. He sucked in air as he appraised my slender body. The desire was raging in his eyes, I could clearly see it. I felt my cheeks go hot. I must have looked like beet at the moment.

Only the doctors, nurses, my mother, and my best friend had seen me all naked. But all of it was nothing like this. Nothing like I felt right now, as he was another person who saw me without anything on and was about to do something else. Something intimate. Something that could create a life I longed for...

While kneeling, Maksimillian removed his own clothing. He looked so comfortable and proud of his body that I could see a faint smile on his lips while I ogled him. His wide shoulders were proud, and so was his muscled torso. His biceps and the bundle of his chest muscles rippled as he moved. My eyes couldn't stay away from his now barenaked body.

I swallowed hard when my peepers went south of his body, taking all in his beautiful abs. His entire being seemed to be imprinted in my brain at the moment, especially that huge rod of his. From my guesstimate, it was way more than half of a ruler, and it was thick. I'd never seen a man without his clothes in real life. In an underwear, yes, since I had swimming lessons and a class when I was in college. It was nothing for me then. But now, it did matter. I had no idea if I could do this now.

My heart kicked my chest once again. I could very well feel my blood travelling all over my system at the moment.

'Am I afraid or just excited?' I tried to analyse myself, as my hands crumpled the bedsheet. On the one side of my mind, I did find him so... imposing!

"I gave you a chance earlier, Zenovia," he spoke slowly, seemingly weighing my reaction to his nakedness. His eyes searched mine once again.

Was it fear that crossed his beautiful orbs as he looked at me now? But why?

I stayed immobile from where I lay, watching him.

"I'm not changing my mind," I told him in a low voice. But I did push the spit down my throat afterwards.

"That's good!" he said with a sexy smile. "I thought you did. And if you did, I'd find a way to make you mine," he added, lowering himself to claim my lips once again.

I moan softly, loving his kiss. A soft gasp left my mouth when his one hand unceremoniously cupped my center. With hooded lids, we both looked into each other's eyes.

"Zenovia…" he murmured in a husky tone. His fingers started to move up and down my already wet femininity. "Ohh… You're so soft… wet… and warm…"

My eyes went round when he lifted those same fingers he touched me with to lick them one by one.

"Ahh… Sweet!" he added and suckled his fingers to my amazement and mortification.

'How can I be sweet? It isn't true, is it?' The heat travelled to my face once again. He may have had noticed it, and he gave me a seductive smirk. On all fours again, he trapped me by his hands and knees. But then, he prodded my knees farther apart by caressing them until he stroked my wet slit. My legs did separate of their own accord, trying to feel more. More of him. More of what he could offer.

My body arched as a moan escaped from my throat; my breasts were pushed forward to him. He caught one peak while I was barely aware that he positioned himself in the middle of my widely parted legs. My hands went up from gripping the bedsheet to grab his head.

I thought I saw my brain in a dark place, as my eyes rolled back with great pleasure. His tongue and lips pleased the left rosy peak of my breast. At the same time, his hand caressed my center, making it wetter and wetter.

Oh, *Doamne!* His fingers felt so good down there. How could this be?

Maksimillian continued to kiss my peaks alternately, as though he couldn't get enough of them. The delicious tingling proceeded to my entire system. I couldn't think of anything else but the way he pleased me. My mind was filled by him, by his touch, and by his kiss.

When his mouth began to travel downwards, my eyes flew open.

"W-what are you doing?" I asked, a bit alarmed and thrilled, when his lips were now close to my V area.

Deflowering

Zenovia

Căcat! Maksimillian was not going further down, was he?

I saw him with a serious face, eyes filled with thick lust. "I'm going to taste more of you, *moye solntse!*" he answered huskily.

The heat reappeared in my cheeks. "W-what?" I cleared my throat and gulped nervously. My femininity was already throbbing with anticipation. I hadn't even got the chance to say something, as his hot mouth descended to plant a kiss on my girly bits. I thought I'd shatter from sudden rapture at that very moment. During which, he practically took my breath away.

While his eyes held mine, he moved his mouth against my center.

"Oh! *Doamne!*" I couldn't help but groan with delectation. My body squirmed, and my back curved as I held his head. His feverish mouth continued to give me something so pleasurable that I'd never imagined before. Or could even imagine.

He continued to move his lips against my femininity. Then, my body shuddered in delicious tingle as his tongue darted out of his mouth to run it along the slit, and it circled around the sensitive bud. My eyes rolled back while I gasped and panted. He continued by flicking the tip of his tongue on my burgeoning apex and sucking it mercilessly.

"Oh! Maksimillian!" I couldn't help but call out his name.

He moaned that sounded like a low sexy growl as he continued to taste me. Not long afterwards, his huge hands slowly made their way from my thighs to the side of my hips, waist, and ribs. Then, he massaged the underside of my breasts before rolling the peaks under his palms. His mouth never ceased its addictive movements against my center in the meantime.

My desire was heightened in each moment. I felt ready to burst into pieces for some reason. I kept on moaning with so much pleasure he gave me. I thought the sound even reverberated in the four corners of the quiet hotel room.

Maksimillian pinched each of my marbled tips that made me moan even more, while my back arched again. He moved his head from one side to the other. He laved my center, and I felt his tongue tease my entrance that made my eyes fly open.

I gasped. My heartbeat's pace increased, and the anticipation inside me escalated. What would he do if he realised he was my first? And what would he do if I'd bleed more than I should during my first time? Would he panic? Or would I panic? Okay, maybe we'd both panic, but I had to be strong no matter what.

My heart quivered because of these thoughts nonetheless. And yet, I was lost again in the pleasure of his mouth. His tongue moved up and down my wet ladyparts and teased the apex, and my fingers buried deeper in his short brown hair.

I was short-winded and had no idea if this pleasure was going to even come down. All I knew was that it had me taken higher and higher. Something built up inside me, gripping and throbbing. My moans went louder by the second until I screamed when I could not take it anymore. My body shook in rapture; I could not even control it. I was breathing in gasps, and I moaned once more.

Maksimillian drank the liquid desire that flowed from my core. He tasted and imbibed it with such intensity of his tongue and mouth that I kept moaning and was quivering with unmeasured delicious feeling. I could not almost contain it.

"O *bozhe, trakhni menya* (Oh, God, fuck me)!" he breathed.

'Oh, whatever that means!'

He kept mumbling in Russian. It was… kind of hot!

My chest rose and fell, as I breathed raggedly. I gazed at him with surprise when he rose slightly to hover above me, looking down at my flushed face. His hands anchored on the bed to support his weight.

My eyes went rounder when I felt the tip of his manhood poke my entrance, preparing to push in. I held my breath, but my heart still pounded so hard. My eyes flickered, and I grabbed his powerful arms. As though it was the most natural thing to do, my legs went to wrap around his waist. I gulped and heaved shakily, preparing myself to feel some pain. But I hoped the pain reliever I swallowed was already working by now.

"Oh!" I panted, as he started his way into my body.

He paused and cussed, looking at me with bafflement. "Y-you're…?"

I nodded, swallowing the spit down my throat. "I-I'm sorry I didn't tell you."

"Zenovia…"

"What? Are you going to back out now? Remember you signed—"

My trap was shut when his lips slammed against mine. The rest of the words I wanted to say went back down to my throat, ending up into a groan.

"You just amazed me, Zenovia!" He gritted his teeth for a moment while he prodded into me. My eyes were still on him, though he already closed his. I could see that he held his breath for a moment when he pushed deeper into me, breaking his way in.

Another muffled moan came out of me, as he covered my mouth once again. He sank into me, deeper and deeper. I felt the strangest thing that shoved deep into me. It pained me but not much that I couldn't bear. Perhaps it was because of the pain reliever.

I groaned softly when he pulled out and plunged into me again. He did it again and again, rocking my body as he did so.

"Oh, Zenovia!" he said and moaned. He panted while he drove in and out of my slick body. Then, he kissed my face and my lips.

As minutes ticked by, I could smell the faint metallic odor of my own blood. I could feel it slopping against my skin, trickling down my butt and further down to stain the bedsheet. But it didn't matter. What he did to and for me mattered. He didn't seem to mind at all anyway.

He dipped his head to catch a marbled peak and suck it. My arms went around him, caressing the back of his head.

"Oh, Maksimillian!" That familiar buildup deep within me started once more, squeezing his huge manhood inside of me. I heard him groan, and he became breathless as ever. I let out a loud whimper when he sent me over the edge, and he burrowed deeper into me. It was followed by his prolonged sexy grunt, and I intuitively knew that he reached his own climax, before I felt his jizz. Some of it escaped and dripped.

We both looked into each other's eyes. I was surprised when he gave me a satisfied and amazed look on his smiling face. Even more so, it was unexpected that he would touch my lips with his again.

"Zenovia," he whispered and took a deep breath.

"Do you have something to say to me?" I queried with a slight raise of my eyebrow.

Perfect For Him

Maksimillian

I did not expect Zenovia was a virgin, and I was the one who had just taken it. Maybe because she was too forward by making a deal with me to be her romp partner until she'd get pregnant. I thought at first she'd been engaged with such an intimate activity for some time, but it proved that I was wrong. Who was sane to make such a deal with a random guy anyway? Besides, forward girls were usually experienced.

Now, still inside her—snugly inside her, that is—I gazed down at her beautiful flushed face. I felt really good for the first time that I've been with a girl... in forever. It wasn't only because she was the first virgin I took but because I felt something for the first time. Something that I could not point a finger on though. At the moment, I had no time to even analyse it.

Despite the air conditioning, it was too hot for me that beads of sweat had scattered on my face and body. Zenovia's beautiful skin was also damp with perspiration. God! She was so exquisite at the moment. More exquisite than anyone—if I had to compare her with anyone. And yet, she was incomparable.

I gently pulled away but thrust deep into her once more. I so loved her tightness, and the wetness that drowned my hard member.

Fuck! It was so good to feel.

For the first time, it proved that I did really want this girl since I saw her at The Black Church. It was the first time I wanted one so much that I'd want to take her again and again—unlike the previous girls I had been with. There was just something about her that I could still not fathom, but it was like she was the sunshine I needed in my life. It seemed that my life had already changed when our paths crossed earlier.

I bent my head to kiss her sweet lips. "What I want to say is that..." I paused, looking deep into her alluring grey orbs, "you're perfect!"

She blinked slowly, and I saw the unshed tears that shone in her eyes. She looked wrecked for some reason that she began to sob. Her shoulders shook, and tears began to spill and run down the side of her face.

"Hey, hey. What's wrong?" I was, of course, alarmed because of it.

I gently pulled out from her body, suddenly feeling void. But I had to know what was wrong with her.

She shook her head, looking sideways when I lay beside her. "Y-you... just said I'm perfect, but I'm not!" she whispered and cried.

I cupped her face and caressed her cheek with my thumb. "But that's what I think. You are perfect to me, Zenovia," I told her with an assuring tone. I was even surprised with myself that I was desperate for her to believe me.

I wiped her tears away by gently running my thumbs on their trails while holding her gaze. I'd never felt an overwhelming emotion just as I did at the moment, like I wanted to protect her so badly and didn't want her to be hurt by anything. Or by anyone.

"Listen to me. Whatever you may think, you are flawless to me."

She laughed hysterically. "Oh, don't sweet talk me, Maksimillian!" She shook her head and looked away from me.

I watched the side of her face as she heaved; her chest went up and down as she breathed. Her beautiful peaks were still on display, and I couldn't help but admire her beauty. My eyes went downward still, and that was when I noticed the bloody sheet.

Oh, fuck! There was more blood than I had anticipated that I sat bolt upright.

"Zenovia!" I cussed again in Russian after that. "I-I'm so sorry. Come here, let me help you with that."

Before she could protest, I already scooped her up in my arms and carried her to the bathroom. She took a sharp breath since she didn't expect it.

I turned the light on after placing her carefully in the white bathtub and turning the faucet on. The water was warm, not scalding. I made sure of it.

She looked up at me when I joined her there. "Hey, get out of the water. Can't you see it's bloody here?" she shooed me away, blushing.

"I know, and I'm the cause of it," I pointed out with a serious face, glancing down at my bloodied shaft.

She sighed when I finally settled behind her and hugged her to me. She relaxed after a few moments of being rigid. We soaked there for minutes while I rubbed her skin with bath gel.

"Why…?" I asked, without saying the rest of the words. I just wanted to know why she stayed untouched by any man until now.

"I don't want to talk about it," her reply to dismiss the topic.

I curtly nodded. Fair enough. We just met, and maybe she didn't trust me if it was some kind of a secret. Her reason, that is. I'd just respect it. For now. But I knew, eventually, I'd ask her about it again. I was really curious. Add to that, she didn't want a father for her child. Who wouldn't be curious by that? Didn't she want commitment? Why? Was she afraid of it? But why? There were a lot of women who even tied themselves to a man they believed they loved at an early stage of their relationship, realising later on that their decision was wrong and ending up in a divorce. Was her reason along these lines? Was she just being cautious or what?

I wanted to know more about her. All at once, as much as possible. However, at this rate, she already clammed up, so it meant she didn't trust me. Yet. I guessed I had to work on it at the duration of this romping relationship. Who knew it would become more than that?

Wait, why am I thinking this? Does it mean I'm really into her since I laid eyes on her? But that's impossible. I'm attracted to her, yes, but…' I trailed off. I didn't want to analyse all this at once, for now, when everything wasn't even sure. But I knew deep inside that I *did* want to know everything about her.

"Why don't you want to talk about it?" I found myself asking her, despite what she said.

First Dinner Together

Maksimillian

Zenovia turned her head to look at me sternly. "Just because!"

I let out my breath slowly. "Honestly, I'm overwhelmed and feel honoured that I'm your first, Zenovia."

She froze and was unable to say anything. I had no idea why. But hadn't she any idea about it or was she processing this in her mind at the moment? I wanted to read her mind, so badly. But it was impossible, of course.

"Why do you need to know?" she asked finally, after I helped her out of the tub.

I dabbed her body with a huge white towel. As much as I wanted to gawk at her naked body, I wrapped the towel around her when she was dry enough.

Our eyes collided and held. Then, I answered, "I want to know all about you, if you let me. I want to know the mother of my future child. Is there something wrong with it?"

"I told you, no strings attached, so I don't think you need to know *all* about me," she stated, turning her back to me and walking away.

I frowned at her reaction, but I remained patient. "Can we have dinner?" I followed her after grabbing another towel to dry my body.

The room was already lit by the lampshade and wall sconces with yellow lights. I found Zenovia already taking off the bedsheet. The blood was more than noticeable, and I winced. Was it because of her reproductive system's problem? I would want to know what it was exactly, which I hoped she'd share to me one of these days.

"Suit yourself," her only answer. She placed the soiled cloth in a corner. She took a deep breath and continued to say, "You don't really have to ask me to have dinner with you, Maksimillian. If you want to go now—"

"No, I don't want to go now. I want to stay the whole night with you, in fact."

Her jaw dropped.

"If you're worried about me taking advantage of you," I said, smirking, "don't."

Her face flushed visibly, and she averted her eyes.

"I know that you should be taken care of, Zenovia. Whatever your reason is to make a deal with me, I understand. I'm blind, actually. But… yes, I will honour that deal." *'If I really can,'* my mind added. Intuitively, I just knew that I wouldn't want to get out of her hair ever. At least, that was what I thought up to this point.

She was quiet once again, and I watched her dress up. When she was done, I remembered to order room service and a couple of fresh linens.

Zenovia looked embarrassed when the hotel maid delivered our order, as well as the fresh linens I particularly asked. The middle-aged staff glanced at Zenovia and me while making the bed. Zenovia pretended to check something on her phone, while I just stood there staring at her.

I could guess the maid's silent observation was because I was still in my towel. Maybe she already presumed that we already did the deed, since the sheet had to be changed. But I didn't care what she thought anyway.

I did not expect Zenovia to arrange the food on the wood table, which was below the mounted flat TV screen. But she did.

The aroma of honey garlic glazed salmon, together with the shrimp stir fry, creamy Tuscan chicken, and *pilaf*, reached to my nostrils.

Zenovia also placed the two canned orange juice opposite each other, near the center of the table.

We began to eat when the maid already left the room, telling as *"Poftă bună!"* (Enjoy your meal!)

"You shouldn't have paid for this meal," Zenovia commented after swallowing a piece of salmon.

I did pay for all of it before the maid could get out.

"Why? Afraid I'd broken the deal earlier on?" I teased her.

"Why are you so nice, Maksimillian?" She unconsciously glanced at my bare torso. "Why aren't you dressed for heaven's sakes? Aren't you cold?"

I laughed at that and shook my head. "I'm not nice, Zenovia. I'm a selfish ass who was born and raised in Russia. And, oh! You should know we take a dip in icy rivers and seas even during winter like penguins."

She snickered at that, making her face shine brighter.

God! She was really like my personal sunshine. She looked so fetching whenever she smiles that it made my heart quaver.

Fuck. Ever since I saw her, I felt like a corny hackney. I was never like this. But this sudden change alarmed me deep inside. And yet, I didn't want to linger on this. Who cared if I turned into a trite? As long as I felt good inside, it didn't matter to me. And she did make me feel great!

"I don't believe you're a selfish person, Maksimillian," she told me with a serious face. But she later on smiled at me—the kind of smile that only she could affect me like a teenage boy whose knees became weak. I only heard about this in the past, but it proved to be true. There was just at least this one person that could make someone feel weak in the knees and make the butterflies in the stomach flutter.

'Fuck! I sound like a girl,' I thought miserably while staring at Zenovia. Ah! She really looked striking to me that I could not take my eyes off her while we ate.

Some minutes later, I could not hold it back. I rose from my seat to lean across the table and capture her chin with my hand. I locked my lips with hers, to her bafflement.

"Hmm… I love the taste of honey garlic glazed salmon in your mouth," I whispered against her lips.

Her big grey eyes went round as she looked at me. "Maksimillian!"

"I did promise not to take advantage of you, but I think you love to be kissed by me. Don't you deny it." I gave her a smug smile, too confident about myself and the way I made her feel.

She rolled her eyes and laughed. "You know what? I can let you have me anytime you want."

Thoughtfulness

Zenovia

Maksimillian looked at me in utter disbelief and shock. *'Doamne! What was I thinking? Why did I even say that?'*

"Given that I... don't... have anything to do," I added as an afterthought.

The corners of his lips started to lift up into a smile. "Okay. What do you do, Zenovia?"

I took my cell phone and thought it was good to send him a copy of our signed deal. "What's your email?"

He chuckled, watching my face. "This... I think this is a good idea!" he said and gave me what I wanted.

I suppressed a smile and sent him the copy of the document. "What do you mean good idea? Don't ask what I do, by the way, because I'm not asking you what you do. I think it's better that way."

He slowly nodded, giving me a measuring but disappointed look. Although he tried to hide it away, I could just read it in his striking eyes.

"I know now where I can contact you, Zenovia."

I laughed. "I can always deactivate my email when this is all over, Maksimillian."

Now his face turned serious as he ground his teeth. I could see how his jaw muscles jerk. But then, to my surprise, he slowly smiled.

"Alright. Let's not think about the end of this deal yet. Do you have any plans for tomorrow?" He drank his canned juice, without bothering to pour it in an empty glass next to it.

I shrugged slowly. "Of course, I have. My friend and I planned this two-week vacation, in fact. In a day or two, she'll join me here," I answered truthfully.

"Oh, a friend? A guy friend?" he queried, an eyebrow slightly raised.

I burst out laughing. I couldn't help it. When I looked at his face again, both his eyebrows were raised.

"What's so funny?" he asked, almost irritated.

I stopped laughing but was still smiling. "She's my best friend actually… and my doctor," I admitted.

My smile faded, and I averted my eyes. I then resumed eating, not knowing why I had to fill him in on the last information. Did I want him to know a little about me even though I didn't want to?

'Căcat. I must be crazy!'

"Oh." It was the only word that came out of his mouth. That mouth that gave me pleasure just a little while ago. Because of this thought, my heart skipped a beat and pounded hard afterwards. I'd never forget how he made me feel.

I had a dull pain in my private area, but mostly, I could still feel the wetness because of the bleeding. I just knew it soaked my clothing now. I should wear a sanitary pad because of it. And I had no idea if it would go away soon. I forgot to ask Antonia about it to be prepared.

"So, where do you want to go tomorrow?" Maksimillian asked.

"I was planning to go to Bran Castle, but I don't want to go if my friend isn't with me yet, since she wants to see it for herself, too."

"The option is?"

"I read a review on Mount Tampa. Since I want to not see hoardes of people, I thought it would be a great change to just head up on the mountain. It's said it's only a twenty-minute walk to the summit where we can see the Brașov sign. So yes, I would like to go hiking, see that big Brașov sign on the mountain up close, and then, just spend a few hours there, I guess, before heading back by a cable car and have late lunch after that."

"Okay. Count me in!" he decided.

My jaw dropped. "Seriously? Are you just going to abandon your aunt?"

He chortled softly. "Trust me, she won't mind at all."

I narrowed my eyes while staring at him. "You're such a bad nephew!"

He laughed at my accusation. "Are you a good niece?"

I pulled my mouth down and shrugged. "Unfortunately, I don't have uncles or aunts. My parents are the only child my grandparents could produce. So… I don't have cousins either."

He slowly nodded, smirking.

Căcat! I just told him more about myself. Again!

I chewed on my inner cheek, thinking what to say or do next.

He smiled, knowing that I realised it. "What will you do after late lunch?" he went on.

I shook my head. I hadn't thought far ahead, since Antonia wasn't with me. But I blushed when it occurred to me that I needed to work on my future baby. With him.

I cleared my throat and just steered my sight away from him. However, I already caught the naughty look in his stunning eyes.

Ah, *Doamne!*

***

Maksimillian

When Zenovia got up from her chair to go to the bathroom to brush her teeth, I noticed the bloodstain in her clothing. I pressed my eyes after closing them and got up to change fast.

I went out of the room, almost running down the stairs to the ground floor, since I couldn't wait for the lift. My mind's eye recalled there was a small *magazin* (convenience store) nearby, so I jogged there, ignoring my bodyguards that watched the hotel and eventually saw me going out.

Glad the small *magazin* was still open, I immediately went to look for that thing Zenovia would need.

There were only a few short rows of products displayed, so I scanned where the tissue papers were. Sanitary pads and wet wipes were usually placed nearby. At least, I guessed that, if they had the same arrangement around here.

From the left, there were chocolates, biscuits, candies, and drinks; the next row had canned goods and other kitchen condiments; right after that was the bathroom products, so I headed there with long strides.

I examined the packs of different brands, not knowing what to buy though. There were thick pads and ultra thin, as well as daytime or nighttime ones. I had no idea what difference would it make.

Chert! I should've asked Zenovia about it. Or would she be embarrassed if I did?

Okh kak nravilas'! (Oh, fuck that!) Maybe the thick one is better, so that she wouldn't have any leak?

The middle-aged man behind the counter stared at me while I paid for a pack. I stared back at him, and he placed the pack in a small plastic bag.

Why was he looking at me like that? Didn't he have a wife or a daughter?

I was about to leave when I thought of buying ice cream for Zenovia. It might cheer her up.

'But why do I want to cheer her up?'

Because she just lost her virginity to me or what? That I didn't want her to feel bad because of her condition? Well, maybe that. But I had no exact idea. I just wanted her to feel good about this.

I went to the right corner of the store and peered at the different flavours of the frozen treats. Now I had no idea what kind of flavour she'd like to eat or if she had any allergies.

Maybe chocolate is safer? Or maybe vanilla? Strawberry?

I frowned, not knowing what to pick.

He's Back

Zenovia

When I went out of the bathroom, I found Maksimillian missing. The table was left abandoned with some unfinished food. It was like he was just gone from the face of the earth. I could not help but feel rejected for some reason.

It hurt so much!

Was he not going to even say goodbye? Didn't he even leave at least a short note or something? Right, there was no pen or paper lying around here, so he could not even if he wanted to.

I took my phone that was lying next to my empty white plate, checking my email just in case he wrote me one. But I was even more disappointed. He did not even send me a quick, short reply for the copy of the contract I sent or just a line that he was going. That he just snatched my virginity and was off into the night.

"He could've just hollered, if he instead not going to spend the night with me here!" I murmured to myself, hating him that very moment.

But why? This was not right. I shouldn't hate him or even get disappointed with him. We only just met, gave me what I wanted, and...

I sighed. Right. I still had to change.

Instead of thinking about him, I went over to the built-in cabinet a couple steps away from the side of the bed. I took a nightshirt and a fresh underwear. I washed before changing, and I examined my reflection closely in the square mirror, which was mounted above the big white sink.

Căcat! I looked miserable. There was the noticeable lifelessness in my grey eyes. The green specks looked dull.

Everything about what my father did to my mother came back to me. I saw my mother cry almost every night. When she'd notice me, she'd go to her room and hide herself there. But I did hear her sobs. It tore my heart at the time.

I really hated my father for leaving her then that I swore I'd never fall in love and marry. When I grew up, I realised I'd need someone with me, to not be alone. To not feel empty living all alone. Just that I still didn't want to have anything to do with men… until this intimate problem came along.

I questioned God why me? How could He do this to me? Why did He give me such a burden that was too much for me to carry? I didn't do anything wrong to be punished like this, so why?

A tear escaped from each of my eyes and raced down my chin. A small sob left my throat, as I continued to stare at my pitiable reflection in the mirror. I cried for a whole minute or so. But I took a deep breath after that. I shouldn't let all these things get to me. I had to be strong. I just had to do what I needed to do, whether with or without Maksimillian's sperm donation!

"I'm fine. I'm good. I'm healthy. I'm going to have a baby even if we just did it once," I told myself like it was a mantra.

I washed my face and dabbed it dry with a face towel. I put it back on its holder on the wall before going out.

I was stunned when I saw Maksimillian standing close to the door that my heart jumped. My hand automatically went up to my chest.

"You startled me!" I complained breathlessly. My eyes went bigger as I gave him an admonishing look. Besides, I didn't expect him to come back! At all! And I didn't expect how my heart jumped with happiness because of seeing him again.

"I thought you might need this," he said, holding out a white plastic bag.

My brows came together as I accepted it. Our fingers brushed, and I peered to check the content.

"Y-you bought me this?" I gaped at him.

"I thought you need it." His eyes assessed me and what I was wearing. The cream-coloured sleeveless nightshirt's hem just reached mid-thigh, while its scoop neckline was low enough to show off some upper part of my breasts.

I didn't expect him to come back, let alone buy me some pads! Oh, crap. I hated thick pads! They always made me uncomfortable, reminding me constantly that they were *there* when I used them.

"You shouldn't have—" I started, shaking my head.

"I may have no idea how it feels for you right now, but I couldn't just let you feel uncomfortable, okay?" He gestured a hand in the air while he spoke.

I opened my mouth to tell him the truth, but I closed it. He was just being thoughtful and being nice to me. How would he know about my problem with thick pads anyway? But he should've told me he was going somewhere to buy me pads, instead of just letting me think he actually left for good, and I'd never see him again.

I gulped and nodded. "T-thanks."

"And… I bought you some ice cream. I thought it'd cheer you up somehow?" He shrugged, and my eyes darted to the two cups of ice cream he bought.

"Wow! Double Dutch!" I exclaimed. "It's my favourite!" I rushed to the table and excitedly opened it, after setting aside the plastic on the wooden chair. I picked up the clean teaspoon placed on the right side of my plate and started digging. "Oh, God! Thank you, Maksimillian!" I said with ice cream in my mouth.

I sighed with contentment. It'd been a long while since I ate this. I tried to stay away from too much sweets, afraid that I'd develop type 2 diabetes.

Maksimillian sauntered closer to me, smiling. I guessed he was happy that I loved the ice cream flavour he bought for me.

"Hey, aren't you eating, too?" I asked him, eyebrows rising as I regarded him.

My heart began to pound harder. He was so close to me than it was necessary. He looked down at my face, staring at the teaspoon that I just put inside my mouth.

I swallowed the ice cream, breathless and eyes unblinking. He held my hand that was holding the teaspoon and removed it from my mouth only to replace it with his lips. I couldn't resist a moan to get out from my throat, and I brushed my lips against his. His hot and wet tongue prodded inside my mouth, tasting and teasing me.

My core throbbed as he went on kissing me. I had no choice but to put the cup down on the table.

"I love and prefer the ice cream in your mouth, *moye solntse*," he whispered and took the teaspoon from my hand. He momentarily parted his lips from mine to dig into the cup and gently fed me while our eyes held. The ice cream melt in my mouth, with his sexy orbs focusing on my lips.

I gasped when he covered my mouth with his once again. "Mmm…" I couldn't help but said softly while he sucked my tongue. At the same time, my mind called out his name.

'Oh, Doamne*! He's really, really good!'*

I was breathless as our lips clung and sucked each other's tongue alternately. His manly taste was mixed with ice cream that it made me more heady.

Barely aware that he placed the teaspoon in the ice cream cup, his hands started to cup my breasts to knead them slowly. He teased my now hardened peaks under the thin silky cloth. His palms rolled them, followed by his fingers that pinched them. The sweet sensation travelled all over my system and was trapped within my core, making me feel hotter and hornier.

"Maksimillian!" I exclaimed softly when his mouth left mine to kiss my earlobe and down the side of my neck. I had to hold onto him, and my hands fumbled with his waistband…

Kisses And Ice Cream

Zenovia

I could not seem to recall when Maksimillian shed all his clothes and shoes off. He was now standing naked in front of me with his hard-on facing me. I swallowed hard, as I remembered how that huge staff of his made me whimper with so much pleasure just a little while ago.

Without a word and eyes smokey with immeasurable lust, he caught me by the waist and passionately ravaged my lips. He seemed to be different from the gentle Maksimillian, and now, he showed me the other side of him. It was curious, since I found it... exciting! I might be crazy, but this thrilled me. In fact, I kissed him back with the same fervour, which made him grunt, and his fingers buried into my flesh through the nightshirt. He squeezed me now and then while kissing me thoroughly, making me breathless.

His one hand suddenly let go of me, as he cleared one side of the table. I felt myself being lifted up effortlessly. My butt found the smooth surface of the table, and he cupped my center, gently massaging it before pulling my now bloodstained underwear down the floor. My feet dangled slightly, and I lifted my eyes to his face.

"Zenovia..." he whispered hoarsely and peeled the nightshirt from my body.

He stepped between my legs while the cool air kissed and blanketed my skin, sending me goosebumps. The peaks of my breasts also hardened, and his eyes seemed to magnetize there. He gently pushed me down, angling my body slightly that made me lean my hands on the surface of the table. My left eyebrow rose when he picked up the ice cream to feed me.

"What's this?" I softly chuckled before eating ice cream from the teaspoon, holding his gaze. Then, his eyes went lower to my lips, and

I laughed a little while kissing him back. "Is it some kind of fettish or what?"

"I just want to eat your favourite ice cream with you like this," he answered, smiling at me sexily. He fed me again and kissed me everytime he did, sharing the ice cream together in this way. It was really sweet, I mused.

Just when I thought he'd go on like that—feeding me ice cream, kissing me, and tonguing me out of my mind—he accidentally, or rather deliberately, dropped a teaspoon of ice cream on my chest. I gasped at the coldness of it that my heart also jumped. I saw him smirk naughtily, and that was when I knew he did it on purpose.

"Maksimillian!"

"Sorry? But I'm not sorry." He gave me a teasing smile, which made him even more attractive.

My mouth opened when he licked the melting ice cream on my chest and sucked each of my taut tips. I couldn't help but throw my head back at the unexpected sensation. His mouth and tongue were cold and warm at the same time. It was a bit weird.

"Oh! *Doamne!*" I couldn't help but exclaim. My one hand grabbed the back of his neck, while the other remained on the table, now at the edge to grip it to keep my balance. My body was slanting back, yearning for more of him. "Maksimillian!"

Without breaking his suckling my right tip, he scooped another teaspoon of ice cream to place it on my flat stomach. My eyes went round, and my stomach made a ripple at the cold sensation. I quivered a little, and his mouth went down to kiss my stomach and lick the melting ice cream. He followed the drip towards the abdomen that made me moan a little.

Oh, *Doamne!* This was sweet torture.

My core throbbed even more because of anticipation.

When he finished licking the semi-melted ice cream on my stomach, his mouth caged my left rosy tip this time, sucking it hard and making me groan. My body shook a little when he dropped a couple teaspoons of ice cream on my V area. I gasped in reaction to it.

While he continued to suckle each of my marbled peaks, I could feel the melted ice cream drip further south. It slowly made its cold way down to my very slit.

"Maksimillian!" I called out to him, panting. My body arched when he sucked hard and nibbled my hardened tip. "Ohh…"

I watched him with half-closed lids when his mouth moved downwards to follow the trail of the melted ice cream. I was already breathless even before his mouth slowly moved against my wet lady parts. His tongue flicked on the little bud before he ran it downwards. I heard him moan lowly, while he laved and licked it. His movements varied from the left to the right and from up north going southwards.

The melted ice cream was cold, but he eventually made it warm with his tongue and lips. He tasted my skin from the V area and back again to my throbbing core. He sucked the sensitive nub there that grew fatter due to increased arousal. I couldn't help but anchor my ankles on his wide shoulders, while one hand caressed his head.

Oh, how I loved to feel his soft short hair against my palm!

Maksimillian nibbled each of my vertical lips down there, making me pant more. I could feel the tensing of my inner walls as the buildup of desire became more intense. More liquid fire flowed down to his sexy mouth. Despite my mortification of knowing I was still bleeding, he didn't seem to mind it and continued to please me. More and more. It was incredible!

I suddenly wondered if he was used to this with other women. Apparently, he was one experienced lover, although he hadn't told me about it yet. For someone as attractive as he, there was no doubt he had lots of women in the past, before meeting me. I may now wonder how many, but I had no business asking him that. I had to remind myself there were no strings attached to this relationship.

If I could call it *that* and not just a crappy insane deal.

But I also wondered if he'd really get on with my craziness after this night was over, although he already said he wanted to go with me to hike on Mount Tâmpa tomorrow…

Hard, Medium, Or Gentle?

Maksimillian

I continued to lap up Zenovia's delicious flower. Her unique and metallic taste combined with Double Dutch ice cream was exotic, and I found it hard to resist.

I moved my lips against each of her meaty petals. Oh, they were so smooth and addictive!

The balls of her feet dug in my back, but I didn't mind. Even her hand that restlessly caressed my head and nape was so good, letting me know she loved the way I tasted her.

I must admit I had never gone down to anyone but her. I had no idea why I started with her and was doing it, but I found it great. With her. Just her. Knowing she loved how I did her was boosting my ego, as I read her body well. She just loved the way I did it.

"Hmm... Maksimillian!" She groaned sexily, again and again.

I lifted my eyes while running my tongue upwards, holding her smokey grey orbs with mine. Her red lips were parted, while she huffed and puffed. She would throw her head back now and again, as I continued to please her. Her delectable flower's nectar slipped out to my waiting hot mouth. I drank from her succulent well, guzzling like a thirsty traveller.

I began to insert one finger into her that made her inhale sharply and grab my head. I slowly plunged deeper before pulling it back. Now and again. And again. During which, my lips and tongue were sexing her burgeoned bud. I stayed there, flicking my tongue and softly nibbling it with my lips and teeth. Her moans grew sexier, longer and higher. Her chest rose and fell faster as she panted.

"Cum, Zenovia!" I urged her with a gruffy tone. I then roughly kissed her fattened nub.

I knew she was nearing to the edge as her hips ground the table. It gently shook with her movements, making the plates, glasses, forks, and spoons clink.

In and out, I moved my wetted finger faster, while I sucked her and flicked the tip of my tongue on her precious bud. My other hand held her by the waist to keep her on the table. I didn't want her to slip and be in any accident.

I felt the tightening of her walls, and she gasped even more when I inserted another finger inside of her. She mewled when I continued to drive in and out of her soaking center.

"Yes, Zenovia. Don't hold back, *moye solntse*." I groaned in return.

She threw her head back again and couldn't help but let out a string of moans. "Ohh... Maksimillian!" She was out of breath.

I did really love to hear her calling out my name hoarsely in such an ardent manner. A loud cry escaped from her when she hit the pinnacle of her pleasure that I gave her. White hot liquid lava ran out of her love canal, which I met with my eager lips and tongue. She was not done quivering when I straightened up from my crouching form.

A sharp intake of breath was heard from her when I plunged my hot rod into her hot and wet depths. Then, I paused to ask her, "How would you like it this time, Zenovia? Hard?" To show her what I was talking about, I squeezed her globes roughly and pulled out from her body just to drive into her hard and deep. Thrice. And more.

Zenovia winced while whimpering my name.

"Gentle?" I asked, slowing down and massaging her breasts gently.

She shook her head. "Show me how's your medium is done," she whispered.

I adjusted my pace in going in and out of her as she requested. She swallowed and breathed fast and shallow, nodding her head.

"You love this pace?" I inquired, kneading her breasts with the right pressure and pinching her hard peaks.

"Vary it. I'll let you know if it hurts me," she said in a low husky tone. One hand was already back on the table.

I watched as her breasts were gently rocked, caused by my continuous thrusts in her hot and tight body.

"Do it harder, Maksimillian," she demanded, and I did so. In and out.

Lentils of sweat appeared on my forehead and chest—I could just feel them. Apparently, Zenovia's chest also glistened with sweat. Her moans and the clinking of the plates and everything on the table were like a beautiful melody that was created for my ears only. I held her small waist with both hands as I continued to thrust into her body, feeling it soaking my huge staff. And it felt so fucking good!

Her blood also stained my hard cock, but it didn't matter. She hadn't told me to stop, so I continued.

"Medium now, Maksimillian," she requested in a panting tone.

"Did I hurt you?" I paused momentarily to be sure she was fine. I was worried. My heart throbbed so hard against my rib cage. I didn't want to add to her pain if she was in it.

"I-I'm fine. Just do it in medium pace for now," she answered, still breathless.

"Okay." I kissed her mouth and sucked her lower lip. It was so soft and tasted good, especially when she moved her lips averse to mine in response. Then, I proceeded as she wanted. My hips moved against hers, my butt and thigh muscles flexing. Now and then, I'd grind my pelvis, pushing deeper into her pleasurable depths and making her grunt.

I thought I was going crazy in being one with her. Never had I imagined I could feel this way. Not in a million years!

My heavy-lidded eyes were watchful of her beautiful flushed face. I knew she was going to be on edge soon. I could feel it. I could feel her tightening around me even more. She was already a very snug fit, and it grew tighter inside by the minute, despite her soaking me.

"Oh, Zenovia, *moye solntse*!" I kept mumbling breathlessly.

"Yes, Maks!" she breathed and moaned.

Oh, I loved *Maks* coming from her lips. It felt very intimate indeed!

I smiled at her and dipped my head to kiss her right peak, suckling it hard. Then, I raised my face to meet her burning gaze.

"I'm going faster and harder, okay?"

She swallowed and nodded. With her gaping mouth, I covered it with mine as I went all out on her. The sound of our joining bodies, clinking plates, glasses, forks and spoons, as well as our mewling was a beautiful song. I wish I could've recorded all of it and could play it whenever I wanted.

I might do it next time. But maybe I'd ask her first to not be a creep or a perv. But yeah, maybe I'd slowly become a sentimental fool for some reason.

'Chert poberi! (Damn it!) Maybe I already am!'

I propelled into her like an angry intruder. She was crying louder and louder. Maybe it even reached outside the door. But who cared? I didn't. And I guessed she didn't either.

Zenovia's pleasing walls compressed around my stroking manhood. My entire groin area then tensed up as my precious sac was already tightening. The excitement was indeed getting intense that I could not even describe it in words. And then, she and I hit it! It was like my brain and everything else shut down, and the only thing that was on was my all physical rapture.

Zenovia's liquefied delight bathed me, and my own cum mixed with hers. It was so damn good to be drowned inside her!

Her body shook in the aftermath while she heaved. "Maks!"

The tender look in her eyes made my heart jump.

'And why does it feel so right?'

Against The Hard Trunk

Zenovia

The weather was good the next day. The sun was all smiles upon the living and non-living things on Earth. I glanced at my hiking companion, who kept on beaming at me toothlessly everytime our eyes met. This made my heart flutter all the time.

Last night, Maksimillian took me the third time in the bathroom, before we finally slept in the bed, cuddling me while we were both naked. I endured the pain, as I realised the effect of the pain reliever died with time. He did notice it, but I just told him to not penetrate deeply. And he did follow as instructed, like my personal slave.

I could not almost believe he was going to though, since he was a bit rough on me the second time—at least, it was to me. But at that time, the pain was dull, and I could take it, mixed with pleasure.

But as mentioned, the third was not the best experience, but he was very patient and considerate. We found the best position that was enjoyable for both of us—the lotus position, as he said. And I did remember Antonia mentioning this to me before, among others, like modified doggy style, reverse cowgirl, sideways, and me on top. She said these would be better for me. Well, she did also show me how these were supposed to be done when she explained to me once. I could only stare at her and at the images with mortification, face burning hot.

But now, it seemed that being extremely embarrassed for doing this sensual relationship with a stranger was totally off the table. Besides, he was one cooperative and understanding partner that I couldn't ask for more. How could I be so lucky? God must've still loved me for giving me this attractive, considerate guy. I wouldn't have dreamt of such a blessing, despite my hatred towards men. And maybe I hated one less man in the world because of Maksimillian.

Earlier this morning, after having breakfast with me, he told me he'd go to his and his aunt's hotel to change. He was back in less than two hours, and here we were, hiking Mount Tâmpa.

The route was completely empty except for us. It was really a nice change for a city girl like me. And maybe for him, too. I could just guess he lived in a city like me. Most probably Moscow. But I won't ask him that. I didn't want to know, to keep his identity hidden from myself. I had no plan of digging into his personal life more than he could offer.

"Are you alright?" he asked when I winced. "Where does it hurt?"

It was uncomfortable using the thick pad he bought, but I wasn't complaining. I had to use it well for the sake of his being thoughtful.

I almost laughed at his question and looked at him with amusement in my grey eyes. "Are you seriously asking me that?"

He opened his mouth and closed it. I could see a pang of guilt in his eyes, but I playfully nudged him sideways. "Hey! It's not your fault, and I did take a pain reliever, so… I'm fine."

"So you're… what? Tired? We can rest here," he suggested, motioning a hand carelessly.

I looked around us. We were past those arrow signs that informed us the way to our destination. The path was narrow; the ground was littered with grasses and dried golden and brown leaves from the previous autums; huge and slim trees, as well as thick short and tall bushes, were on either side of the trail. The leaves were in different sizes and shades of green, from light to dark. To our left was the downwards slope area, whereas to the right was the higher ground.

Far down the left side was the city of Brașov. We could see the rust-coloured roofs of houses and establishments—the dominant colour of medieval edifices, especially. The sky was blue with thin stratus clouds that scattered way up above us.

When I laid my eyes on Maksimillian, I noticed his perspiration. Mine was also obvious now, but I pulled out a wet wipe from the package to refresh my face. I offered him one, and he took it to wipe his face and neck. I couldn't help but chuckle. We didn't really care about it when we were in the *act*, but this was different since we were outside. Or it was just my opinion.

I shoved the package back to my small backpack and offered him some water. He declined, since he had his own backpack and supplies. He, in fact, drank the blue-coloured energy drink like a thirsty camel. I just watched him guzzle it with fascination—his Adam's apple bobbing up and down his throat.

I didn't know what came over me, but I tiptoed to kiss his neck. He froze when he felt my warm lips on his heated skin. He swallowed the last of the liquid and inserted the empty bottle in the pocket of his backpack while staring at me.

Before I knew what he'd do next, he pulled me close to him, half carrying my body to his. He scooped me by the back of my thighs, walked a few steps, and rested my back against the giant trunk of an unknown tree. It was hard, and the gnarled bark was uncomfortable against my back, but I didn't mind at all, since my thoughts were merely on Maksimillian while my legs wrapped around his waist.

"I shouldn't have let you wear these jeans!" he whispered, kissing the side of my jaw and neck.

I chortled a little. "I should wear at least some decent clothing to hike. I can't go around naked, don't you think?" I purred at him.

He groaned and chuckled without mirth though. "You're such a tease, giving me that naked picture in my mind," he uttered huskily. He slightly nibbled the skin of my neck and sucked it tenderly.

I shivered in response to his playful kiss. "We can't do it here anyway. What if others are on the trail?" My eyes closed, and I sighed in surrender to him.

"The bushes are thick enough to hide us, and this tree will most definitely give us the right ambience. What do you think?" His suggestive husky tone was teasing and alluring. He glanced at the giant tree that could positively hide us from anyone's eyes, since it could hide at least three people. Besides, it was on a higher ground and a few steps off the trail.

My eyes went round, looking at him in disbelief. "Seriously?"

"Well, I'm just suggesting. Let's face it, Zenovia. You're horny as I am," he elaborated bluntly in a whisper. Then, his tongue trailed down my throat, before kissing my chin and covering my lips with his.

And I was lost in the moment.

He put me down the ground to unzip my jeans and his. We also put our bags down to be more comfortable. Right after that, he turned me around with my jeans halfway down my thighs. He guided my body to bend over slightly, and he unceremoniously drove his hard and huge member inside me without foreplay, hands holding me by the waist.

We both groaned when our bodies united once again. He was careful not to penetrate too deep, and I was touched by his thoughtfulness.

"Oh, Zenovia!"

"Maks..." I whispered back.

The birds' chirps and our low moans were the only sounds we could hear. I thought it was the most natural thing that could happen at the moment.

I felt him go faster and deeper as time went by. At least, it wasn't painful because of the medication I took before we hiked.

Maksimillian's hand went down to my front to tease my bud. He stroked me there while he pummelled my body with his delightful hot rod. Oh, *Doamne!* I felt like I was going to burst anytime soon.

"Maks!" I groaned louder when I reached the peak; my hands grabbed the tree bark so hard that I thought my nails dug into it.

I heard him grunt, knowing that he already sprayed his seeds inside me. I felt it even more when some of it dripped down my thighs.

We were both panting when he pulled out. He picked up my bag to take out a couple of wet wipes to clean me and himself.

"Are you fine?" he asked in a gentle tone and eyes. Then, he kissed my lips softly.

Keepsake

Zenovia

We stood behind the Braşov sign about ten minutes or so later. The picturesque views across the hills were truly amazing.

"This is worth the little effort we had," I told Maksimillian smilingly.

I had no idea if what I felt right now would have been the same if I went alone.

He put an arm around my shoulders and kissed my temple. At the same time, he took a selfie of us, with the city below us as the backdrop. I didn't actually expect he'd do it. I wanted to tell him to delete it, but maybe he would after this. He wouldn't keep it, would he? Especially after the deal. We agreed, and he signed it.

"I have a favour to ask you, by the way. It may sound weird."

I stared at his face. His arm was still around me as he gazed down at my face.

"What is it?" I asked, almost anxious for some reason.

He gave me a naughty grin of his. And then, he whispered into my right ear, "I want to record your moans."

Heat rushed to my face, and I blinked many times with my mouth gaping open. "W-what did you say?"

"I can't resist it. I want to record the moment if you'll let me."

"Why?" I asked him, face beet red. I even pushed him away.

"I want a keepsake from you, Zenovia," he articulated with a no-nonsense tone.

I stared at him for a minute long before shaking my head. I could not believe he was asking me this. Wasn't it like a creepy idea? I mean, yes. There were many pornographic videos, of course, but him having to keep such a record? I was astounded!

"Zenovia, look. You'll have my child. It's more than a keepsake from me. But me? What about me? I'd want something from you, too."

I blinked many times while staring at him. I could not believe he'd put it that way. It was sort of a blackmail or maybe a trade to put it lightly. But then, why? And I did ask him again.

"Because I love the way you moan, all right? I want to hear it even if we're far apart, when the time comes. I want to at least remember you."

"Maksimillian…" I could only whisper.

The wind blew and carried his name to somewhere. My heart was beating so hard inside my chest. I tried to push the lump in my throat, swallowing hard and averting my flickering eyes.

'He wants something to remember me by? In that way? But why? Can I let him?'

My sense of seeing swept the rust-coloured buildings down below us. Some streets were busy, with cars and other vehicles lining up. A barking of the dog from somewhere broke the silence between us.

I thought of his request for a long moment when my cell phone rang. As it was, this area was blessed with great coverage for communication by four major service providers in the country.

Maksimillian took a deep breath and looked away as well. I fished out the cell phone from my jeans front pocket. He absently regarded the view before us, while I answered Antonia's call.

"Hey! Have you found a man yet?" she asked me directly, as if she had eyes somewhere here.

"Uh… yes." I couldn't lie to her even if I wanted to.

She squealed, so I put the phone far from my ears for some moments. "Oh, my God! So? How is it? How is he? Tell me, is he a shower or a grower?"

My brows creased, while I listened to her bombarding me with questions such as these. "Antonia, what does it even mean?" I inquired with frustration and irritation.

"Hey. Didn't you listen to me before? If he's a shower, his member is the same size as his normal one. If he's a grower, you know, he's way bigger than his original size." She giggled after explaining it to me.

I sighed, rolling my eyes. "Why would you even want to know? Besides, what reason do I have to tell you that? *Doamne ferește!*" I answered, gesturing a hand and shrugging helplessly.

She laughed at me. "I was just asking, hoping you'd share your experience. Can't I even be curious? So, how was it? I'm sure you already did it!"

I cleared my throat while I felt myself blushing. I chewed my inner cheek and looked away when my eyes met Maksimillian's. There was no hiding that he listened to my end of the conversation. I only stood a couple feet away from him.

'But he doesn't understand Romanian, does he?'

"We're... uh... hiking. In fact, we're now behind the Brașov sign!"

"Oh! Really? You went there without me?" she gasped. She hadn't mentioned she wanted to come here, too.

"What am I supposed to do without you here?" I put a hand on my waist, looking up at the blue sky.

"Sure, of course, of course! You can also go to Dracula's Castle with him if you want."

I caught bitterness in her tone though. "What do you mean by that? I thought you were coming tomorrow or the next day after that."

"Total change of plans! At least for me, Zen. I can't go there and have a vacation with you at all. My colleague's health suddenly deteriorated, and I have to take care of her patients in addition to mine. So, that's why I actually am calling you now, to tell you this."

My face fell. "What?"

"I'm so sorry, Zen. You have to take this vacation without me. But, hey! It's not so bad. You have him... What's his name, by the way?"

"Um... I call him Maks."

I saw Maksimillian smirk when he glanced at me, hearing his nickname. What could I do? I couldn't lie to my best friend. I couldn't tell her about Maksimillian's manhood though—that it was really huge. It was personal for heaven's sakes! *Doamne fereşte!* Besides, I didn't want to go into details with her. But could I get away with it when Antonia was my OB-GYN?

'Oh, God!'

"Anyway, as long as you have lubricant, that is if you're dry... it would help you enjoy your *time* with him," she said, before telling me she'd hang up.

Căcat! Right. She did tell me that. Maybe I should use some, since she put it in my travelling bag herself, just in case. I had forgotten about it. How stupid could I be? But maybe I didn't need it. For now. I was soaking when Maks and I did it anyway.

I looked at Maksimillian guiltily. After his request, I didn't even look at him properly. Now, I had nothing to do after the call.

I prodded the invisible lump in my throat and spoke, "I-is it really important for you t-to record... me?"

He stepped closer to me and tilted my face by holding my chin with his strong fingers. He blocked my view of the blue sky when he bent his head to capture my lips with his own.

"I wouldn't ask if it wasn't," he whispered, looking deep into my eyes.

Lunch Date

Maksimillian

Zenovia and I went down by a cable car ride. The stunning view of Brașov City was a memorable one, especially that I had the most beautiful local girl with me, all to myself. We did drink some refreshments at a bar on Mount Tâmpa. We stayed there to take in the beautiful landscapes. We took pictures and videos to document our time there.

Now, I watched Zenovia's face. She watched the details of the cityscape from this angle. We passed by over thick and dark green conifer trees. The dull yellow and brownish red buildings were so close to each other; their heights varied. Some castle towers with conical roofs looked imposing even at this distance. There were also scattered buildings on nearby hills. I guessed some of them were old fortresses and some establishments or private residences.

Romania was rich, especially historically speaking. It had undergone a lot of wars in the past, and everything was just interesting in my point of view. Its people's origin was said to be an ethnic mixture, the Thracians with their Geto-Dacian branch and the well-known Romans. Hence, we could obviously see the unique and different features of Romanians even nowadays.

Although the economy is somewhere in the middle, the country had nearly forty percent of population that was at high possibility of being trapped in poverty—thus the reason why many Romanians were expats. They were scattered all over the world, working their asses off to put food on their family's table.

I helped Zenovia out of the cable car when it stopped. We hailed a taxi to bring us to a Japanese restaurant. I guessed she would want to have something different, so I thought of it.

I was glad she looked excited to try some *sushi* and other things. She especially loved all the *sushi* and the *shabu shabu* (soup with udon noodles, rib eye steak, cabbage, mushrooms, and other spices and vegetables).

I was somehow touched when she took pictures of the food we ordered before she helped herself with everything. She also took some photos of the place, specifically the unique interior design. There were hanging plants near the wall.

To the left side of the restaurant from the entrance, dim white lights were aimed from the floor upwards to the wall where the hanging plants were. On the opposite wall, it had an aquarium-like graffiti, with some seaweeds, colourful fish of different types and sizes, and shells. Meanwhile, the rectangular tables were set in three rows to the right of the establishment. However, Zenovia and I took one of the VIP cubicles to the far side opposite the doorway. It was a small square room with an open doorway that faced the main entrance. A table was in the middle, and Zenovia and I sat opposite from each other.

"Let me," she said when the bill was given to us by a dark-haired girl in her twenties. She had a light makeup on and was mostly staring at me than at Zenovia. But I didn't mind it. I was already used to women gawking at me even in Russia.

Zenovia took her wallet to pay half of the bill. I gave her a look of disapproval.

"Zenovia, I am the one who's taking you here—"

"Remember our deal?" she pointed out.

My jaw hung. "This has nothing to do with it," I protested and ground my teeth. I did my best not to raise my voice.

Zenovia was adamant. She put half of my money back on the table, put hers on the small basket and gave it to the server with a smile, saying her thanks in their language—at least, I knew that much. I knew of some Romanian words, but I mainly knew how to speak German, French, and English, so that I could use them when dealing with international clients.

"*Mulțumesc mult* (Thank you very much)!"

"*Cu plăcere* (You're welcome)," the woman replied, glancing at me before turning on her heels to leave us.

I stared at Zenovia with an irritated look. "Where do you want to go after this?" I asked instead, trying to make my voice steady.

We both stood up and started to leave the restaurant, with me holding a plastic with a couple of takeaways for our dinner. We chose the different types of *sushi*: *hosomaki, nigiri, maki, chirashi, temaki, uramaki,* and *mekajiki.*

"I'll buy something, so you can just go get your rented car in the meantime," she suggested.

I raised an eyebrow while tapping my fingers unconsciously on the plastic I was holding. Her eyes went there, but she did not comment.

"Where am I going to pick you up?" I queried, recalling that we left the car near where we started to hike.

"Maybe at the Irish pub we went to yesterday?" she told me.

I saw the heat crawl on her cheeks, and she looked away, chewing her inner cheek. I chuckled lightly and caught her small waist. "I'll see you later then," I whispered and gave her a peck on the cheek.

She quickly glanced around us, slightly embarrassed. However, other people who saw us just smiled and got on with their own business.

***

As I drove the rented car, I noticed my bodyguards following me. During the hike, I instructed them not to bother. I wanted to have Zenovia all to myself. And that was lucky enough. I got time to have sex with her in the woods. It wasn't I'd normally do, but I couldn't just resist her.

Now I was looking forward to another night with her.

Aunt Marisha did tease me this morning when she met me in the wide hallway of the hotel when I returned there to change. She was on her way to have her breakfast at the restaurant. She rarely had room service sent up to her suite. She wanted to meet other people. Well, that was her. She loved to socialize, which was a headache for my cousin. She was just a social butterfly.

"Why don't you check out and just check in to her hotel instead?" she suggested playfully with a grin on her beautiful face.

I took a glimpse of the two bodyguards I assigned for her protection. They wore casual clothes and were discreetly standing in a corner, talking to each other in hushed tones. My aunt glanced at them, and there was a knowing look in her eyes. Okay, she must have already learned these were her security details but just didn't complain to me.

"I just might do that. Thanks for the advice," I answered her and went into my room.

I shook my head when I recalled that scene earlier.

Now, I scanned the street where I was supposed to meet Zenovia. I wondered where she'd gone to after our lunch.

My hands held the wheel tighter when I saw her near the Irish pub, talking with a man and laughing.

'Chert poberi! *Did she get rid of me in the pretext of fetching my car, so that she can be with another man?'*

Forced Shopping

Maksimillian

I turned the hazards on and parked the car, ignoring the glances of some people at the vehicle and me. I strode quickly and held Zenovia's arm. She gasped, did not expect I'd be there.

"Maks!" she breathed and turned to the man she was talking with. She was talking fast in Romanian, while the man in his early thirties was staring at me. A small grin curved on his lips before saying something to Zenovia.

I didn't get what they talked about. I only knew a few words, and they definitely weren't included in their conversation. He then walked away reluctantly, seeing me still holding Zenovia's arm.

"Let go, Maks." She took her arm back almost roughly.

I did let go, afraid I'd bruise her. "Who was that? Did you just spend your time with him while I took the car for almost an hour?"

She gave me a confused look. "What are you talking about? Florin is my best friend's ex-boyfriend, and he happened to see me here. He just told me he moved here for personal reason."

I gave her a measuring look. That was when I noticed she held a black plastic printed with a known brand's name on it that sold sexy underwear. She held it together with her navy blue backpack.

"You... were shopping underwear?"

Her face turned scarlet. "Obviously. What did you think? That I—"

"Why didn't you tell me? I should've gone with you," I cut her off.

Her jaw dropped. "Maksimillian!"

I sniggered and crossed my arms on my chest, giving her a teasing and naughty look. "Do I get to see you wear any of them? I'm sure there are at least a few of them in there." I glanced at the plastic to make a point.

"It's none of your business!" she hissed.

"Should we get in and have some drink before going back to the hotel?"

"You can't park your car there!" she admonished me, eyes bulging upon seeing the car with its hazard lights blinking continuously.

"It's your fault. If your local authority demands that I pay—"

Her round eyes kept scolding me. "Let's go back to the hotel!"

Actually, I didn't care if I'd shed some hundreds or even thousands of *lei* for traffic violation and whatnot.

I smiled diabolically to tease her more and opened the door for her at the front passenger seat. I went around to get behind the wheel and maneuvered the car out of that street and back to the main road, going to my hotel instead of hers. But before that, I was planning on taking her to a boutique to buy her some clothes.

"Where are we going?"

"I thought I'd show you my suite," I answered with a grin.

"Why? Are you planning on something that's—"

"Since you didn't let me pay for our lunch date, I thought I'd buy you clothes and shoes instead."

"What? I don't need you to buy me clothes or shoes. Besides, it wasn't a lunch date," she disagreed.

"You're not asking me to buy you clothes or shoes, but I'm going to. So, it has nothing to do with our deal. Got it?" I glanced at her with warning in my eyes.

She clamped her mouth and stared at me for a few moments before looking away, heaving. She didn't like the idea of me buying her anything. That was more than obvious. But why didn't she want it? I was giving her things out of the goodness of my heart, not to make her feel indebted to me or anything. Did she happen to think it this way?

"But before that, let's go to a notary office," she said, glancing at her wristwatch. She took out her cell phone and searched for the closest one that was open at this hour. She gave me the address, so I entered it on the GPS.

***

It took us almost an hour to have the documents printed and notarized. At least, we did not have to come back to retrieve the papers.

The office was small and was near a shopping mall. Beside it was a row of other establishments, such as a photocopier, a flower shop, and a school supplies store. The front wall was made of glass, where the name of the notary office was written in bold and in red colour— *Popa Elena, Birou Notar Public* (Popa Elena, Notary Public Office).

When we were back inside the car, where it was parked just across the street of the notary office, Zenovia gave me a copy of the notarized document. I slowly accepted it while looking at her and before glancing at it. I had no idea what I felt then, but it was some kind of surreal. That I was into this agreement officially and legally.

'Will I never see her again once she got pregnant with my child?' I wondered.

I didn't want to analyse what I was feeling at this very moment. They were mixed, so I guessed I couldn't identify them so well and might be wrong.

***

Approximately fifteen minutes later, I found the boutique near the hotel I checked in. I parked in front of it, ignoring my bodyguards that tailed us.

I held Zenovia's hand. I guided her inside the well-known French fashion brand store. Since the front was made of glass, we could clearly see all the rows of racks where dresses, shirts, skirts, and others were displayed. It was air conditioned inside when we stepped in. I swept my eyes to the left, where the dresses on hangers were arranged on the racks.

I ushered Zenovia there, holding the small of her back. She turned her head to look at me.

"You want me to choose the dresses?"

"I can tell you only wear a dress when it's necessary. I've already seen you in it, and it seems you're more comfortable in jeans and shirt, just like today. But I prefer you to wear dresses." I bent my head to whisper in her ear, "At least, while we're in this deal, I want to see you in dresses I bought for you." I straightened and smiled at her.

Zenovia's face turned pink. "I don't need dresses!" It was the second time she hissed at me. When she realised what she just said, I chuckled at her embarrassment. She must have realised she implied being naked in that statement. "You know it's not what I meant, Maksimillian! *La naiba* (Damn it)!" she protested to supply her previous line, giving me an irritated stare. "I just don't want to—"

"To be indebted to me. Is that it, Zenovia?" I asked her promptly with a serious face this time. There was no more teasing on my end.

She stared at me, and we both ignored the salesladies that cast their concerned look in our direction. Maybe they thought we were fighting. And I believed we did!

"Yes!" She gritted her teeth without looking at me. Her breast went up and down as she breathed.

I held her by the nape, so she was forced to look at me. "Are we going to make a scene here? Because I don't mind."

"Maksimillian!" She looked alarmed and afraid for some reason. Definitely, she didn't want to cause any scene.

"Are we going to shop you dresses or not?" I questioned her once and for all.

"All right!" she answered through gritted teeth.

I knew that I blackmailed her, but I wasn't sorry. I just wanted to gift her something. Was it wrong?

And yes, I admitted to myself. I was doing this, so that she would not forget me easily.

Withdrawal

Maksimillian

I waited for Zenovia to try on the dresses I thought would look good on her. Well, maybe every dress was going to.

She came out of the thick gold-curtained fitting room to show me. Her two hands were on her waist. Obviously, she was not into this shopping spree at all. But still, she tried to just go along with it to avoid any consequences.

I roved my eyes up and down to appraise her beauty in a light blue backless short lace dress. The hem was about three inches above her knees. The mirror showed me her uncovered back, making me think of her nakedness and her writhing body beneath mine while calling out my name as if in a litany.

"You look perfect!" I smiled at her with great satisfaction and admiration.

My phone suddenly buzzed, so I took it from the left front pocket of my jeans. I saw it was my cousin, who was calling. I immediately wondered what was going on.

I raised an index finger at Zenovia, and she sighed. She marched back to the fitting room where a dozen more dresses waited for her to be tried on. I watched her swaying round buttocks and small waist that I could span with my two hands, until she disappeared behind the gold curtain. That dress was really perfect on her.

"*Da, Rurik, chto takoye* (Yes, Rurik, what is it)?" I asked him in Russian, eyebrows meeting.

"There's something you need to know."

"What?" I almost snapped. It wasn't like him to drag a subject, unless he had a reason for it. In his opinion, that is.

"We... lost a couple of Turkish clients over Chinese steel suppliers. They're not renewing their contract with us. Our sales will surely plummet next month, and until we find new ones to replace them."

We were supposed to meet these clients next week. My cousin promised he'd take care of it while I was having my vacation with his mother. We were confident everything would push through then. But now, it all went down the drain.

"What? *Chert poberi!* (Damn it!) All of a sudden? Those Turkish clients have been with us for years!" I could not believe it. Something must have happened or just came up that they decided to opt for another steel supplier. Good thing about these specific Turkish clients, our contracts always ran two years at a time, not just a year.

"Well, true. But business is business, cousin. You know that so well. The largest steel exporter apparently offered better prices as we all know it, and the Turkish clients decided to go in different direction this time. I guess the temptation is too strong!" Rurik concluded.

I cursed in my head a few times, rubbing my face with my free hand. My cousin suggested some things, which I thought was fine, so I gave him my approval. After all, he was the co-owner of the Frolov-Usmanov Inc. He would want nothing but the success for our company just as I do. We both always did what we thought was good for it. Just that he asked me to do my part as well, which I would despite the fact that I hesitated because of my current predicament with Zenovia.

If I told her I'd go for now and would come back in a few days, would she wait for me and not cancel our agreement? After all, it was already notarized. We were already legally bound by it no matter what.

But what if she wouldn't get pregnant despite our efforts? It hadn't occurred to me just yet. 'Til now. We hadn't talked about this matter, so I must bring it up to her later.

Just after I finished talking with Rurik, Zenovia stepped out of the fitting room to show me a dusty green floral print maxi dress—if I was not mistaken, as the salesladies discussed it earlier. The dress had breezy ankle-length maxi skirt, which had mid-thigh high side slits and an elasticized back. The top part of it was elasticized as well, with ruffled and off-the-shoulder straps. The dress brought out her perfect figure and sensuality.

I smiled at her to let her know I loved the dress on her. She protruded her lips and chewed on her inner cheek again, giving me a semi-hostile look. She still didn't enjoy this shopping thing with me. Now I wondered what type of new underwear she bought. I would like to check them out if she'd let me. But well, maybe I needed not to, since she would most probably use them while we were together.

She went back in and out of the fitting room the next half an hour or so. I didn't mind waiting though, because everytime she emerged, she looked stunning!

"So, which one are you going to buy for me?" she asked after fitting the last dress, which was a sleeveless beige crochet lace mini dress. It had pierced accents that were eye-catching and had spaghetti straps.

Instead of answering her, I called the attention of the salesladies. Both came up to us, leaving a couple of clients that were still busy checking out some items.

"We'll take all of these and the shoes, too." I gestured at everything that Zenovia tried on.

They were both quick to take the items to the cashier, while Zenovia gaped at me as though she'd seen something baffling.

"Y-you...?"

"Yes. I can very well afford to buy you clothes and shoes, so don't fuss, okay?"

"B-but—"

I held her by the nape and shut her up by kissing her lips. She tried to resist but eventually responded to me, which made me smirk. I left her mouth to gaze at her beautiful grey eyes.

"Just stop arguing with me, *moye solntse*," I whispered. Our lips were just an inch or so away.

I held her hand and led her to the cashier. The cashier took off the anti-theft tag of the dress that Zenovia wore. The clothes she wore earlier when we hiked were in one of the shopping bags. One of the salesladies helped us out to place the bags in the backseat of my rented car. I gave her a tip, for her and her co-worker.

The pretty saleslady in her twenties gave me a wide smile and thanked me, telling us to come back. Well, I doubted it. My shopping companion was not so eager. Besides, she was not from around here. Her real address said so in the notarized document. If not, I'd just pull some strings to get it. I did not need to anyway.

"So, you seem busy," Zenovia commented.

The car sped to the hotel where I checked in. She looked at me when I turned my head to glance at her.

'Oh, is she starting to get curious about me and what I do?'

"Oh, that! My cousin called and told me some serious problem at the company, so we have to send an employee to Finland. Just that I thought I'd better go there myself. While we're on this matter, I'm letting you know that I'm going to be out of Romania for a few days. Will you be here when I come back, Zenovia?"

Just To Be Clear

Maksimillian

"What? You're leaving?" Zenovia's brows furrowed.

"Are you concerned I may not come back? That I'd break our deal even if you now know my address in Russia?"

I slowed down and parked the car in front of the four-storey hotel, which overlooked most parts of the city. The glittering golden and white lights that formed into random curvy or straight lines were breathtaking.

Zenovia's eyes wavered when I looked at her again. The engine of the car was already off, but the overhead lights were still on.

"I can't… I won't and I don't have the means to come after you despite the notarized agreement. It's the reality for me. I was just hoping you'd be a man of your word, and you'd honour our agreement."

"Which I still have to prove to you." I nodded. "You'll see then."

Zenovia stared into my eyes, and I held her gaze. I had no plans of looking away. I wouldn't. It was almost like I could see her heart in her eyes. At least, how she felt at the moment. It was reflected in those intense-looking grey eyes of hers that seemed to pull me to her. Her fear. Her doubt.

I cupped her face, still looking deep into her striking orbs. "I just need to do my job, Zenovia, but I will be back, okay? I promise."

"But you said you have an employee that you can send to Finland, so why do you have to go?"

The corners of my lips slowly lifted into a smile. "Are you being clingy right now?" I teased her.

She smacked my hands away. "Of course not! I'm just asking. You can go to hell for all I care! I can just find another man to give me a baby! Someone who's not as complicated as you."

My smile faded instantly. She was about to get out of the car, but I held her fast before she could even open the door.

"Don't you dare find another man to give you that baby you want, Zenovia! We have a deal! *I* will give you what you fucking want! Okay?" With one hand, I held her jaw firmly but not to the point of hurting her. I just wanted to make her look at me and let her see how serious I was.

Without any other thought, I slammed my lips to hers and darted my tongue inside her mouth when she gave me access to it. I could feel my member go rigid almost immediately, upon feeling her kiss me back.

"Maks..." She sighed in surrender.

"Zenovia! Never doubt me again, all right?" I spoke through gritted teeth when I paused kissing her.

I saw tears spill from her peepers, and they raced down her cheeks.

"Why are you crying?" I asked, even more concerned.

"I-I don't know. I... I just want you, Maksimillian..." she whispered and cried.

God of heavens!

I quickly got out of the car to open the door for her. I grabbed the takeaways and a couple of paper bags I could get from the backseat with one hand, and the other held Zenovia by the wrist. We marched through the open entrance and the cozy lobby, going straight to the lifts. There was nobody at the reception area, but I didn't care, though it was a wonder why. Anyway, inside the lift, Zenovia was quiet and did not look at me. Instead, she just stared at the number of the floor as we ascended to the last floor, where my suite was.

As soon as the lift dinged and opened, I almost dragged Zenovia down the hallway. Our steps echoed in the quiet well-lit place, passing through closed doors. Before ending up to the last room, I stopped and put the bags down to open the door of my suite.

She looked around us, taking all in the cream-coloured walls that were bare and the red-carpeted hallway. The recessed cool white lights on the ceiling lined up in interval, with a distance of a meter or so. The doors had a uniform colour of mahogany.

Noticeably, two doors opposite to mine had "Do Not Disturb" red sign hanging on the doorknobs. When I glanced at my aunt's room, it was bare. It only meant she was out to explore the city or some tourist spots near or outside Brașov. At least, she entertained herself even without me, and she had not burdened my conscience for leaving her all alone.

As soon as I slid the keycard, the door opened. I pushed it open and switched the lights on. With it, the air conditioning turned on automatically. I slightly pushed Zenovia to go inside while I grabbed the shopping bags. I dropped them on the floor to take the red sign to hang it on the doorknob outside to let the staff and others know to not disturb me.

Or rather, us.

Zenovia stepped back to admire the spacious rectangular suite. The king-size bed was in the middle with its headboard almost against the wall. The huge bed was covered by silver-grey bedsheet. The pillowcases were also of the same colour, leaning neatly against the headboard.

The walls were in pastel yellow. Above the headboard of the bed was a rectangular Japanese painting of some colourful landscape with trees and flowers. It looked airy, breezy, and sunny. I could feel the happy and positive vibe of the painting. It was also what I felt right now while I was with Zenovia.

I watched her sweep her eyes to the left, where the bathroom was; next to it was the dressing room with the walk-in closet. On the opposite side, to our right, was a white living room set, with a couple of single couches that faced a long couch. These had white leather upholstery, with three grey-coloured throw pillows arranged neatly in a line. The center table was made of glass, and a small crystal flower vase stood in the middle with a white tulip in it. Meanwhile, a flat TV was mounted on the wall that faced the long couch.

Zenovia turned away from me to face the glass wall, after checking out everything in the room. The white curtains were not drawn, so we both could see the stunning sight of the night cityscape of Brașov. The hills had occasional, scattered lights that came from some edifices or homes. The golden and white lights that formed random lines and curves were lively and could take anyone's breath away.

"It's so beautiful here!" she whispered happily.

I was already behind her and encaged her gently between my arms. I bent my head to kiss her left cheek.

"We can leave the curtains open while I'll please you. Or not. Your choice. No one can see us up here anyway," I whispered into her ear before nibbling the lobe.

She slowly turned her head to hold my gaze. "Yes, we can leave them be." Her lips parted, and she closed her eyes to wait for my lips to cover hers.

Hot Moans

Maksimillian

I was about to kiss her when her phone rang.

"*Căcat* (Crap)!" she whispered an oath.

I didn't even know what it meant, but I got the gist. Her eyes went wildly to her bag that she was still holding. I recalled she transferred it there before trying on the dresses earlier. Now, she fished it out of the pocket of the bag and signalled me to not speak.

"*Da, Mămică,*" she answered.

'*Ah, her mum's calling.*' I rubbed my face with my hands and let Zenovia talk with her mother. I crossed the carpeted floor; my steps were quiet. I took the plastic with takeaways and placed them on the center table instead. After that, I went to the bathroom to take a quick shower.

Zenovia was done talking to her mother when I stepped out of the white-tiled bathroom with only a grey towel wrapped around my hips. She appraised my look before averting her eyes.

"Are you hungry?" I asked her.

"No, not really. I just need a drink and maybe a shower. I feel sticky," she answered, looking embarrassed.

I chuckled and went to the minibar to get her some canned drink. I opened the peach juice can to pour the content into a tall glass. I beckoned her by my finger to come to me to get her drink, which she obliged. I stole a kiss on her lips before I handed her the drink. Certainly, I could not take my eyes off of her, and she smiled.

"Thanks for this," she murmured and drank half of the content.

She gasped when I started to take off her dress. However, she did not protest and let me continue doing it. She finished her drink at last, and she was all naked, except for her undies that she wanted to keep on. I definitely knew and understand the the reason why.

Her medium-sized breasts were perfect; so were her small waist and round hips.

Just how exquisite she is!' I thought helplessly.

"Should I join you in the shower? I don't mind taking it again," I suggested to her with a seductive smile on my peach-coloured lips.

She just smiled at me toothlessly. Something in her eyes told me to follow her when she turned around to head for the bathroom. Before I forgot, I took my phone with me. As soon as she saw me with it, she did not comment. Anyway, she already gave me her permission to record the sound of our encounter, as I requested.

"Did you take a pain reliever?" I asked with concern, knowing that she needed it before our contact.

"Yes, with the drink."

I calculated the time she'd be fine then. I would need to give her a long foreplay to be more comfortable.

We both soon forgot that I tapped the button to voice record. I placed the gadget near the sink, and I started kissing her while cupping her face. My already rigid member was grinding against her belly. We both moaned softly at the delicious sensation we felt right now.

I removed my towel to put it on the tiled counter that was connected to the sink. Not long after, I helped her with taking off her undies that had the sanitary pad without really looking at it. Instead, I just dropped it into the trash bin.

I then slowly guided Zenovia into the shower cubicle and turned the valve on. I helped her with soaping and rinsing her body under the running warm water, taking care of cleaning up her center as she preferred. At the same time, I was already stroking her erotically, arousing her even more.

I turned off the warm water of the shower and resumed kissing her lips. I thrust my tongue inside her mouth to explore inside and to duel with hers. I caught it and sucked it mercilessly, making her mewl.

"Maks..." she whispered breathlessly in between kisses.

My already hard cock poked her abdominal area while I played with her lips. I sucked and nibbled her lower lip. Again and again. During this time, my one hand went down to caress her already damp sex, and it had nothing to do with the shower. I separated her lips down there with my fingers. I moved my hand up and down, teasing the small nub with my fingers time and time again.

I felt her knees wobble, so I scooped her behind the knees and back to carry her out of the shower cubicle. I sat her gently on the counter of the sink with my towel underneath her butt.

Almost without any ceremony, I pulled her legs up and pushed them apart, planting the balls of her feet on the edge of the counter. She was wide open for my admiration and inspection. I could see the glistening part of her womanhood.

She was apparently aroused. But I needed her to be more ready than this. It was too soon. I did not want her to moan in pain but in pleasure.

I bent forward, holding and stroking her inner thighs to keep her legs apart while I kissed her center.

"Oh, Maks!" she exclaimed, as soon as my lips touched her wetness.

I sucked, nibbled, and kissed her there, earning me hot and sexy moans from her. Her hands went to hold my head, fingers burying in my still wet hair. I ran my tongue over her slit, laving and nipping it.

"Ahh!" she moaned louder. It echoed in the four corners of the spacious bathroom. Her heavy breathing told me she was close to the edge.

While kissing her center, my thumb found the apex part and teased it lightly by making circles on it. I continued to stroke it while my tongue teased her entrance.

"Oh, *Doamne!*" she whimpered. I loved her panting and squirming.

But it was not enough. I wanted her fully aroused and near the highest peak of her desire. And then, I could let her hold it to prolong her sweet torture, before I would let her cum around my thrusting member.

I went on to lick her delicious femininity. I sucked one vertical lip and nipped it, like I had all the time in the world. I transferred to the other lip, giving it the same affectionate attention. It made her body quiver, and another set of sexy moans came out from her throat. Oh, how I so loved that sound coming from her!

I stroked intensely her now plump bud that resulted to her endless wiggling. But I did not let her cum by pressing that nub. Her body still quavered though, and her core throbbed. I could feel it against my lips that were wet with her nectar and my own saliva.

"Maks…" Her tone was begging. "Ohh…"

I lapped up her moistened femininity. Then, I nibbled, nipped, and sucked it in varied pressure. I teased her entrance again with the tip of my tongue, earning me a sexier whimper. She really wanted me inside her now—I just knew it.

With hooded eyes, I met her own smokey ones. Our lips were parted, and we both breathed unevenly.

I straightened up a bit but dipped my head to give her a hard kiss on the mouth. I let her savour her own nectar mixed with my own taste. She moaned while kissing me with equal passion.

As she was busily kissing me back, I poised the head of my cock at the entrance of her core. She moaned deeper when she felt my tip and moved her hips, urging me to push inside. Apparently, she could not wait any longer.

To not be dismayed, I gave her what she wanted. I sunk my furious rigid manhood inside her very depths. She was hot, slick, and wet. It was great, for both our pleasure.

"Ahh! Maks!" she whimpered sexily. She grabbed me by the shoulders.

I pulled out and entered her with a single stroke. And then, I paused to look at her face.

"Are you okay?"

When she nodded and swallowed, I withdrew again and plunged deep into her.

"How about now?" I asked her again.

"It's okay. Don't ask me every single time, Maksimillian. I'll tell you if and when it's painful, okay?"

"Alright, alright. I just—"

She grabbed me by the head and kissed me hard, to shut my mouth. I could not help but smile while kissing her back. She was one fiery, horny woman!

And well, I could not complain about that.

I thrust into her again. And again. And again. Numerous times. It was hard and fast like I wanted—and the way she loved it.

I pumped harder into her sexy body, pulling up her legs up to rest against my shoulders. My left hand came up to touch her right breast, kneading it while basking in its softness. Oh, how good it was to touch her like this. Her moans got louder and louder with the intensity of my plunges.

"*O, Bozhe* (Oh, God)!" I exclaimed, panting hard.

With it, she whimpered more and more. And yet, my hardness stroked her tight inner walls continuously, creating delicious friction.

I pumped harder, countless times.

Until she screamed upon hitting the apogee of her pleasure.

I felt her hot lava envelop my steely manhood. But I did not stop thrusting her, so she continued to cry, body squirming. She grabbed my shoulders tighter, telling me it was too intense for her. We both breathed hard. And yet, I kept on pumping her hard and fast.

After some more moments, I buried my rod to the deepest I could. "Ughh!" I grunted when I released my load inside her. "Zenovia!" I bent my head to lock my lips with hers, though both of us were still short-winded.

'Oh, God! I think I'm fucking in love with her already…'

Surprise?

Zenovia

It was the second day Maksimillian was out of sight. I had been with him for what? Just a couple days? I could not believe myself that I was already attached to him, like we had known each other for years, and I missed him like this.

No, it wasn't just about sex. It was his presence. His companionship.

I missed his voice... the way he talked...

I missed his eyes... the way he looked at me... the way he closed them when he reached his climax.

I missed looking at his lips... the way he smiled at me... and of course, the way he kissed me, either the upper set of my lips or the ones down south of my body.

"*Căcat* (Crap)!" I cursed in a whisper.

Erase. Erase! I said nothing about sex, but it all came down to it. And yet, I knew it was more than that, I promise. And I shouldn't, should I? After all, I shouldn't think much about the man who would eventually become my child's father, as I was the one who proposed the no-strings-attached relationship!

"Oh, *Doamne*!" I groaned, rolling to the other side of the bed in his hotel room.

It was already past nine in the morning, but I did not feel like going out today either.

I inhaled deeply, and I could still smell him on the pillow, his expensive musky cologne and his unique masculine aroma. I closed my eyes and just let myself drown in it.

Maksimillian told me to check out of my hotel, and he managed to find someone who sent all my things in his suite. He said he wanted to find me in his room when he's back. If this was being a pushover, maybe I was. But part of me wanted to do this for him, to wait for him where he wanted me… where he could immediately—I don't know—track me, reach me, or something? Because I still didn't give him my phone number, although he gave me his.

"No, I won't call him!" I said aloud, though my voice was drowned in the pillow, where my face was buried.

He had no idea when he could come back, so I was sort of pathetic like a lovesick puppy.

"No! I can't be like this! I have to enjoy my vacation! I have only ten days left to enjoy the city and around it."

I sat up quickly and ran to the bathroom to take a quick shower and change. I decided to wear one of the dresses that Maksimillian bought for me and the underwear I bought. Luckily, I wasn't bleeding anymore.

I planned on having breakfast at the restaurant below while applying a light makeup.

My phone rang suddenly. I was about to go out of the room. Oh, God! My mum was checking up on me again. She had been like this lately, ever since she learned that I had been to the hospital to diagnose what I have. I did not tell her, but my best friend did, because she could not trust me to tell my mother. Antonia thought I would never tell my mum. Well, she was right. I had no plans on telling her, so my doctor took the matter into her own hands, as a concerned friend and my mother's *first* daughter. Insert eye-rolling here.

"*Da, Mămică.* Don't you have any summer class to teach?" I answered in one breath and chewed on my inner cheek.

I remembered to grab my purse. After breakfast, I planned to come back up to brush my teeth and call a taxi while trying to decide where I would want to explore all by myself next. I guessed it would not be too hard to find something interesting. There were a lot of places I could go around here.

"I'm still worried about you, Zenovia," my mother countered right away. "And no. My next class will be this afternoon, so I have a lot of time to talk to my daughter."

"Well, sorry, *Mămică*. I don't have much time. I'm about to go out!"

"Where? I heard you're still in Brașov and that you met a guy! When are you going to tell me this?" she confronted me.

I didn't actually tell her I wasn't in Iași, because I knew she would fuss about it. And I was not wrong. Here she was.

"Antonia told you?"

"Antonia sponsors your vacation. At least, I can tell that much even though she had not told me but only your whereabouts. And this guy. Who is he? Where is he from? Can you tell me?"

"*Mămică*, it's not what you think, okay? I just…" How could I tell her I was merely using this guy to have a baby? She would go mad!

"You're getting to know this guy?"

"Uh… sort of?" I winced at the white lie.

I heard her laugh. "*Bine* (Good)." She was actually happy about this new development in my life. "You just take care of yourself, all right?" She was about to hang up but said, "Text me his name, will you?"

"*Mămică, nu!*" I protested, groaning.

"*Bine, bine* (Fine, fine). *Ai grijă* (Take care). *Pa* (Bye)!"

I blew my breath as a sign of relief.

I opened the door and noticed that the red tag "Do Not Disturb" was still hanging there. I could just gape at it but didn't get to touch it, as a woman's excited voice startled me.

"Oh! You're that girl!" she exclaimed in her Russian accent.

I blinked, recognizing the older blonde woman. She was slim, tall, elegant, and beautiful as I remembered her in The Black Church. She wore a pair of flare-type slacks of colour brown and paired it with the same shade of sleeveless blouse. Her makeup was light, but her thin lips were painted with fuchsia. Hence, they could get attention right away.

"H-hi!" I stammered in a single word.

La naiba! (Damn it!) She saw me going out of her nephew's room with the red tag on the door! Oh, God! Could the floor swallow me now?

Her eyes darted to the said red tag, and she smiled knowingly. I could not define how hot my face was right at this moment.

"I'm Marisha Frolova, Maksimillian's aunt." She went over to me and offered her hand.

I immediately noticed the rings on her three fingers, as well as the glittering bracelets around her wrist. They were all gold, with diamonds as accents and decorations. I could just guess they must worth thousands and thousands of euros. Or more?

'How rich is Maksimillian really?' I began to wonder. Not that I really cared, because I didn't really care about his money. Besides, we only had an agreement to make a baby, and nothing would really matter afterwards, would it?

I did shake Marisha's hand. It was so soft like a baby's. I bet she never worked in her life. Her floral perfume was obviously expensive but strong for my taste. I was glad I didn't make a face because of it. But I was astounded when she suddenly embraced me and kissed me on both cheeks. She then cupped my face and looked at me in the eye.

"You should know I'm thrilled to have you all to myself!"

My jaw dropped. "E-excuse me?" I asked in a low tone, confused.

About Maksimillian

Zenovia

Marisha did not exactly answer my question, but she just dragged me towards the lifts, and we got into one.

"You haven't had breakfast yet, have you?" she asked with a wide smile.

I looked up at her, since she was almost a head taller than me. She wore gold-coloured high heels that were obviously expensive, whereas I wore the golden flat sandals that went well with my printed red-and-gold floral dress. It was a pair that Maksimillian also bought for me.

I shook my head.

"That's great! I wondered when I could talk to you." Marisha smiled sweetly.

"Y-you knew I was in Maks' room?"

She chortled that startled me because of its loudness. I didn't expect she would laugh that loud. Was it natural or she just found something hilarious in what I had just said?

"*Dorogaya* (Darling), I know everything that my son or my nephew is doing!" she told me with amusement in her knowing green eyes.

I felt the heat creep up my face once again because of it. I was speechless and could hardly look at her.

"I may be always out of their sight, but I just know where they are, what they do, who they're with, where they sleep, or what they eat or drink." She gave me a sweet smile, again. But I thought there was something more to it. I must say this woman was scary. And yet, she looked rather charming. It was crazy.

And that somehow chilled me to the bones. For some reason.

"But don't be embarrassed, *dorogaya*. I think you're one special woman for my nephew. Otherwise, you won't be staying in his room," she added, after the lift sounded to warn us that we had reached the ground floor, and its door opened.

My brows met, suspicion growing. Maksimillian must have had a lot of girlfriends.

"May I know what you mean by that?" I tried to clarify while we walked through the lobby and the hallway towards the restaurant. The wall on our right was painted with light blue, while the opposite one that faced the parking lot was made of glass, so there was natural light that streamed in.

"Well, my nephew is a virile man, Zenovia."

What the hell? She knew my name, even though I hadn't told her yet, I just realised.

"So, he had a lot of women. But they were all his pastimes. Ergo, he had numerous one-night stands. Now, I'm wondering why you're not discarded after his first *use*? Forgive the word. I don't mean to offend you, but that's the word that comes to mind, considering my nephew's taste," she explained hurriedly.

I glanced at the restaurant, which smelled of bacon and coffee. The walls here were painted with a brighter tone of yellow. The square wood tables glistened, spotless. They were arranged in rows of threes. There were about twelve of them, and every one of them was a four-seater. The chairs were high-backed with intricate geometrical design, which gave them a nice look.

Marisha guided me to the one in the farthest corner. As we sat facing each other, two bulky men came in and took a table opposite us. I noticed Marisha's stare at them but hadn't said anything. She instead took the menu that was lying on the table and studied it. I had no choice but to do the same.

"Well, I have nothing against you in case my nephew is—"

"I'm sorry. Please hold it." I put a hand in front of me. "I don't think we are what you think we are," I told her honestly. I shook my head with a shrug of my shoulders.

She slightly put the menu down, still holding it, to give me a measuring look. Her big round eyes seemed to search mine.

"Okay, I will hold it. But let me ask you, do you like my nephew?"

It was my turn to laugh. But it was not loud as hers, of course. However, it was enough to get some attention from a few people that were present there.

"I wouldn't be here if I weren't. But rest assured, this is not what you think it is," I emphasised again, just in case she missed it the first time.

Her curvy eyebrows rose. "What? Do you mean you're playing my nephew?"

Now that made my jaw hang open. "Uh, no. I don't mean it like that," I slowly drawled. "It's something I can't explain, I'm sorry." I shrugged.

Her eyes narrowed. "What did you two do in a public notary office?"

Doamne fereşte! She knew about it, too? But I had hoped it was not the content of the notarized file. I would not know how she'd take it and what she'd think about it. Or think about *me* for that matter.

"I prefer not to say, I'm sorry. I hope you'll respect that."

She stared at me for a long moment before she smiled at me toothlessly. "Well, if my nephew is clinging onto you, he must have a *special* reason. I won't be meddling with your affair, whatever it is, but I hope none of you will get hurt. You see, I'm an understanding person. I love *love*. You know what I mean, *dorogaya?*"

"Of course." I nodded curtly and gave her a small smile.

'*There'll be no one that'd get hurt. We only have a deal, Maksimillian and I,*' I mused.

"Tell me, what is your plan for today while Maksimillian is away for an emergency business trip?" Marisha asked after we got our order minutes later.

She had a Romanian breakfast composed of smoked ham, sunny sideup, *zacusca*, sliced tomato, a few pieces of sliced cucumber, green onion, and toasted bread, whereas I opted for mashed potato and sausage. She also ordered a cup of black coffee, while I chose fresh orange juice as my beverage.

"Hmm… I haven't decided yet—"

"That's perfect!" She clapped her hands that it startled me. She never ceased to do that to me.

I looked at her with confusion. "I don't see why it's perfect," I slowly expressed, before drinking half of my orange juice. Then, I put the glass down on the table, looking pensive while chewing on my inner cheek.

"You and I are going to Cetatea Râşnov," she stated with a wide smile.

That was part of Antonia's original itinerary, next to visiting the Bran Castle.

"Oh! Well… I don't really—"

"Like to go with me?" she tested.

'Yes! Because I know you'll tell me just anything about Maksimillian. And I'm afraid. I'm afraid I might fall for him if I know more,' I desperately thought.

Value

Maksimillian

I waited for Zenovia's call since yesterday. She had my number, as I gave it to her the morning before my almost three-hour flight to Helsinki, by private jet. There was no time difference between the two cities, so there was supposed to be no problem about it at all.

It did not matter whether or not she was in my hotel suite. I could easily have her tailed, and I would see what she does and ensure her safety. For some reason, I was cautious—*smotret' v oba* (to be on the lookout)—about it. I knew she could be a target to get to me. After all, being one of the Russian billionaires had more than one downside. It was not all cheery days in my world.

My cousin and I had to always keep our eyes open. Otherwise, we could end up like my parents or his father, as well as our grandparents. Until now, my parents' case had not been resolved. The helicopter crash was not just an accident. I knew someone was behind it. But no one could say who, even the authorities that investigated it. Not that I believed them, of course. If some other powerful oligarch would have been behind the incident, then justice would be obscured. As for my uncle, he was poisoned by an unknown enemy. We did not even have any idea who to suspect.

All their deaths were puzzles to me, my cousin, and my aunt. We had no one to point a finger to, thus the reason why we had to be vigilant at all times.

Now that I had someone I started to care about, I could not and would not want to lose her. But what the fuck was with her? Why hadn't she called me yet?

'Is she busy entertaining herself while I'm away?' I mused with irritation.

If she wouldn't call me within the day, I'd call her tonight. Right now, I was meeting my potential client, thankful enough that the short notice of my presence was acknowledged. Looked like this Finn still wanted to have business with Frolov-Usmanov Inc.—if I was not mistaken.

I just hoped this meeting would go smoothly, as Rurik and I had hoped, just like the first client I talked with yesterday. If not, I would need to spend another couple days or more here to get another potential client.

Yesterday, I was lucky Mr. Korhonen of Korhonen Steel Ltd. was delighted to add us as one of their suppliers. We did reach to an agreement instantly, and the man in his fifties was happy I came over and was able to talk to me personally. He said he admired my father even before Frolov-Usmanov Inc. diversified to steel industry over twenty years ago.

I straightened the jacket of my dark green three-piece suit. My two bulky bodyguards, wearing black three-piece suit, were behind me as we walked down the narrow silver-themed hallway of Finnkin Industry. The executive lady secretary was waiting for us by the door; her desk in a corner was behind her. She was already informed by the receptionist at the lobby when I entered the building and was instructed to go up here on the top floor. The fifteen-storey building was modern, and I could not find fault in it.

The blonde, mid-thirties executive secretary, greeted us with a professional smile. I took a quick mental note of her beige slacks paired with the same coloured blazer that showed off her slim figure. She looked professional with her tight bun and stud earrings.

"Welcome to Finnkin Industry, Mr. Usmanov. Mr. Mäkinen is waiting for you. May I offer you something to drink or anything?" she offered in a husky feminine voice with a gesture of her well-manicured hand. I immediately noticed her wedding ring with a shiny stone.

"No, it won't be necessary. Thank you," I answered formally.

She nodded curtly and opened the door for me. One of the bodyguards stayed behind, while the other followed me inside.

My eyes met the spacious but minimalist office, which had a cream-coloured carpeted floor, thus making our steps quiet. The office had an L-shape table at the farthest part of the room, with a closed glass window. It was not the only three-by-three feet window, as there were other four. Their blinds were up, giving a natural light inside. Hence, there was no need for the small recessed lights in a circular formation in the ceiling to be on.

Mr. Mäkinen got up to meet me, almost jumping from his grey swivel chair. He was a man in his late forties and was half-bald with average high-bridged nose and thin blond-and-white brows. He was a head shorter than me but was stockier that the buttons of his white dress shirt appeared to separate anytime soon. His black slacks were silk and were also in the same predicament.

There was a small sitting area for visitors opposite his desk. There, he gestured for us to sit after shaking hands. Meanwhile, my bodyguard remained near the door.

"What do I owe you this visit, Mr. Usmanov?" he asked directly, blue eyes regarding me with curiosity. His Finnish accent while speaking in English was noticeable—just like my Russian accent.

"I'm sorry again for the short notice, and I'm grateful that you spare me your precious time at your working hour, Mr. Mäkinen," I answered and began to tell him honestly what was going on with my company. I had to, since there was no hiding it. Sooner or later, the Turkish companies would release the information that they no longer renew their contract with us. Besides, business dealings were built with trust. Therefore, honesty must prevail.

The way his round face turned from serious to concern while listening to my business story and watching my presentation that I played through the laptop I brought with me, he nodded. He injected some questions, and we talked about government policies for exporting and importing the goods, among others.

"I see." He pursed his lips, making a thin line. "I'll have to talk with my people about this matter."

Right. In normal circumstances, there would have been a supplier bidding to win customers. But being one of the most powerful suppliers, it could be flexible. Albeit all these, I was ready to negotiate price-wise. It would all boil down to it anyway.

"Of course, Mr. Mäkinen. I'll be here for a couple more days," I informed him. I knew I gave him a tight schedule, which I didn't have the right. However, I couldn't afford to stay longer and just leave Zenovia in Braşov, as I already did. "If you haven't reached a decision by then, it's all right. You know where to contact me. In the meanwhile, I'll talk to others while I'm in the city," I bluffed.

His brows knitted upon hearing it. I knew he was already weighing this chance to grab my offer, and I hid a smile. After all, they did want our high-quality products. These had been highly recommended and were competitive with other suppliers, not only from Russia.

I got up and shook his hand again. He walked me to the door and invited me over dinner to his own home.

Well, I could not turn him down, since he was the only potential client left that I needed to talk to. But I wondered what time I could get away to call Zenovia up, and would she be in the hotel during that time?

Bonding?

Zenovia

As much as I wanted to decline Marisha's offer to hang out with her—er exploring Râşnov Fortress—she was eager to have me with her, so I decided to just give in. At least, I would not be so lonely to explore a place alone. Maybe it would be more enjoyable to have a companion. And I guessed she was not a boring one.

It was more than a twenty-minute drive to get there from the city. The fortified place was located on the limestone hill, surrounded by a forest with green conifer and other trees. It is said to be one of the best preserved citadels in Transylvania and had the oldest structures maintained since the fourteenth century. The entrance had an arch shape with a sort of colonnade on top of it.

There were actually many buildings inside the entire fortress. They were made of stones and bricks. It was amazing to see these. The pathways were made of stones, as well as the stairways, since the whole place was not flat.

The triangular shaped roofs of the buildings were brownish red, while the walls were somewhat between the colours dull yellow and light beige—whatever it was called. Anyway, the sturdy thick fences of the citadel was really old. There were imperfect square holes where I believed the inhabitants used to peep to see where the enemies were and release their arrows and whatever weapons they used then.

The citadel had two courtyards—the exterior and the interior. The outer one was called either "the garden of the fortress" or the "the courtyard in front of the fortress" that was in the eastern part of the citadel. It had an entrance for food and weapons at the time. The other entrance was under the square tower for the cattle.

Meanwhile, the inner courtyard was where the inhabitants were housed. During the sieges, it served as pantry and shelter. We were informed by the tour guide that Marisha hired for us personally that the rooms had names, such as "priest," "school," and others. In fact, there was a school built on the top of the hill. In 1650, a chapel was constructed, and its walls were the ones seen today. Noticeably, there was a large crucifix on the exterior wall of it.

I must say I felt and breathed the medieval air here. It was very interesting. I heard that in 2002, the Râşnov area became popular after some American directors had chosen to shoot the movie titled "Cold Mountain." It starred Nicole Kidman and Jude Law, and it was awarded an Oscar. I should say it was awesome and deserving, as I watched the movie myself. And I now noticed some of the parts in the citadel were familiar, because some of the peasant scenes were shot here.

A couple hours later, we checked out the Râşnov Fortress' feudal art museum that exhibited some antique furniture, weapons, armors, tools, prints, galleries, ports specific to the century, and different photocopies of documents from the thirteenth century.

In the museum, some unusual objects were displayed, such as a yoke that was used to transport prisoners and a torture mask. Boutiques were set up in the houses that were occupied by the old inhabitants of Râşnov centuries ago. Here, I bought some semi-precious stones and books that tell about the history, as well as the tradition of the place, whereas Marisha bought some various souvenirs, like art objects and others that caught her fancy.

There was a bar-terrace in the center of the citadel. We took a rest and had some refreshments after a considerable long walk among the ruins.

"Ah! Maksimillian surely missed having a tour in this endearing place," Marisha commented. She placed the glass on the table. The personal tour guide talked with the driver, as they were both Romanians.

"Well, he can always come here if he wants," I replied, and she just smiled while regarding me. I drank the refreshing peach juice. Its cold and sweet liquid soothed my parched throat. The sun was high and scorchingly hot.

"Maksimillian is always working hard, you know? That's why I dragged him on this vacation." She told me after a minute.

I just nodded, did not want to ask anything. I just knew she would talk about him while we were here.

"You don't happen to know who he really is, do you, *dorogaya*?" Her beautiful brow arched in question.

I slowly put down the sweaty glass, looking at her in the eye. "Do you think I care who he is, Marisha?"

She shrugged, still smiling. "Why wouldn't you want to care? He's a very powerful man in Russia. One of the powerful men, I must say. He's influential, extremely rich, one of the most sought bachelors, and—"

I held a hand to stop her. "Please, don't tell me anything more. I didn't come here to actually fish some information from you about Maks. You see, I don't ask you questions, Marisha. I hope you understand this."

She laughed hard, drawing attention to our table, but she didn't care. I could feel a subtle heat crawling on my face, but I tried to ignore it. I supposed I should get used to her loud laugh. At least, for the entire period of being with her.

"*Dorogaya*, I can now see why Maks is taken with you. You're... different." She smiled at me with a knowing look.

"Is there something that you want to imply here?"

"Why? Is there something that I should? Besides, is it bad?"

I shook my head. "Be assured that I am not going to trap Maks into a relationship, which you might be thinking right now... that maybe I'm just playing some cards to get him because I don't. Okay?"

She stared at me for a long minute while I finished my drink. Her eyes were condescending if I'd think about it, but I didn't care about her or Maks at all.

"Are you rich, Zenovia?" she suddenly asked to my bafflement.

It made me laugh, actually. "No. I'm just a simple hotel receptionist who once dreamed to become a famous painter!"

"Oh! You wanted to be a painter? What stopped you?"

I dropped my gaze. "The question should be *who*. It was... uh... my father. When he left me and my mum, I just... stopped painting."

"Oh, I'm so sorry to hear that!" There was sympathy in her eyes as she regarded me. "How long has it been? But haven't you got the urge to paint again?"

"It's been a long time now, and no, I don't have the urge to paint anymore," I lied, looking away.

"Well, maybe if you found the inspiration, you can paint again," she murmured and finished her drink as well. "I heard artists can't really turn their backs on their passion."

"Anything left for us to check out?" I asked instead. I didn't want to linger on the subject. It was a painful one.

"Hmm. I heard there's an archery area around here, where one can practice their skill and precision. Would you like to try it out with me, *dorogaya*?"

"What? You're going to do archery?" My eyes went wider. I couldn't believe she was up for it. With her style, she didn't seem to look like... sporty.

"Well, if you stick with me, you might discover something more about me and my family," she answered meaningfully.

I chuckled softly. *'Sorry, I don't want to know more about you or your family. I just fear that I'd get attached to you if I'll do that, and I can't let it happen.'*

Deets

Maksimillian

I made some calls to my cousin and had emergency meetings with our staff. I asked for the papers to be sent to my official email, so that Mr. Korhonen of Korhonen Steel Ltd. and I would sign the contract in the next two days. He was going to make it a big event.

By the time I was done with work, it was already time to get ready for dinner with Mr. Mäkinen of Finnkin Industry. While on my way to his home, in the backseat of the rented car, I received a report from the security details of Aunt Marisha through email. I would receive this type of report at least once or twice a day, unless there were important ones that happened or were happening. As for emergency ones, my line was kept open for it.

I read the detailed report quickly.

"Subject A went to have breakfast at 09:37 with Subject New. Subject A ordered smoked ham, sunny sideup, zacusca, sliced tomato, a few pieces of sliced cucumber, green onion, and toasted bread with black coffee, whereas Subject New had mashed potato and sausage with fresh orange juice (Main conversation topic: You)."

I scoffed upon reading the first part of the report. I couldn't believe Aunt Marisha and Zenovia went to have breakfast together and talked about me. I wondered why my aunt approached Zenovia. Maybe she wanted to know more about her, since I housed her in my suite.

A lopsided smirk then appeared on my lips, before I continued to the next part of the report.

"Subject A and Subject New went back upstairs to their respective suites at 10:06, came down together at 10:30 and went to Râşnov Fortress."

I learned that they had a tour guide while exploring the citadel, had a refreshment at a bar-terrace, talked more about me, and my aunt learned that Zenovia wanted to become a painter. They went to do archery, where Zenovia wasn't good at. My aunt beat her every time. Well, my aunt was an athlete, so it was only natural. She had a fair share of callus, which she had scraped then and had some therapy to keep her hands soft before marrying her late husband. She only picked the bow and arrow once in a blue moon after that.

"Current status: Subject A and Subject New went back to their respective suites after early dinner at 18:58. Will send an update later."

I shoved my cell phone in the secret breast pocket of my dark blue three-piece suit. I checked my watch; it was 7:35 PM. I was told dinner was at 8:00, so I had more than enough time to get there.

***

Dinner with Mr. Mäkinen, his wife, and two children proved to be enjoyable. His modern manor made of glass and concrete was beautiful. It had three stories, and they had no neighbors to keep their privacy. The premises were surrounded by a high fence and were filled with CCTVs. There were a couple of guards at the front gate and a handful around and inside the house.

It took us more than a couple hours to dine, talking about some personal things about me, the business, and my family.

"We heard you're a very busy man, so it was a great surprise to hear you were coming over yourself to have a meeting, Mr. Usmanov," Mr. Mäkinen said truthfully.

I nodded. "I thought it is very important to meet you myself, considering the pickle I'm in," I humoured.

He laughed, as well as his wife, who was a blonde. She had blue eyes, too. So were their two sons that were ten and twelve years old. Their bald middle-aged butler, on the other hand, was in and out of the dining room to see to it that we lacked nothing and that our needs were satisfied.

As for my bodyguards, they stood just right behind me, which the couple understood very well. As it was, their own bodyguards were not far away from us, too.

"Arvo, enough talking about business," his wife, in her late thirties, gently chastised him, touching his arm.

I smiled at the woman who was seated across from me at the rectangular glass table; her two children were to her left, eating silently.

Aside from my *lihapullat* (Finnish meatballs) plate with mashed potatoes, gravy, cucumber pickles, and lingonberry jam, a lot of food was served in front of us. These were mainly Finnish dishes, such as *lohikeitto* (creamy salmon soup), bread, whole fried Baltic fish with garlic sauce, and some desserts, like *runebergintorttu* (a small, cylinder-shaped treat with a combination of almond flour and wheat. This cake had strong flavours of ginger and cardamom, with the essential addition of a dollop of raspberry jam that was enclosed by white icing) and *mämmi* (a traditional Finnish porridge or pudding typically seasoned with dark molasses syrup). I just knew from the look of them, as I studied the menu back in my hotel.

I turned my head to the left, where Lotta's husband was seated, at the head of the table.

"Why don't we ask him about his personal life, which the media haven't so much to report about?" She turned to me with a coy smile, batting her blue eyes.

'What's going on here?' I mused.

Well, she was pretty and sexy, I must admit. However, I wasn't attracted to her the way I would have in normal circumstances. If she wasn't married, that is. I had no problem with women's age even before I met Zenovia, for as long as I could just fuck them without any responsibilities afterwards.

I pulled my mouth down and curtly nodded to her. "Well, what would you like to know, Mrs. Mäkinen?" I asked with a formal tone. I glanced at her husband, who appeared to be interested as well.

"If you have a future wife that we know nothing about," she answered bluntly with a little careless gesture of her dainty well-manicured hand. I noticed her long nails were painted with pink.

I chortled softly. I did see it coming, noting how she looked at me. "Well, that… remains to be seen. I'm working on it at the moment, you see?"

Her mouth formed into an "O," while her blue eyes rounded. She then turned to her husband. "What did I tell you? There's nothing on the news about his personal life, Arvo!"

Her husband just shrugged. "He's being careful not to spill anything about his private life, Lotta. It's good that he could keep it at that."

"May we know who she is?" Lotta further asked me. Her excitement seemed to die down. However, she tried to keep her lively aura, to be the perfect hostess.

I glanced at Arvo first, and he shook his head. I thought it would be better to keep Zenovia out of this. Not that we had a deal. Even without it, I would still keep her identity in the dark as much as possible.

"Well, I should keep her identity hidden. You'll know in time," I replied without offending her.

Lotta asked me about my cousin and my aunt after that. "What about your parents' deaths? I heard it's still an open case," she probed.

"Yes, but there's no progress. Just like my grandparents' or my uncle's," I answered with a heavy heart.

My grandparents' deaths were already a cold case, but I had my parents' and my uncle's kept open. I had a private investigator look into them. But so far, there was nothing new. No leads had turned up just yet. Still, I did not want to give up.

Raining Bullets

Maksimillian

It was about ten minutes after we left the Mäkinen manor. It was in the outskirts of Helsinki. We followed the asphalted road where trees and grasses were on either side of it—as I could remember it.

It was suspicious. The streetlights were on when we passed by earlier, when we were headed to the Mäkinens. Now, it was dark except for the rented vehicle's headlights.

My heart pumped hard in alarm. "Floor it, Sacha!" I barked my order to my bodyguard behind the wheel, and I dialed the Finnish emergency number.

Sacha was confused for a second but did as told. He increased it to full speed, while my other bodyguard, Oleg, beside me in the backseat took his gun from his holster and cocked it.

The operator that answered spoke in Finnish, but I spoke in rapid English. I was not even done delivering my sentence when she asked me why I called, and I felt the tires of our car take a hit. I was not sure if it was the front or the back, but it resulted to our vehicle's imbalance. It spun around while bullets started to rain on us. I was just grateful the car did not turn upside down.

My bodyguard quickly pulled my head down, while the three of us let out some Russian oaths. Even though the vehicle was bulletproofed, it was not a hundred percent safe. Apparently, whoever was after my life did not know that I secretly rented this type of armoured car. If they did, then they might have had used RPGs. Or was this just some kind of an attempt merely to shake me?

I tried to peer outside when the car was put to a halt. The windows cracked, but still, the bullets had not penetrated. It looked like we were surrounded, as the bullets came from all sides.

Oleg was about to retaliate, but I held him back by pulling his collar. "Don't you dare go out or you'll die!"

"But, sir—"

I didn't let him finish and addressed Sacha. "Let's go! I don't fucking care even if we run with the busted tires!" I ground my teeth, eyes flashing.

The sound of bullets fired continued, hitting the body or the back of the car. I could just imagine how the ruined car looked like at the moment or how the iron wheel may have made sparks against the road.

Still, we could not see the people shooting at us. They were either crouching or hiding behind the trees, as I saw some faint muzzle flashes from there now and then. I could just guess there was at least a dozen of them out there. Who knew if there were even more?

Sacha tried his best to manoeuvre the car in spite of it being in its hellish form at the moment. The car speedily moved in a zigzag, and it was definitely a bumpy ride until we reached a more populated area.

"*Chertovy ublyudki* (Fucking bastards)!" An expletive came out of my mouth when we were shot at no more.

Who could've ambushed us like that? I thought we were a goner back there.

The call I made was already dropped. I had no idea when. We dropped by the nearest police station to report it. We stayed there for hours, and we had to show my bodyguards' license to carry firearms. These were scrutinized before we were released and were assured that they would investigate what had happened. However, I did not put my trust in that. It would be pointless. As long as I had reported the matter, I did not care anymore.

I contacted my private investigator, gave him some instructions, and he promised to do his best to drag the culprit into light. I had not much hope for that either. But still, it was better than nothing.

Everything was frustrating.

I was exhausted by the time I was back in my suite. My bodyguards were on high alert. One of them had already contacted for backup from Russia more than an hour ago. They would be here for my duration in Helsinki. They would arrive in less than an hour.

My cousin was alarmed upon learning what happened. "Are you all right?" his immediate question when I answered his call.

"Yes, I'm fine. Don't worry. What about you and Aunt Marisha?"

"We're fine. We're fine. I'm just relieved you're safe," he answered, sighing.

"Well, I'm lucky I made that decision to be cautious."

"That's good, that's good," he agreed, knowing that I was referring to the armoured vehicle. I could imagine him nodding right now. "I sent a dozen people there. The ones we trust the most, of course, so I can be sure you're okay."

I chuckled at that. "I don't need a dozen, Rurik."

"What? You were almost killed!" he protested.

"Almost, but it didn't happen, so chill!"

"What? Are you crazy? How can I do that when you were almost killed?" he shouted, repeating what he said. "I'm going to flay that person once he's caught!"

I laughed at that. "Flay? Seriously?" I took off my jacket, tossed it on the couch, and loosened my tie.

Oleg eyed me but was quiet. Sacha was outside the door of my suite, guarding just in case. And as usual, I stayed away from the windows even though the thick curtains were drawn. Who knew if the assassin would use thermal imaging radar to get me?

Oleg and Sacha were loyal bodyguards I had for years, since I started to work at the company. They were assigned to me by my uncle. As for the bodyguards that my cousin now sent my way, they were the ones that our family had in our payroll for years, so we knew them already, personally.

"Who knows it's the same person who's behind the death of our grandparents, my father, and your parents, huh? What do you propose we do to that person then?"

"We're not criminals or some savage people, Rurik. We do it by law, if possible." I knew I was being a hypocrite, but I had to stand by it no matter how much I wanted to avenge the deaths of our family by my own hands.

"I can't believe you're saying this to me again. You know who's manipulating the law, cousin!" Rurik pointed out.

I could just imagine his flashing eyes right now. The anguish he felt when his father was poisoned, I could just understand it.

I closed my eyes tightly and took in a sharp breath. He was right. The most powerful one was in charge of it. Right now, we had no power despite the money we had. We already used some of it to get the justice we needed, but nothing happened. We had a few suspects, who were in the elite circle, but we had no concrete evidence. Bad blood would just be earned if we proceeded with it. Rurik didn't care, but I did, for the sake of peace no matter how temporary it was. Because I knew it would go in a cycle of bloodbath if we acted rashly. I just wanted him and Aunt Marisha to be safe. They were the only family I've got left.

I sighed. "Let's just be rational, Rurik, okay? We don't want more enemies."

"We didn't do anything to them, cousin! So, why are they doing this to us?"

I shook my head, one hand on my hip. "I don't know. I don't know, cousin." A sigh of defeat left me again. "Just take care of yourself there, all right? I have your mum covered."

"Oh, she knows that even if you don't say." He sniggered though.

"Well, she's no fool. But, at least, she's not complaining and understands the necessity."

"Well, she's gotten used to it."

"Aunt Marisha's a strong woman. She stands up for herself when uncle died. I know that what she's doing after that is just to dull the pain away."

"Well... that's her," he agreed quietly.

After our talk, I took a quick shower and slumped in my bed. Oleg and the other bodyguards were outside my room, taking turns after they arranged their shifts and plans to keep me safe.

I then decided to dial my suite's number in Brașov.

Phone Sex

Maksimillian

I missed her.

When I thought of Zenovia while we were being ambushed, I thought I'd never see her again. Or hear her soft voice again.

Right now, I just wanted to hear it. I wanted to assure myself that I was still alive and that she was safe where she was supposed to be. I had no alarming call from anyone who was watching her, so I figured everything was fine.

"*Da, allo* (Yes, hello)?" she finally answered the phone.

"Expecting some Romanian to call you up at this hour?" My mind drifted to Florin, who was her best friend's ex-boyfriend. If he was interested in her, it would be a no-brainer. Zenovia was beautiful inside out. I could tell regardless of the short period of time we got to know each other.

"What? I thought it was someone from the lobby or something!" she answered with a high note. Naturally, she was pissed about my subtle accusation. "You can't expect me to wait for your call and guess or know for sure it was you!"

I punched one pillow and put it behind me to lean against the headboard. "Why didn't you call me? I've been waiting." I scowled.

"Why would I call you?" she shot back.

"Because I gave you my number."

"You said you're on a business trip. Why would I disturb you at your work?"

O, Bozhe! She had all the answers to throw right in my face!

"You think I'm doing work at night, too?" I pointed out.

"Well, aren't businessmen do that?"

Just as I've said, she never got short of answers. If only she knew what I had undergone just a few hours ago, I wondered how she'd react.

"If we ordinary people work hard, businessmen work harder. Why? Because you don't want to lose money!" she added. "Am I wrong?"

Oh, God! She was just... spunky!

A big sigh left my system. "Let's not talk about my business trip, all right? I just want to hear your voice." My voice became gentle.

"Well, I was going to ask how it went. Is everything fine?" She lowered her tone, too.

I could not resist a smile then. "Are you concerned about me or my business?" I joked.

"Okay, don't answer that. Just sleep. It's late."

I cursed softly when she was about to hang up. "Hey, hey! I'm not sleepy or tired. How was your day, by the way?"

"Well... It was great actually! Your aunt and I went to Cetatea Râşnov, and she actually is a great archer! I couldn't have imagined it!" And then, she went on to tell me how Aunt Marisha taught her how to do it.

I was smiling widely while listening to her. She told me everything she saw there that I could already picture it in my mind.

"So, have you been thinking about me?" I asked, voice dropping lower than usual.

I heard her gasp on the other end. "Uhm... I guess? Your Aunt Marisha talked about you whenever she could find the chance, so it's hard not to."

I laughed at that. "You don't like her?"

"Well... she laughs hard, she's pretty, and she's... a bit nice actually."

"Only a bit?" I teased her.

"Well, she's really nice. She would have snubbed me if she wasn't, right?"

I grinned upon hearing it. "No one has ever said she's a snob. But… she's actually picky sometimes when it comes to personal companions."

"Oh, really? And are you implying that I'm lucky?"

I grimaced a little. "You can say that."

She laughed and told me she was embarrassed for being there. "You can just imagine my uneasiness when she saw me come out of your room! Oh, crap! I can still feel my face heat up because of it," she murmured.

A soft chortle escaped from me. "Why are you embarrassed? I wanted you to be there."

"I know, and I let you." Her voice dropped again, sighing.

"I miss you, Zenovia," I confessed with a serious tone.

Right now, I really wanted to hold and kiss her. But I didn't hear any answer from her. I just listened to her increased breathing, which made my manhood go rigid.

"Zenovia, what are you wearing right now?"

"My nightshirt, of course," she answered.

I smirked at that. "What's the colour of your underwear?"

"What? Why are you asking me these questions?"

I didn't answer to that and waited if she'd really tell me or not. I was already aroused just to hear her breathing.

"Well, it's a…" she paused and cleared her throat, "uh… lacy red one."

"I haven't seen it yet. Is that one of those you bought the other day? Can you take a picture and send it to my email?"

"What? Are you mad?"

"Come on, *moye solntse*. Can you let me see it? Just this once, I promise," I pleaded, still testing if she'd do it. It wasn't being a perv, but I did want to see her in it.

I waited for a minute or two, and she did send it to my email with an email subject of "DELETE THIS IF YOU DON'T WANT TO DIE!"

I decided to check it out on my laptop instead of my phone to be bigger, and I grinned from ear to ear. Excitement ran through my system.

O, Bozhe! When I opened the file, that was when I realised she took a picture of herself with nothing on top but her hands covering her breasts. She looked so seductive with half-closed eyes. She also bit her lower lip. Her toned thighs were closed, almost overlapping one with the other, emphasising the inverted triangle at the center of her exquisite body more. Her sexy lacy red underwear was lowcut, and I could see the flesh underneath the lacy fabric.

Chert poberi! I really wished I was there with her and take it off from her.

"Zenovia, are you there?"

"Yes! I'm here. H-have you seen it?" she stuttered, breathless.

A Russian expletive left my mouth before I answered, "You look like a goddess, *moye solntse*." My heart was beating so fast, I could hardly breathe. "Can you take it off for me?"

"What? No!" she protested.

"Just do it for me, please. How I wish I'm with you right now, *moye solntse*," I honestly told her with a husky tone.

"M-Maks…"

"I really want to touch you down there and kiss your fucking sweet flower until you'll lose your mind and you cum hard, Zenovia!"

She gasped and groaned.

"Touch yourself, *moye solntse*. Imagine that I'm the one touching you there, caressing that little bud of yours. Oh, I miss your taste. I really want to lick you and suck you there right now. I want my tongue to run along those crevices and go around the apex of your sweet flower. I want to suck your nectar there," I whispered in a breathless tone.

Her heavy breathing was too clear to me. She was affected by my words, and I couldn't just stop. And damn it! I began to stroke my own member under my bathrobe, wherein I was naked underneath.

Looking at her picture, I continued to move my free hand up and down my huge full-blown erection. Actually, it was my first time to do this phone sex, but it seemed to be going well between us at the moment.

Zenovia panted and called out my name. I could just imagine how her body was thrashing on the bed right now, with her flushed face and body. I wanted to ram her with my huge staff, wanted to drown into her hot depths, wanted to be squeezed by her tightly, and then let my precious jizz spurt inside her and give her the baby she so desired.

"Maks!" she called out and a prolonged hot moan followed it, telling me she came.

"Oh, Zenovia!" I grunted, as I unloaded myself, too.

We were both breathing so hard, and my heart's deafening thumping sounded in my ears.

"Fuck, *moye solntse*! I so love your moans!"

Thinking Of Him

Zenovia

Some minutes after my body exploded with Max on the phone, he let me go, to go to sleep. And yet, here I was, thinking about him.

I didn't know what came over me. When he asked for a picture of my red underwear, I wanted to resist it. But he was so… persuasive that I couldn't let him down. And I thought that maybe… maybe it could take away some of his stress at work, so I decided to give him what he wanted. Besides, I trusted him.

I knew I shouldn't have because we were practically strangers. But after everything that had happened, I did trust him. In just a few days, he earned it. I supposed it was because he was one reliable person. He took care of me ever since we started having this sensual relationship. Still, I had no high hopes over this. I knew that I had to stop, as per our agreement if and when I got pregnant.

I sighed and decided to watch TV when I couldn't sleep. Maybe I'd get sleepy while watching some boring news. Not my favourite channel, but I stopped when I suddenly caught a picture of Maksimillian on TV. My eyes almost bulged, and I sat quickly to see if I hadn't imagined it. But it was gone, and I didn't hear a thing, since it was muted.

Maybe I did just imagine it, because I was thinking about him.

I lay down again on the bed after I put my nightshirt and underwear on again. I rolled to my stomach and breathed in Maks' faint scent on the pillow. *Doamne!* I must be going crazy over this guy I just knew for over a few days!

'It can't be!' my logical mind bellowed.

***

The TV was still on when I woke up. It was past eight in the morning when I peeked at my cell phone that I placed on the side table. There was a text from my mum, asking me about Maks' name. Of course, I didn't reply to her about it. Instead, I told her about the fortress I visited yesterday. I didn't tell her I was with Maks' aunt. I supposed it was better to skip that part and not fill in my mother some details. She wouldn't know anyway, if she wouldn't see the pictures that I took. Marisha made a point that she and I had at least a picture together, on my phone!

She was nice to be with, actually. She taught me some pointers on how to use the bow and arrow. It was kind of a great experience for me. In fact, it put a smile on my face when I think about it now.

I turned the volume of the TV on, a little bit higher, to not be deafeningly quiet inside the room. I opt to order room service, trying to avoid Marisha, just in case. What if she'd drag me somewhere else to go with her, and then, she'd tell me more about Maks?

I shook my head. I couldn't let her. I didn't want to know more. The little I knew about him, the better.

"Finnish authorities are still investigating what happened to Russian billionaire, Maksimillian Usmanov. According to the report released last night..."

My eyes went round when I heard Maks' name on TV.

"What? Russian billionaire?" My jaw dropped; my grey eyes were fixed on the flat screen.

There was no mistaking it. Maks' picture was on the upper right corner of the TV!

The anchorman continued to speak, but all I could gather was that Maks was ambushed in Helsinki and was lucky to be alive. There was no other information that registered in my brain as my hands shook.

Doamne fereşte! He almost died, and I didn't know!

I was heaving when I grabbed my phone and dialled his number with slightly trembling hands. I paced near the foot of the bed while his phone rang on the other end. I guessed he was still sleeping. I hoped he was. I hoped nobody entered his suite in a Helsinki hotel and killed him in his sleep! *Doamne fereşte!* I was so worried.

I had no idea, but my eyes felt hot. My hands trembled even more when he didn't answer the fourth, the fifth ring. My heart was quivering, too.

"*La naiba!* Why aren't you answering the phone?" I yelled.

I sniffled and realised I was already crying. The tears had already damped my cheeks.

I dropped the call without him answering it and dialled it again with still shaking hands. I put the phone on my ear and listened to the ringing of the phone again.

"Hey! Good morning!" He was breathless.

"What the hell's going on with you? Why didn't you pick up right away when I'm calling? Where were you? What were you doing?" I demanded, voice high.

And I broke down, even though I didn't mean it.

Oh, *Doamne!* I was so relieved to hear his voice and to know he was okay.

I dropped my butt on the bed and cried.

"Hey, hey! I was just taking a shower, so I didn't hear you call. As soon as I heard it when I was done, I dashed to get my phone!"

"How could you do this to me, Maksimillian?" I sobbed and felt stupid for feeling like this.

"Hey, Zenovia! Why are you fucking yelling and crying?" He sounded alarmed. "What's happening there? Are you all right?"

My free hand caught the sheet and fisted on it. "Why? Why didn't you tell me you almost died last night?" I confronted him.

"What? Where did you hear that?"

"I saw it on the news! Don't lie to me!"

There was silence on his end before I heard him sigh heavily. "I… I wasn't going to lie. I was just wondering how you knew. And I certainly didn't know you'd react this way." He chortled softly.

My brows met, thinking he must be crazy. There was nothing funny about what had happened to him.

"Why are you laughing?" I almost squeaked.

"Are you worried that your sperm donor almost died?"

I ground my teeth, and a string of Romanian oaths left my mouth. He heard it but didn't understand the literal meaning. He got the gist, though. He must have because of the tone.

"It's not because of that! It's about your life, Maksimillian!"

"Okay. So, you already know who I am."

I swallowed hard and took a deep breath, wiping away my tears with the back of my hand.

"You know what? I don't want to be entangled with you anymore, Maks. This is all a mistake. What I did was a mistake."

I was about to hang up when he warned me, "Don't you dare hang up on me, Zenovia! And don't you dare tell me that the deal we have is going to be cancelled because I won't let you. You hear me?" There was danger laced in his voice, although he wasn't shouting at me.

My heart jumped because of it. It was not fear. I was not afraid of him.

But why did I feel like this? Was it because he cared about me even though he did not say it in words?

My throat went dry, and I did my best to swallow some spit.

'Maybe he just didn't want to lose an overly willing romp partner,' a part of my mind suggested.

I ended up the call without saying a word, and I took a deep breath.

'What now, Zenovia? You're in damn big and billionaire trouble!'

Crap! How did I get myself into this?

Touched By Her

Maksimillian

I was definitely touched when Zenovia called me up. Even though she was shouting and demanding me where I had been, at least, she called me upon learning what happened last night. She did not really say goodbye and just hung up, but I did not mind. I knew how conflicted she was with herself at the moment.

But fuck! She said what we had was a mistake, and she did not want to be "entangled" with me. The hell she didn't want to! She was already tied to me even if she'd destroy the notarized document! She was not going out of my life that easily.

I called up the security details that were assigned to her, and I gave them the instructions to look out for her. Closer than ever. She might or might not run away from me today. But there was really no telling. Who would know what she'd do while I'm not there? I didn't want her to hide. I absolutely didn't want any problem with her right now while I dealt with my job at the same time and in a different place!

Chert poberi! I would be powerless if she would just disappear from my life, and I couldn't find her in spite of the address on the agreement paper. But hell! I hoped it wouldn't come to that or I'd go fucking crazy! Even thinking about it at the moment, it was already reeling my head towards insanity.

I called Rurik, and he already saw the news. It was a bit crazy over there, as some of our family friends called him up to ask what really happened to me and if I was fine. Well, I almost could not believe they cared. Or was among them the traitor, just trying to get some information? Well, it could be possible.

Mr. Mäkinen called my hotel to talk to me and asked if I was doing all right. He was shocked that something happened to me while I was on my way to my hotel last night. It seemed that he wanted to let me know that he had nothing to do with it. Of course, I didn't even suspect him. There was no motive that he'd do something like that. I was one hundred percent sure he had nothing against me. He did invite me over to his home, but it was not to get me killed.

He asked me to extend my stay for another two or three days if possible while he spoke with his staff. I knew he'd ask me for an extension. Just like Mr. Korhonen, he did want us to be one of their suppliers for steel. It was not only for our good reputation but for the high quality of the products produced and delivered.

Stainless steel (pipe fittings or tubes) was the main Finnish steel import. In the trade flow statistics, the Russian Federation came in fifth in 2018. By 2019, my country became second as Finland's main partner in the overall import main supplier.

I was confident that the demand for steel products would increase just like we had locally. We would need to expand into new markets to develop significantly and thus earn more. By that, we also have to consider and apply some strategies, such as production upgrades, implement advanced technologies, innovate and increase production.

I sighed after talking with Mr. Mäkinen on the hotel phone. Looked like he had someone on me, since he knew the number. Most probably, he pulled some strings for it.

***

I was busy the next couple of days in Helsinki, but I kept calling Zenovia at my suite in Brașov whenever I had the time, as I already had her number when she called me, crying. I was relieved she did not leave. Yet. Or just as she planned. I was afraid she would leave and go back home.

In the meanwhile, I gave another job for my private investigator (PI), which was to get some more information about Zenovia and her family. I knew it was me being a creep, but I couldn't help it. It was just in case she would run or hide away from me.

It turned out that she had a broken family. Her father had a second family living in Bucharest. Her mother lived alone in their house in Iași, whereas Zenovia lived in the same city as her but in an apartment building. According to my PI, her home was about twenty minutes away from her mother's. She seldom visited her and that their relationship was normal as it could be.

I learned that she worked as a hotel receptionist in Iași. It was a four-star hotel. But I already knew she wanted to be a painter. I still have to know why she stopped painting, though. Would she trust me enough to tell me the reason why?

Aside from these, I also learned she actually had no boyfriend even before she met me. So, that was the reason why I was her first. I did feel very lucky indeed. Even though we were strangers, she trusted me with her maidenhood, which I did not expect at all.

I tried to talk some personal things with her when she picked up my calls, but she would just clam up and not speak. Because of it, I felt frustrated, but I tried my best to be understanding. She had her issues, all right. I wouldn't and couldn't force her. Just that I really needed to know more about her from her own sexy mouth. If she would only let me…

"When are you coming back to Romania? Or are you going to bail and just go home to Moscow?" Aunt Marisha called me on my private number the night before I was going back to Brașov.

"You'll never know until the time comes, Aunt Marisha," I told her with a grin.

"You be careful, Maksimillian," she reminded me.

"Yes, I will. You, too, Aunt Marisha," I replied to her.

I looked out of the window of my suite, which was on the tenth floor. Helsinki was a beautiful city. The scattered lights of gold, white, green, purple, blue, and others were just so fascinating. I even wished Zenovia was here with me right now to see all this. I wondered if she had the inspiration to paint whenever she sees beautiful things. Wouldn't she ever paint again and why?

I decided to take a picture of it and sent it to her.

"Sir?" Oleg took my attention, reminding me to stay away from the window.

I nodded and walked away from there. Just then, the glass window cracked when the bullet went through from where I just stood a mere second ago.

"*Blyad'* (Fuck)!" I cussed, while Oleg pulled me and covered me with his bulkier body.

Whoever it was really wanted me dead!

Lube It!

Zenovia

My heart thumped so hard inside my chest when I saw Maksimillian in the suite just when I came up after dinner. I had no idea he would be back tonight. After all, he said he was not sure when he could come back.

Our eyes held for some moments before he crossed the room to where I was. I had not even closed the door yet, and here he was, caging me in his muscled arms.

"Zenovia! I missed you so much!" he whispered.

His arms were tight around me that I could barely breathe. I wriggled out of his warm embrace to look at him. He was truly here. For real. Safe and sound.

"I saw on the news there was another attempt on your life!" I roved my eyes up and down his body, but he seemed to be in perfect health. "Were you wounded?"

He shook his head and smiled, pushing the door close and locking it. "Were you worried about me?"

'Who wouldn't?' my mind screamed.

I was ready to say something else, opening my mouth, but he covered it instead with his. It made me gasp and moan. He unzipped my blue-green sundress and peeled his own shirt and pants, leaving nothing on our bodies. Then, he effortlessly carried me only to gently push me against the wall with my legs wrapped around his waist and my arms encircled his neck.

"Ahh! Maks!" I tore my lips away from his. "I'm not *ready*!" I told him.

The tip of his hard length was trying to enter me, but I was not wet. Yet.

Yes, I was excited, but my body was just… not!

Maksimillian paused and kissed my lips aggressively instead. "What are you suggesting now?" he questioned in a whisper.

I could feel the urgency he felt to sink his hot and passionate manhood into my body. *Doamne!* He did not lie when he said he missed me. I missed him, too. But I was just not aroused yet. At least, not now.

"I-I have the lubricant Antonia gave me. I can use it," I indicated and chewed my inner cheek as he stared at me, a little breathless.

"Okay, if you want."

"I *need* it, Maks."

"Zenovia, tell me honestly. What's really your problem?"

"I already told you."

"No, you didn't tell me the details. You just told me you have a problem with your body but not the whole story. Or the details."

"I have endometriosis. It's chronic. I'm told there's no cure, but there are treatments."

His brows furrowed.

"It means, I have implants of tissue outside my uterus, and they formed as scar tissue. It's mild and had been taken out over a month ago. You might have noticed I have a small scar on my belly. But who knows what'll happen next? That's why I want to get pregnant right away because time will come and I'll eventually become infertile, Maks." My eyes stung, as I explained to him. "I-I just want this baby so bad! Please!" *'I don't want to be alone!'* my mind added silently, over and over again. I could feel the weight in my heart, as well as the fear of being alone in the future.

Tears rolled down my cheeks, while I stared back at him; my lips and chin quivered. I had no idea what was on his mind right now, but he looked at me with sympathy.

"Zenovia," he whispered that my heart trembled.

I swallowed and blinked fast. He kissed my tears slowly, and I was barely aware that he brought me to the nearest furniture, the long couch. He sat down with me on his lap. He looked at me with such tenderness in his sea-green eyes. His hand gently caressed my face and cupped it.

"We'll try and try until you and I will have that baby, all right?" he murmured softly, looking deep into my eyes.

I gulped again and nodded. "But I think I need that lubricant right now, Maks," I reminded him.

"Okay. Okay. I'll get it for you. Just tell me where it is," he said, standing up after letting me sit on the leather upholstered couch.

"It's in the inside pocket of my luggage bag. It's a blue-and-white box with an English label, so you won't miss it." I watched his naked ass go to get the lubricant. It was the one that could help me get pregnant actually. I just hadn't tried it with him yet.

He was back after closing the walk-in closet where I placed the luggage. In his hand was the rectangular box, and he inspected it while walking towards me. I thought he looked funny as he did it, with his now semi-hard-on displayed. Seriously, he still looked huge to me.

He knelt in front of me, between my spread legs. My back was leaning against the couch, and I was watching him.

My heart drummed in my chest, with my face growing hot. It was kind of embarrassing with my current predicament. My life was really crap! Not normal at all! I couldn't have sex like any other normal women my age.

When he finished reading the instructions, he chose 2g to fill the tube in the applicator. Then, he looked at me. "Ready?" The applicator was prepared to be inserted inside me.

I pushed down the spit in my throat and nodded to him. "You can enter the tube now," I told him.

I heard him cuss, as he slowly inserted the tube in my core. My hands gripped the edge of the couch, and he raised his eyes to look at me.

"Fuck, Zenovia. I wish I'm the one that's inside you right now, not this fucking thing!" he mumbled.

"Damn you, Maks! Just you wait after this and you'll be inside me, okay?" I felt the coolness of the lubricant inside, announcing its presence there.

Maks slowly withdrew the applicator and put it aside, on the center table where the box was placed as well. He leaned forward to kiss me.

"Sorry, I can't wait. I just want you so much, Zenovia!" he apologised, kissing me hard that took my breath away. With it, he raised one of my legs against his shoulder and knelt one knee on the couch.

When I looked at his member, I saw that it was more erect than a little while ago. I could just gasp at how fast he was aroused again. And I moaned when he prodded into my core. He paused for a moment and slowly moved inside me, staring at my face. I guess we both were feeling at the strangeness of the lube at first.

Maksimillian fully pulled back and sank again. This time, he grunted. "Fuck. It's a little odd, but it's really good, *moye solntse*," he said, smiling.

I bit my lower lip, feeling his massive erection slip in and out of my femininity. It was good, and I began to feel aroused, as he drove in and out. I bit my lower lip and suppressed a groan when he went deeper.

"Are you okay?" he asked, pausing a moment.

I nodded. "You can make it rough if you want. I'm fine," I told him.

He did so, giving me a grateful look, with admiration. "Ohh... *moye solntse*!" he grunted, panting. He shook my body with his every powerful thrust. "I really missed you!" He pinched one peak of my breasts, never letting it go and continuing to pump me. It seemed to be harder every time. "I thought I'd never see you again... or feel you again... like this!" He buried his hard staff so deep and ground his hips. Once. Twice.

I couldn't suppress my moans any longer. The quiet suite was filled with our heavy breaths and moans.

Our eyes held as he continued to plunge in and out of my body now. His free hand caressed my leg and thigh. His abdominal and thigh muscles flexed, as he pumped his hips, thrusting in and out continuously. Without growing tired. It appeared.

Oh, *Doamne*! He looked so marvelous as his body grew damper. I could feel it and see his skin glisten under the lights.

He shifted my position that I now lay down on my back on the couch, with my two legs resting on his shoulders, and he knelt in front of me. His hands were on each side of my hips, and he entered so deep and good. My mouth was ajar, and the moans came out freely when he began to move in and out of my core. Again.

"Maks!" I kept calling out his name, moaning and puffing.

He sure hit the most pleasurable spot I have at the moment in this position.

"Yes, Zenovia. Cum now if you want, *moye solntse*!" he urged as he mercilessly rammed my body.

"Ohh! *Doamne*!" I mumbled repeatedly. He drove in and out harder and harder, taking me higher and higher.

A scream tore at my throat when I reached that beautiful climax that only he could take me, and he was just right close me. It was tremendously pleasant to hear him grunt when he sprayed his seeds inside me. Both of us were breathless and filled with perspiration.

He carefully gathered me into his embrace and kissed me on the lips.

"Will you date me tomorrow?" he asked with a charming smile that was so contagious.

But it did make me think for a minute before I answered him.

What If...?

Zenovia

But, of course, before I could even answer Maksimillian's invite to have a date with him, my phone rang. I pushed him to get it, although I wondered who was calling at this time, after dinner. I ignored his groan of complaint when I shoved him aside. I did feel hollow inside when his manhood was pulled out of me. He stayed in the couch, as I hunted for my phone, which was among our clothes on the floor, in my purse.

I frowned when I saw the name on the screen.

Mihai.

'Why is he calling me now?'

I glanced at Maksimillian, still thinking whether or not I'd answer the phone. His eyes were questioning me who it was, and he gestured for me to answer it. After all, I pushed him away to check who was calling.

I swiped the screen and placed the phone against my ear. "Yes? Why are you calling me, Mihai?" I asked in rapid Romanian.

"Can't your brother call you up now?" his answer.

I rolled my eyes. "Half-brother! Remember we have different mothers?" I shot back.

"We have the same father, so it's the same. I'm still your brother," he countered in a hoarse voice.

"Why are you calling?" I asked in irritation, resulting to the creasing of my forehead.

Maksimillian looked concerned and came up to me, hugging me from behind and kissing the side of my neck and cheek.

It was really good to have him back.

When I saw the news today, all things had crashed into my mind. What if he had died? Would I be happy once I'd not be entangled with him any longer? Although I did tell him that, I didn't mean it, because I still wanted him... wanted to be with him... wanted to be kissed and held by him. And it was the first time I realised that I wouldn't want any man to father my baby but him. I did not want to analyse why, but it was just it. I could not imagine myself being with someone else. It didn't feel right either. For some reason.

"Who is it?" he whispered. His hot breath tickled my ear.

"My brother," I whispered back.

"Who are you talking to?" Mihai asked. "I can hear you whisper there. Is it Antonia?"

"No! It's not her. And I wasn't whispering," I lied.

"I heard you. I have good ears. I can hear well!" My brother was such a nitpick. I hated him. "I heard you took a leave from work at the hotel. I called you there, because you won't pick up any of my calls," he continued to grumble.

I raised an eyebrow. "You what? You called at my workplace? What's wrong with you?" I reprimanded him.

"Why are you always angry with me? There's nothing wrong with me. I just want to get close to my sister. Is there something wrong with it?"

I sighed and didn't answer him. There was no use telling him about my anger. He had no idea. Maybe it was wrong to just be so angry with him, too... when it wasn't his fault to be born by a different mother... that it was our father's fault. It was just that I really hated... everything... everything that had happened in my life.

Bottom line, I loathed my father to death! And all men...

No, not all men. I had no hate for Maksimillian. It was even the opposite. I wanted him. I couldn't hate someone I wanted, could I?

"*Tati* said we're going to Iași tomorrow."

I heard Mihai continue to speak.

"I was thinking if we could hang out! Maybe watch a movie or have some ice cream the day after tomorrow? You love Double Dutch! My treat, I promise," he added.

What if I gave him a chance to be close to me? But then again, I'd see our father if I'd let him. And I didn't want to.

I ground my teeth. I hated to be in such a dilemma. "I'm not in Iași, so I'm having a rain check."

"What?" he sounded disappointed. "Where are you then?"

"I-I am on vacation, all right? You can't just tell me to hang out with you."

"You're not lying to me, are you? Because I can call Antonia anytime and ask her," he threatened.

I chuckled but without merriment. "You have Antonia's number?"

"Yes! We're even friends on social media!"

"What?" I absolutely had no idea about this. Well, I wasn't fond of social media. Maybe that was why. But him having my best friend's number? She didn't even tell me about this. I wondered what they also talk about behind my back.

"So, where are you?" my brother asked while Maksimillian licked my earlobe and sucked it gently.

I tried to suppress a moan despite the sensation it sent throughout my body. I turned my face to give him a warning glare. But the gorgeous imp just smirked and continued to run his tongue on the side of my neck and nipped it gently, making me shiver.

"Ohh..." A moan escaped from me, forgetting I was still talking with my brother. So, I cleared my throat while feeling Maksimillian's smile against my skin. "I-I'm in... Ahh!" Crap! I just moaned with my brother still on the phone! *Doamne!* Maksimillian just won't stop kissing me, and now, his palms rolled my two peaks and kneaded my flesh. The tips instantly hardened from his touch, and I cussed, realising belatedly that my brother heard it.

"Are you upset with me again, Zen?" My brother's voice dropped.

"I'm in Braşov, okay? So, I can't see you or meet you if you go to Iaşi with *him*." I couldn't say the word that I call my father. Never would I ever again in this lifetime! I so hated him with all the fibre of my being that my heart was so heavy, my chest went tight, and my eyes began to water.

I hung up and sobbed, dropping the phone. It created a soft thud as it landed on Maksimillian's pants on the floor. That was when Maksimillian stopped kissing and caressing me, frozen. He moved from behind to face me.

"Hey, hey. I'm sorry."

I shook my head. Plump tears ran down my cheeks. I looked at him, who appeared blurry in my vision.

"No, no. It's not you," I whispered, shaking my head. My hands grabbed his forearms as I broke down.

"What did your brother want?"

"H-he wants to see me. But I don't think I can. I hate him, too!" My voice cracked while Maksimillian looked at me with confusion.

He held my chin up gently by his fingers to make me look into his eyes. "Why? Tell me everything, Zenovia."

Preggy Topic

Zenovia

I barely recalled when Maksimillian carried me to the couch where he cuddled me. I was seated sideways on his lap, leaning against him. We were both still naked. One side of my face rested on his chest, and his arms were around me.

I was like drugged by him, and I spilled everything to him. "My father cheated on my mum since I was seven," I began, listening to the strong and steady beating of his heart.

Somehow, it made me feel something indiscernable at the moment. Maybe this was too intimate for me? It should frighten me, but still, I continued to speak.

"My mum didn't know he already has a son with another woman during their marriage. It turned out, when I was nine, Mihai was born. When my mother learned about it, they had a huge fight. You can just imagine he already had a five-year-old son when she discovered it. He cheated on her for a long, long time!" I sniffled, tears starting to flow again.

Maks sighed and kissed the crown of my head.

I continued, "It devastated my mum. I was fourteen at the time. I was blinded by everything until then. I thought we had a happy and perfect family." I sobbed, shoulders shaking. I felt him caress my arm up and down and kiss my hair. "I thought everything was beautiful like my paintings... My father loved them, you know?" I sniffled but sobbed again. More tears raced down my face. I even wetted Maksimillian's chest. But he didn't mind at all. Instead, he embraced me tighter and kissed the crown of my head.

"I'm so sorry to hear it, *moye solntse*," he whispered and kissed my forehead.

I blinked fast, trying to clear my eyes from the tears. Maksimillian gently wiped my tears away with his gentle thumb.

"At the time, I so loved painting and thought I could become a famous painter someday, if only I'd pursue my dream and passion. Many thought I would become one. They believed in me and my talent, since I started at five.

"But then... my parents divorced. My perfect father was actually not perfect. He was a monster, who betrayed and hurt my mother and me." I shook my head. It was so hard to speak because of my constricted throat.

"Oh, Zenovia..." he whispered and squeezed me a little.

"It hurt so much that I thought my world crumbled then and there," I added. "I could see no more beautiful things. Everything was gloomy. My mother kept crying every night that it tore my heart into a million pieces! I can't even describe how bad it hurt! It's when I started to hate my father even more. And the rest of the male population. I hate men, Maks!"

He shook his head. "No, you don't, Zenovia. Don't say that. You don't hate me or your brother. Yes, I'm certain that you don't hate me. You just think you do hate your brother, too, because you were hurt and maybe because he's the living proof of your father's betrayal."

I tried to absorb what he said. I had no words to grasp and throw at him at the moment. Instead, I just cried more.

"If your brother wants to meet you, then I think you should. If he makes such an effort, I believe he loves you, his sister. Don't take this away from him. I mean, you can't be so bitter to a kid who's innocent, can you? I know what you must feel and maybe I don't really know anything about it, but in my point of view, you're a good person, Zenovia. You can't hate your brother. You just think you do because of your father, because of what he did to you and your mum, because you're just hurting so much. But remember that your brother is a different story. He has no fault in all of this. It wasn't his choice to be born out of wedlock, and he just wants to have his sister and be loved by her. Can't you do that?"

I bawled when he said it. His arms went around me once more, squeezing me a little.

"Come on, *moye solntse*. You don't really hate men. You just think you do. Look, what if we have a baby and it's a boy? Don't tell me you're going to hate him?"

"Of course not!" I snapped at him and slapped his other shoulder. "I'll love my baby more than my life, Maks!"

He chuckled. "See?"

He had a point.

I swallowed and sniffled. He cupped my face and wiped my tears with his thumbs while looking into my eyes. He really looked so adorable right now that my heart flipped.

"I have a concern, though. It may not be the right time to ask you this, but I have to know, Zenovia."

I slightly nodded.

Then, he went on, "What if… *we're* not going to get pregnant, what will you do?"

I actually went still by this question. It did not occur to me, because I always thought it would be doable. But, of course, who was I kidding? There was this possibility that even though I was not on the stage of being infertile yet, there might still be a chance that I won't get pregnant due to some reasons. Stress could be one. I was already stressed when I found out about the diagnosis. Or what if Maksimillian couldn't do it in spite of being healthy?

There could be other factors that I couldn't get pregnant even with this deal, even if we both wanted it. I had to face it.

This was my super sad reality.

My heart became heavier by the minute as I stared at Maksimillian. I didn't want him to be bound to me, with our deal forever. I couldn't, could I? He had his own life to live for Pete's sakes!

"If… I don't get pregnant—"

"We'll try again and again," he cut me off with gentle eyes.

"Maksimillian, you yourself asked me what if I won't get pregnant," I pointed out in a firm but low voice.

He smiled and gave my lips a peck. "I know. What do you think if we don't get pregnant in let's say a year or two?"

I was horrified to hear it. I didn't really think that far ahead. I just thought it was just like a month or two. Or maybe a little more than that. But a year or two? That meant something! How stupid was I to bind him in such a deal? I was so selfish and self-centered! I was too engrossed in my own problem that I hadn't thought about the other party. What if he really couldn't make me pregnant because *I* was the problem in the first place?

"Maksimillian," I started.

"I'm up for it. I don't care how long it'll take for you to get pregnant, if you do get pregnant—"

"And what if I won't ever get pregnant at all?" I cut him off this time.

He stared at me for the longest time. My heart drummed so fast and hard against my rib cage that I thought he could hear it.

"I'll take responsibility for you," he slowly said, eyes searching mine.

"W-what? What did you say?" It came out as a whisper, eyes wavering.

"I will honour our deal until my death," he replied without reluctance.

"What?" I exclaimed in disbelief. "You must be joking, right?" My voice went a little higher.

By Her Side

Maksimillian

I watched as Zenovia slept peacefully beside me. She was on her side, facing me. The morning sun aided me to have a pretty good look at her. The light freely came in through the glass wall. The curtains were not drawn as usual, since this part was safe from any long-distance attack or attempt on my life. The hotel was near the edge of a cliff. My bodyguards downstairs had this side covered as well, just in case.

Zenovia's beautiful grey eyes were close, but this didn't make her less exquisite. After her breakdown last night and our talk about the baby, I helped her cleanse first and cuddled her to sleep. I just assured her that I'd do anything for her, which she looked uncomfortable for some reason. I had no idea what was running in her pretty little head, but for sure, I'd know later on. I just hoped it wouldn't go as bad as I suspected.

I was careful not to wake her when I went to the bathroom butt naked to take a shower. It was already past eight in the morning. But I thought she might need some more rest after that emotional breakdown.

I stepped out of the bathroom with only my towel wrapped around my waist. My hair was still damp from the shower. I glanced at Zenovia, who was still immobile in the bed, just as I left her less than fifteen minutes ago.

I texted one of my bodyguards to order some food for us to be sent in the suite. I didn't want to talk over the phone to not disturb Zenovia's sleep.

Her phone on the bedside table suddenly rang, which made her stir and wake up. I watched her feel for it by her hand, eyes still closed. I couldn't help but smile as her hand kept reaching for the ringing cell phone. I quietly moved and pushed the phone near her hand, and she got a hold of it.

"*Allo*," she answered with a groan. Her eyes slowly fluttered open, squinting as she listened to the caller.

I didn't get who it was, since I didn't peer at the screen, but she appeared to be sour-looking. She spoke in Romanian. Of course, I could only guess a few people who ever called her.

"Mihai!" Her voice sounded like a warning. She sat bolt right up while I crossed my arms on my chest, gazing at her.

So, it was her brother calling.

"*Ce* (What)?" She looked around, like in panic, the sheet covering her naked breasts. Then, she caught me standing just by the bedside table. "*Nu* (No)!" Not long afterwards, a string of Romanian words left her mouth rapidly.

I had no idea what she was talking about, but I could only guess. She was against whatever Mihai was talking about.

"Hey. What's wrong?" I asked her when she ended the call. I sat on the edge of the bed, facing her.

She covered her face with her hands. "Mihai said they're not going to Iaşi to see me."

"Oh."

"But…" She rubbed her face and looked at me, shaking her head. "They're coming here to see me. It's easier and a shorter trip actually than going to Iaşi. From Bucharest to here, it's just more than a couple of hours drive compared to almost or more than six-hour drive to Iaşi. My father sometimes prefers to drive than to take the train or the plane."

I nodded and smiled at her. "Then, I guess you have to get ready before they arrived."

She stared at me. "They're almost here."

"That's good then. So, what are you waiting for?"

"I don't want to see my father, Maks!" she snapped.

I blinked a few times. "Okay," I slowly said. "Then, tell your brother where you can meet him. Your father will probably drop him off there, and we'll see your brother. I mean, you. I'll send you to wherever it is in the city."

Her jaw dropped. "There's no way my father will just drop off his son in an unfamiliar place, Maks!"

A wicked smile appeared on my face, which weirded her. "Then, I'll meet your dad and your brother."

***

Zenovia looked uneasy when she saw her brother and father enter the hotel restaurant. Instead of cancelling the food for room service, I had the bodyguards eat them instead in their room, since they hadn't had breakfast yet. They usually had it at nine, as they would have coffee before that time. A couple of them though were at the restaurant, blending naturally with other customers.

"Zen!" her brother excitedly called out.

He was tall for his age, lean, and had short dark brown hair, wearing a white shirt and blue ripped jeans, as well as running shoes. He actually had some similarities to Zenovia. They shared the same eye colour, where they took after their father, who had an average height and a bit stocky in build. He had average looks and looked… kind.

It must be hard seeing herself in the mirror, reminding her all the time that she had the same eyes as her father, whom she hated so much. She told me she last saw them three years ago.

I saw how Zenovia's eyes waver when she tried to smile at her brother. It came out as a little grimace. Then, she met her father's eyes.

"*Hei. Ce mai faci* (Hey. How are you)?" her father asked in a gentle tone. He looked at her with concern in his eyes, sitting down across from us.

"Just order anything you want, my treat," she said in English instead to her brother, who kissed her cheek.

"You're not going to introduce him to us?" he asked in English as well, eyeing me.

She glanced at me and then at her brother and father, feeling awkward. I understood why she was in this predicament, though.

"Uh… This is Maksimillian. Maks, my brother Mihai and… my father," she said, voice lowering at the last phrase, as if she didn't want to say it.

I held out a hand to her father first, with a formal smile on my lips. "Nice to meet you, Mr. Cuza."

He looked at me straight in the eye and nodded, taking my hand for a brief but firm shake. I did the same to her brother, who was staring at me.

"Hey. I think I know you," Mihai observed. Recognition dawned in his eyes, and they lit up.

"Shut it, Mihai. Don't even say it, okay?" Zenovia warned her brother.

He looked at her with open mouth. "Seriously? He… he's…"

She gave him a warning glare this time.

"Zenovia! It's good to see you here with Maksimillian, *dorogaya*!"

And I stared with jaw hanging open at my grinning aunt. She glanced at the two men seated across from us.

O, Bozhe! Aunt Marisha may just complicate Zenovia's position at the moment.

Hot Seat

Zenovia

Doamne fereşte!

Of course, it was around this time Marisha would have her brunch. I took a quick glimpse of Maksimillian, who was also unprepared for this. He looked at his aunt with his mouth gaped open. He then turned to look at me, trying to act normal.

"Hi! I'm Marisha, a new friend of Zenovia's." Standing close to where my father sat, Marisha politely and elegantly offered her hand to him, who seemed taken by her beauty. But I thought she already knew him, since she had once displayed her "power" in knowing things about me and others anyway.

"I'm Daniel, Zenovia's father," he said with a charming smile. "Pleasure to meet you, Marisha."

She looked sophisticated in her black slacks and cream sleeveless top. Her hair was in a bun, and her daylight makeup was perfect. Still, she wore that fuchsia lipstick that seemed to be her signature colour. Plus, her perfume just wafted to our noses. My father seemed to like it and stared at her more than necessary, as though in subtle flirting.

'Căcat! Don't tell me he's also cheating on his second wife?' I seethed, giving him a scathing look. It was not like I cared about his current wife, but him being so unfaithful might never ever change! *'Oh, dear God! I just so hate him!'*

"And you beautiful young man are…?" Marisha turned to my brother. "Is this your younger brother?" She briefly glanced at my father, who blushed visibly.

I almost rolled my eyes, and Maksimillian chuckled.

"Aunt Marisha, that's Mihai, Zenovia's brother," he stated the obvious, and his aunt let out a loud laugh.

"Oh, my bad! I'm so sorry for my mistake!" She put a hand on her face, as though she was embarrassed, but I knew better. She was just being... charming.

"You're his aunt?" Mihai looked at me, at Maksimillian, and then at Marisha.

Maksimillian slightly shook his head. "Sorry. She's just... too—"

"Loud? I'm loud, Maksimillian?" Marisha prompted, eyebrows rising and eyes daring her nephew.

"I was going to say friendly, Aunt Marisha," his gentle answer, and he deadpanned.

"Please join us, if you're not with anyone, Marisha," I invited her politely with a small smile.

Maksimillian stood up to give up his seat to his aunt, who thanked him with a kiss on his cheek. He took a free seat from another table and placed it at my other side, almost squeezing me between him and his aunt. I almost sighed when they started to check the menu. We talked about trivial things, such as the weather, how long the Russians were going to stay in Romania, and so on.

I caught my brother glancing at me and Maksimillian now and then while waiting for our orders to come. Meanwhile, my father seemed to weigh my relationship with the Russians. Still, he appeared especially charming and a gentleman to Marisha, giving her extra attention like giving her the tissue paper stand when she needed it. She accidentally spilled her latte on the table.

Under the table, Maksimillian took my hand that was balled into a fist.

"So, what's your actual relationship with my daughter?" My father had the nerve to ask Maksimillian, before he glanced at Marisha who had a small smile.

"How long will you stay here? Are you going back to Bucharest after this?" I questioned my brother instead to not let Maks speak, and it seemed that my father got the hint.

Mihai grinned at my inquiry, showing his white and perfect teeth. "We're going to stay for a few days. *Tati* said we can explore Braşov together."

"What?" I almost squeaked. I threw my father a glance.

"*Mami* is busy with a big project, so she's not with us right now. She's working hard on a new plan. It'll take her a lot of time like weeks or even months 'til she finishes it, so…" My brother shrugged after sharing this information.

Maksimillian, who was at my left, turned his head to me in silent query.

"His mother's an architect, so she and my father who's an engineer work at the same company. But it appears that they are not working on the same project anymore," I spoke meaningfully, thinning my lips afterwards.

As it was, their relationship started when they worked on some projects together in the past. No wonder why it took my mother a long time to know the truth, since everything just seemed normal in their marriage. She did not even suspect that he had an affair with his co-worker because she trusted him. She just thought they worked together. But on the side, they were actually working on another *project*, where my eyes transferred at the moment. To my half-brother.

"So, how did you and my sister meet?" he asked Maksimillian straightforwardly. He could be that sometimes if not all the time.

"Oh, I actually caught them having eye-to-eye in The Black Church," Marisha shared before her nephew could or would even answer my brother's question.

Maksimillian and I stared at her, but her eyes were fixed on my brother and father, with a smile on her lips. It was almost devious.

Ah, *Doamne!* She could be a piece of work.

"Oh!" Mihai could only say.

"So, anything else you can tell us about you two, Zenovia?" my father prodded.

I didn't really want to talk to him, so I just ignored him.

"They're dating, if you ask me," Marisha remarked, chuckling.

I chewed on my inner cheek, trying to not say anything to her that might prove rude. Well, I reckoned it was better that she answered for me and Maksimillian, since we didn't know what we had between us anyway.

I couldn't tell my father I had a deal with Maksimillian until I'd get pregnant, could I? Besides, he had no business in my personal life. He stopped being my father after all, when he and my mother divorced. He was never there for me after that. He was only a father to Mihai. I was not his daughter anymore.

And I hated him! So, so much. 'Til now.

I felt Maksimillian's hand gently caress mine under the table. He placed it on his muscled thigh and tried to make me calm. I could understand that he just let his aunt do the talking for us while I was in the hot seat. It seemed. Anyway, there was nothing alarming yet in what she said to my brother and father, if she did know what was really going on between Maksimillian and me.

"How long has this been going on?" my father asked me. He looked so serious that I thought he acted like my real father now.

Walking Away

Zenovia

"What gave you the right to ask me that?" I couldn't control myself now. I glared at my father. My tone went higher, making Marisha and Maksimillian stare at me, speechless. Some other people already had their attention on us. On me, specifically. "I didn't come here to be questioned by you. I'm just here because your son wanted to see and meet me! You are not originally part of this meeting, so you have no right! You have no right to act as if you're a good father or whatsoever because you're not!" I stood up almost violently.

The wooden chair made a harsh scraping sound on the tiled floor. I didn't even mind that I barely ate my food. I just wanted to be out of here. I was oblivious to other people's stares that followed me.

My eyes stung. I almost ran away from the restaurant. Maksimillian and Mihai followed me. I didn't even know where I was headed, as long as it was far away from my father.

"Zenovia!" Maksimillian called me, at the same time when my brother yelled "Zen!"

My tears already raced down my cheeks. I was barely aware that I was near the lift, where a few people came and went.

"Just go back in there and be with your father!" I told Mihai through gritted teeth.

"B-but... we're supposed to have your favourite ice cream!" His voice croaked.

I faced him, not looking at Maksimillian, who let us talk for a bit. But I could feel his being edgy right now, not too sure about what he'd do or how he could even comfort me.

"I will not see you or meet you again if you're with him, all right?" I shook my head, sniffling. "I can't bear to be in the same room as he. And I don't want to talk to him *ever* again!"

"Zen…" My brother's eyes shone with unshed tears. I knew he was torn apart because I was not on good terms with that… *nenorocitule* (fucker)! And I saw him appear behind my brother.

"Zenovia." My father uttered my name like I was a little girl again. He used that tone when I made a mistake, but what mistake did I do now? He was the one who even committed a sin! He lied; he betrayed my mother; he had an affair for God's sake! And now? He had such a thick face for showing up here when he already knew I didn't want to see him even after all these years.

I decided to ignore him.

"*Tati, te rog, nu acum* (Dad, please, not now)!" Mihai snapped at him to my surprise. "I told you to not come with me, because she said she doesn't want to see you! You just don't listen! Now, look what you've done! She's not even going to hang out with me anymore!"

Plump tears started to roll down his pale face, just like mine. I never heard him talk to our father like that. Or cry. Well, maybe because we hadn't lived in the same house anyway. But even before, I did notice he was such a nice young kid, who wanted to have everything lively and agreeable because of him. He was not the type that wanted to have any fight with anyone. He was good at lightening up the atmosphere. But now, he couldn't, and I didn't even let him.

Mihai turned to me. "Can you give us another chance, please? Just the two of us. Just to stroll… maybe in Old Town?" he suggested with hopeful eyes.

I began to sob harder while Max gently rubbed my back. I looked up at my brother, who was a head taller than me. I slowly shook my head.

"I don't know. I don't know, Mihai. I-I just want to be alone for now," I mumbled and gently shoved Maksimillian's hand and left them.

***

Maksimillian

I felt rejected when I tried to comfort Zenovia, and she pushed me away. Not literally pushed me, but it seemed that she didn't want my presence either.

It was the first time I was hurt for real. I knew she was hurting deep inside, too—the reason why she did it and walked away. And I tried to be understanding, in spite of the pain in my heart. I even asked myself why I felt this way, again, when we just have this deal between us. But yes, I was falling for her hard and fast than I could imagine. Never had I imagined it actually. It never occurred to me that I'd even fall for any woman in this lifetime.

But instead of wallowing in this emotion of being torn and got rejected, I tried to man up. I turned to Mihai, who pressed his eyes with his fingers to stop his tears. I was touched by his ardent brotherly love for Zenovia. It reminded me of Rurik's care for me. We were cousins, but we treated each other more than that. We were like brothers, in fact.

In the corner of my eye, I noticed Aunt Marisha stand behind Daniel. She gave me a look of sympathy. I bet she already knew what was going on with me. I could hide nothing from her anyway.

"Do you love my sister?"

I was caught off guard by Mihai's question.

"We… are on the stage of getting to know each other, Mihai," I told him honestly. At least, that was what I wanted to believe. Zenovia and I were starting to open up to each other, weren't we? She even told me about her father and everything she went through after his affair.

He swallowed and nodded, staring at me. "Then, you're not her boyfriend yet?"

"It's… complicated." I had no choice but to say it. It came out bitter, though.

He scoffed upon hearing it. "Right. My sister's complicated, so I'm not even surprised!" He gulped once more, looking at me in the eye. "But can you... Can you tell her that I'll be around until she makes up her mind?" He slowly shook his head. "Can you tell her I'm not going back to Bucharest without spending some time with her? Please?"

I let out a heavy sigh. "What makes you think she'd change her mind if I'd tell her?"

He shrugged. "I don't know. Maybe you're someone special to her. You must know she's never dated anyone yet. You're her first, right?"

My heart somersaulted when he put it that way. I knew it was the innocent "first" about the first guy she was with, not literally the one who actually devirginised her. Or was it? He could not possibly know it, could he?

'Chert poberi. *I must be overthinking and overanalysing things!*

"I'll tell her your message. But try to call her, too. Maybe she'll answer. Okay?" I put a hand on his shoulder and squeezed it a little.

He nodded and sniffled. "I'm sorry you're caught into this."

"It's okay. I did half-anticipate all this, after what she told me about your family history."

He chuckled bitterly. "It must be hard for her to tell you about it. My sister doesn't just open up to someone who's not close to her."

"You seem to know her very well despite the fact of your distance from each other."

"I keep tabs on her. Please don't tell her that. She'll be mad," he added quickly.

I chortled. "Are you free some time? Just the two of us?"

He looked at me before he nodded. "Sure. I'll give you my number then."

A Chance

Zenovia

I found myself back in Maksimillian's suite. I was in the bathroom, facing the mirror after washing my face. My eyes and nose were still puffy and red, but I guessed I shouldn't care about it anymore. I was in no mood to go out and explore some medieval castle, though I was excited to see Dracula's Castle for the first time. But now, Bran Castle was not on my priority list anymore.

When I went out of the bathroom, I saw Maksimillian come into the suite and close the door.

"I'm sorry," I apologised in a quiet voice.

"For what? Rejecting my comforting you?" he asked slowly. He walked up to me.

I frowned at him. "What? I didn't—" I began, but he cut me off.

"Yes, you did, Zenovia." His eyes were accusatory.

I played in my mind what transpired earlier. And yes, he was right. I did reject him, but I didn't mean it.

I slowly gulped down the invisible lump in my throat. "I'm sorry, Maks."

He was now right in front of me. He held my chin with his forefinger and thumb. He tilted it, so that I could meet his intense sea-green gaze. His masculine scent and expensive cologne enveloped my entire being, making my heart and stomach flutter.

"Zenovia, in case you haven't noticed, I care for you. In spite of knowing each other for just a short time, I want you to know that I do care about you. Do you believe me?" He said it almost in a whisper-like tone, increasing the pace of my heartbeat and making me breathless as a result.

I did believe him, but something held me back, and I didn't know what exactly. Was it because of my fear of another man that could hurt me in the future? As it was, no one could tell what the future holds. And no matter how much he cared for me right now, I wasn't sure it'd be the same in the next days, weeks, months, or even years. Just like how my father loved my mother while it lasted. I wanted to believe there was something that could last for a lifetime at least, since we couldn't live forever in this world.

His gaze held mine, and I couldn't look away. It remained that way while I was breathless. His eyes caressed my face as he waited for my answer. Another minute ticked by, and he pressed his lips on my brow.

"All right. I understand. I understand," he said, sighing in defeat. He touched his forehead on mine, and I closed my eyes. A tear escaped from each of my peepers, slipping down my cheeks. He wiped them away and then encaged me in his powerful arms. "Mihai asked me if you and he can have a date? He doesn't want to go home until you give him the chance."

I sobbed when I heard it.

***

Mihai and I walked around the Council Square the following afternoon. Maksimillian did his best to put my mind off my family troubles by pleasing me with his mouth before taking and pumping my body hard. I didn't have to use the lube this time, as he did more wonders to my body. But I knew it was like a switch, considering that I had a reproductive issue. My life was a complete mess entirely. But I just loved the way he cared for me and for being patient with me. I did realise it had nothing to do with the signed deal between us, but I refused to even think it. I just let my body be one with him, trying to protect my heart nonetheless.

Mihai and I chose a nice café where my brother ordered Double Dutch ice cream, *clatite Brasoveana* (pancake filled with beef, mushroom and cheese), and *placinta cu mere* (essentially a sheet cake with shredded baked apples in the middle, with raisins added to it and topped it with powdered sugar).

"These are all sweet. You know it, right?" I commented, looking at each serving we had of these Romanian desserts in front of us. I glanced at him from across the small square table and made a face.

"Sweet things make you feel good." He stated a fact.

I started to eat my share of *clatite Brasoveana* after the ice cream, and he did the same as though copying me. He grinned at me and took a selfie of us to document our sibling date. He then posted it on social media.

Antonia called when she saw the picture of us, but I didn't talk long. Besides, she had an emergency. She was just happy Mihai and I found time to be together during my vacation time in Brașov.

"I don't want to ruin this time with you, Zen," Mihai began.

When he said it, I gripped my fork tighter. I was in the middle of eating the apple pie, and I knew what he was about to say.

"Did he put you up to this?" I gently confronted him, looking straight into his eyes.

"No, no." He readily shook his head. "*Tati* told me he wanted to see you actually. That's why he originally planned to go to Iași. To talk to you, Zen."

"Are your parents getting along well?"

He nodded. "I believe so."

I scoffed and dropped the fork to sit back on my chair. I let my eyes roam around us while I thought of my father. I barely took note of the hanging plants of the café. These had pink flowers with lines of white on each petal. The tourists and local people roamed the Square; some took family photos by the clock tower. Others were happily having chitchats with friends in nearby cafés and pubs. I could faintly hear some different languages spoken to their companions. Some were in German, French, and some others I couldn't tell or even guess.

"Why would he want to talk to me?" I settled my eyes back to my brother and took a deep breath. He did not miss the bitterness and anger in my tone, even though it was low. I crossed my arms just below my breasts, regarding Mihai carefully.

I believed he was thinking about how to put the words aloud while he drank the cola. And then, he answered, "He didn't tell me. But I think he wants to say sorry. I overheard him mentioning it to *Mami* while they talked in our living room, believing I was already asleep." He looked with great discomfort when he conveyed it to me. "It was a long time ago, though."

There was nothing to swallow, but I gulped and considered his theory. Was he right about it? But why just now, after all these years? He did not even try to talk to me. Well, I could remember he did visit me in our house one time after the divorce. But he watched me destroy my own paintings, in front of him due to my uncontrolled anger.

I did regret why I did it. It wasn't fair to myself. It took love, effort, and inspiration for me to create those paintings, but in the heat of the moment, I just did it.

Yes, I remembered now. He did try to talk to me, but I shouted at him, telling him to leave our house, since he didn't live there anymore.

I could just feel the heaviness of my heart when I recounted that scene in my head. Bile rose to my mouth that I had to drink my own cola to get rid of it.

"Y-your mum and dad talk about me often?"

"Not very often, but yeah," he answered truthfully. I could just see it in his eyes.

I swallowed one more mouthful of cola from my glass.

"Can you give him a chance to talk to you?"

"I don't know, Mihai," I quickly replied to him with a shake of my head.

"We'll stay some more days. We're going to explore Bran Castle, too. Can you come with us then?"

I scoffed. "No. Certainly not!"

"But, Zen…"

"No! I'm not going there with you and him, okay?"

"Then, bring along your boyfriend!" He groaned.

It made me still for a couple of seconds. "No." I shook my head again and continued to eat the Romanian apple pie. "And he's not my boyfriend!"

"Do you even know who he is?"

I stared at him and pointed the fork in his direction. "Don't you ever tell a soul!" I warned him.

"Ah, so you know him," he concluded and ate the rest of his dessert.

"Not really. We just met almost a couple weeks ago."

"What? He didn't tell you he's a billionaire?" He frowned.

"No, because I didn't ask, and I've just found out," I reasoned.

"He seems to be a nice guy and has a lot of money. Why don't you make him your boyfriend?"

I snorted at him. "What? Just because he has a lot of money, I'd want him to be my boyfriend. It doesn't work like that for me, okay? Besides, I'll be going back to Iași in a few days. My vacation's over, so you and I are not going to have another bonding time."

"Unless, you go to Bucharest or I go to Iași."

"Right." I smirked at him.

He nodded with a tight smile, staring at me with such gentleness in his eyes that it made my heart jolt. "I love you, Zen."

I blinked back the tears that threatened to fall.

"Just finish what you ordered, and we'll go."

"What? I still want to hang out with you!" he protested.

The 3 PM sun was still bright and hot, and I squinted my eyes. "I didn't say we go back to the hotel. I was going to say we can still check out the White and Black Tower. We have time before dinner."

"Are you going to treat me to dinner then?" He gave me a sly smile now.

I sniffled and shrugged. "I'd think about it 'til dinner time."

"You're going to treat me to dinner, aren't you?" he pressed on the subject.

"If I'd think about it, you were the one who wanted to hang out with me. Maybe you should be doing that instead of me. After all, you have more money than I do. I'm just a hotel receptionist."

"Yes, in a big hotel."

"Well, it's a four-star hotel but enough to make a decent living out of it," I concurred. "Wait, don't you hang out with your friends? You seem clingy to me," I teased him, trying to lighten up the atmosphere even more. I was just feeling so tired of feeling the hate inside me.

"My friends and you are different, and I can be clingy all I want. You're my sister," he retorted.

Well, what else could I do? He was unfortunately born like this.

Traumatic

Zenovia

I didn't have the heart to turn down my brother after all. I went to Bran Castle with him, Maksimillian, and my father, with an extra person. Marisha.

There was a long line of tourists at the ticket booth, near the gate. A few steps from there, a souvenir shop was set up. Shirts, mugs, bags, key holders, and other stuff with a vampire's face or simply "Bran Castle" with the picture of it printed on them.

A group of people, young and old, took photos with someone who was dressed as Dracula. The actor wore the signature cape of black colour on the outside and red on the inside. He had a makeup on and fake fangs as well. It was quite fun to watch.

After Maksimillian paid for our tickets, he took my hand. We started to get in line at the concrete slope area, where the tourists waited to get into the castle. Meanwhile, the vast courtyard in front just below us had been taken care of. Its well-cut green grass was a beautiful sight. There were at least two paths I could see that would take to a park, where there were a few benches that tourists could sit and enjoy having snacks, and the other led to the pond. The pond had water lilies floating. Their pink flowers were just amazing! The place simply looked perfect as if in a picture.

We explored the interior of the castle, where I felt goosebumps for some reason, somewhere in the living room. There was a bear fur splayed on the floor. Weapons and other stuff were also displayed on a wall. Some were in a display glass boxes. The old unlit chandeliers were hanging on the ceiling, and I could feel the old atmosphere, like I was brought in the past.

I noticed a narrow passage, which led downwards. It was off-limits, and I thought it was going to the dungeon.

Maksimillian and I exchanged glances. He looked ready to explore it, but I firmly shook my head. He just rolled his eyes that made me giggle.

Meanwhile, my father was busy looking at some other stuff with Mihai and Marisha. I just tried to ignore him.

We moved on to the interior courtyard where there was a well. And the wall some meters away from it had some bars and torture instruments. I could just imagine the number of people crying in agony in this area. It must have been so horrible at the time.

***

For some reason, we lost Marisha, my father, and Mihai. Maybe it took some time for them to check out some souvenirs in the shop near the courtyard. So, Maksimillian and I decided to walk towards the pond and took some pictures with us there. I could see him happy for being with me, and it moved my heart. Still, I didn't want to linger on this feeling.

I realised we explored the vicinity for about three hours, and it was quite an experience.

"Come on, let's go check where they are," I urged him.

"You can call Mihai on the phone and ask him where they are. You can also tell him that we'll wait for them here," he answered, pulling me back.

We were pulling each other while giggling when a crack sounded in the air, and I saw one of the leaves of floating water lilies had a hole, making my eyes grow bigger.

Maksimillian let out a Russian cuss and ducked, pulling me down with him. "Get down!"

Screaming and frantic running ensued. We searched where the gunshot came from in the midst of panicking people.

Oh, *Doamne fereşte!* Were we going to die here now?

I tried to think if I was ready to die with Maksimillian beside me. Maybe it wasn't so bad. But what if he died?

My mind was in a riot, and my breathing was fast and shallow. My heart ached just thinking about him dead right before me. No! I couldn't take it for sure. God forbid and knock on wood. I just couldn't find the wood right now though, as more gunshots sounded.

We were actually in the open, but maybe it was because of panicking people that the shooter couldn't take me or Maksimillian down. In fact, one was shot in the shoulder, as he passed by us, while we were crouched near a bench. It wasn't really safe there, but we had no choice at the moment rather than just stand there and let the bullets hit us.

And then, I realised that the one who was shot was not only a passing person but Maksimillian's bodyguard in civilian clothing. That meant casual wear, not in a three-piece suit. More of them came to cover us and retaliated.

I suppressed a scream when another bodyguard fell down, hit in the chest. Oh, God! I believed he was dead!

My body shook, hands and body grew cold, and heart seemed ready to burst in my rib cage as it pumped violently. Never had my life been threatened like this. It was terrifying! I was petrified.

Local police officers came to our rescue, shooting at Maksimillian's enemies. I just covered my ears and closed my eyes, afraid to see anything. But, at least, he was there to assure me I wasn't alone and that he'd protect me. I just noticed he had covered my body with his bigger one.

I heard the policemen hit the shooter in the shoulder, and they were after him. It seemed that he was working alone.

The chase went through the courtyard and past the gates, where the people stayed out of their way. A couple of bodyguards went to follow as well.

With a shaking hand, I dialled 112 for emergency, since it seemed that no one cared or knew what to do out of panic.

***

My father and Mihai hugged me, while Marisha ran her hand up and down Maksimillian's arm. She mumbled something in Russian, so I had no idea what she was saying. But I could just deduce it was about Maksimillian's life being threatened, and that they would do their best to find the culprit.

We went to the police station and gave our statements. I was trying hard not to be afraid anymore, although it was traumatic. I found myself breathing in and out slowly to calm my nerves, with Maksimillian holding my hand to assure me that everything was fine now.

His bodyguards needed to be hospitalised. At least, the one hit in the chest had an emergency surgery and would recuperate. I was so relieved he wasn't dead, as I had initially thought. It would be terrible for his family if he died then. I could just imagine how hard it would be for them. Thank God he was fine.

Antonia called when she saw what happened on the news. I hadn't expected it was released immediately. Well, social media was the first to cover it actually, because some people uploaded videos that showed what happened. But thankfully, my face was not on the news, as she said. But she knew we were in Bran Castle at the time.

Mămică also called, but she had no idea I was at Dracula's Castle when it happened. I just didn't want her to worry and demand that I cut my vacation short and be safe in Iași. I already rolled my eyes at this possibility. I wouldn't cut my vacation when it was almost finished anyway. Besides, it wouldn't happen anymore, would it?

Or it was just my wishful thinking...

Forgiveness?

Zenovia

"Why are you here?" I asked blandly when I saw my father, after opening the door to Maksimillian's suite. Obviously, he learned about the suite from Mihai. Well, if not from Marisha or Maksimillian himself.

Maksimillian was out to talk with his aunt in her suite, and it was already after dinner. He and I had just arrived from eating out at a Russian restaurant on *Strada Mureşenilor*. I did enjoy eating *pelmeni* (dumplings served with either vinegar or sour cream, and I chose the latter) and *khvorost* (brushwood crunchy cookies).

It was my last night in Braşov, and I'd go back to Iaşi the following morning, so that I could have enough rest and go to work the next day. I'd be back to my reality after this vacation. As for my and Maksimillian's deal, we hadn't talked about it yet. I had no idea how to make this work, since I now had a dilemma over this entire thing. It wasn't because of my life being threatened, but it was because of my growing feelings for Maksimillian. Fact: I was more afraid of my feelings than my life in peril. It was a twisted logic if I'd think about it.

"I know you're mad at me," my father began in a soft tone.

"I think that's an understatement," my cold retort. I turned my back on him.

"Zenovia!"

I stopped and slowly turned to face him, trying to not scream at him with all the hatred I felt inside and kept for so many years. My hands were in tight balls at my sides.

"You have no idea how much I hated you all this time," I began with a tight jaw. "You have no idea how *Mămică* suffered because of what you did… You just don't know she was in great pain because of you! Right." I laughed ruefully. "Of course, you didn't because you weren't there, but I was there to witness it! She cried every single night, and it went on for a long time. Even though she tried to hide it from me, I heard her every sob that she tried to suppress! And then, in the morning, she's smiling to show me she is fine. But her puffy eyes couldn't lie to me. She tried to be brave and strong in front of me. And you know what? I told her to stop crying over you, because you don't deserve her tears. Neither one of us did!" I shouted at him, not minding the open door and my voice reaching the hallway.

"Zenovia, I know what I've done was wrong." He looked at me with pleading eyes. "If only I could turn back—"

I raised an index finger, gritting my teeth as I said, "You can't! You can't turn back time and undo what you did. We were a family, but you threw us away. All of us here on Earth have only one chance at life. You blew it off right in our faces, and it hurt!" My voice croaked, and I sniffled, trying hard to blink away the tears that formed in my eyes. "The pain you inflicted us is still there. You don't even deserve to be called my dad. You don't also deserve Mihai's love and respect!" I derided, tears already spilling from my eyes.

"No, you're wrong! We have many chances in this world, not only one. If you just give me another chance, we can still be a family—you, me, and Mihai."

I scoffed at him. A family, the three of us? He was unbelievable.

Sniffling and wiping my tears angrily, I shook my head. "You think it's easy for me to just… forgive you now and be family again? It's not even the same! You ruined our lives!"

"Zenovia…" he paused, blinking his teary eyes. "You just don't know how hard it was for me to stay away from you. Remember when I went to our house after the divorce?"

"Don't," I warned him. Memories flowed in my mind. My tears just didn't know how to stop falling.

"I wanted to tell you how sorry I was, Zenovia. And I still am. But you didn't give me a chance then. I wanted to tell you that I'll never stop being your father even though your mum and I separated ways, but you were adamant about not having me around. You even destroyed all your paintings—the paintings that I loved so much! It was like you ended everything between us at that moment. And I thought…" He breathed hard. "I thought it was best to stay away as you wished, because I didn't want to hurt you more than I already have. And yet, I didn't know I even hurt you more by staying away then and for not being there for you all these years. I regret listening to your angry words at the time. I wished I knew what was the right thing to do for you to let me into your life, to stay there, and be there for you as a father should. I wasn't and am not a good father, but let me make it up to you now, Zenovia. *Te rog* (Please)!"

I uncontrollably bawled when I heard these words. More hot tears ran down my cheeks, my lips and chin quivering. My shoulders shook, and I could not breathe well, as if my chest was pressed by something invisible while my throat was constricted.

I swallowed hard and cried hard. That was when I felt my father's embrace. It was warm and gentle. His subtle woodsy and unique scent was too familiar that my heart beat strongly against my rib cage.

I did miss him. A lot. I missed his embrace and affectionate kisses. He was a sweet father and used to kiss my cheeks and forehead. He was also actually a hugger. Whenever I achieved something, I was kissed and hugged by him, telling me how proud he was of me. All of this just rushed into me again. After so many years that I shut off all those happy memories, they came back to me now. And my eyes were like a broken dam.

I didn't even notice Maksimillian right away when he stood by the doorway, watching us father and daughter, crying each other's eyes out.

The Next Step

Maksimillian

"What? What did you say?" Zenovia's jaw hung.

She was ready to leave that morning, and so was I.

After her and her father's dramatic and touching scene last night, they miraculously made up. I couldn't be happier for her. After years of bitterness, anger, and hatred she had held and kept inside, they were finally a father and a daughter again. A family once more.

"Maks!" She slowly wriggled out of her father's embrace, tears wetted her face.

I immediately sauntered towards her and dried her tears, while her father watched us, wiping his own tears.

"I... uh..." she began but couldn't make out the words. She then swallowed hard, and I nodded.

"I understand." I kissed her gently on the forehead. "It's great. It's great. I'm happy for you both."

"Thanks for giving us some time to talk, Maksimillian. I owe you this for lifetime," Daniel told me.

Zenovia's mouth opened in surprise, looking at him and at me. "You deliberately went out so we could talk?"

I simply nodded.

"I asked him, so don't get mad at him, Zenovia," her father defended me.

Zenovia just stared at me, speechless. I could just guess that she was still trying to absorb all this and that she was now actually on good terms with her dad.

Well, that was a great achievement for me. Not that it'd go to my head because I did a good thing for Zenovia. But I just needed this. I just wanted her to be less… *unhappy, because I knew how hard it must be for her, especially that she had a chronic condition.*

Daniel left after bidding us good night. And, of course, I couldn't resist the pull of my desire, so I kissed Zenovia that left her breathless.

And so naked and moaning afterwards.

"You heard me, Zenovia. I'm coming with you to Iaşi. You're still not pregnant, are you?" I pointed out.

She closed and opened her mouth, looking at me with utter bewilderment. "But you have to go back to Russia!"

"I will, in due time," my calm response.

"But—"

"Let's just be together," I persuaded her. When she winced, I immediately added, "For now. For now, okay?"

She let out a big sigh.

I still had no idea why she did not want to give us a chance. But maybe I should just take it slow with her. One little step at a time.

***

Zenovia

I couldn't believe we'd take his private jet to get to Iaşi faster. It was my first time to be in such a high-class air transportation, and it was my first time in Braşov-Ghimbav International Airport. Its terminal was made of concrete floor with metal braces, sturdy concrete pillars, metal beams, and glass walls all around, so it looked really modern.

I had heard that the Irish singer and songwriter Ronan Keating was the first one to use the runway in 2019. Too bad I wasn't there to see him. I was one of his fans since his Boyzone time up until now when he had his solo career.

"Can I get you a drink?" Maksimillian offered as he poured the expensive champagne in his glass, looking at me from across the big cozy seat he was in. It had cream-coloured upholstery, so it looked elegant and spotless.

I pulled my gaze from the oval window. I was entranced by the cottony clouds down below. We were already cruising by noon, and it was faster than commercial planes.

"You know I have zero tolerance in alcohol, Maks," I replied, eyeing the champagne.

"This is non-alcoholic, *moye solntse*. Besides, I have some other drinks to offer you other than this if you don't want champagne," his smooth rejoinder. He smiled at me and sipped at the amber liquid, eyes holding mine nonetheless.

I stared at him. His Adam's apple moved up and down, as he imbibed his drink. I didn't know what got into me, but I imagined his lips working on my femininity at the moment that I started to feel hot. I shifted in my seat, trying to not think about it.

"What does *moye solntse* mean, by the way?" I questioned slowly to distract myself. Otherwise, I'd jump on him, and maybe one of his bodyguards would walk in on us unexpectedly. It'd be a hell lot of embarrassment!

"My sunshine. That's what you are to me, Zenovia."

I furrowed my brows but smiled at him. "Why?"

"Why do you have to ask that? It's just how you are to me, bringing sunshine to my gloomy skies!"

I laughed at his being cheesy. I could not almost believe he was a bit poetic. And yes, trite. It never occurred to me when I approached him in The Black Church.

"Surely you have a more logical reason for calling me that."

"There's nothing logical when it comes to you, Zenovia. You have to know that you're the only woman I've ever dated. Surely, Aunt Marisha already spilled the beans, hadn't she?"

I chortled softly and nodded. "Yes, when we had this girl bonding, if you want to call it that. Apparently, she did it to talk about you. I don't know though if she was selling you or she wanted me to stay away from you."

He took a deep breath and let it out slowly. "Hmm." He put the empty glass down. "I can just guess what else she said."

"Well, she talked about your late parents and uncle. And I think, she misses them."

He slightly nodded and rubbed his lips with his fingers. "I do, too." He went on to tell me how much he learned from his late uncle, Rurik's father. He also talked about his cousin, who was always supportive and affectionate to him.

"You are very lucky to have them, even though you don't have your parents anymore. But are you sure your parents were killed? Maybe it was just plain accident, Maks."

He looked at me straight in the eye. "It wasn't, Zenovia. I'm telling you it wasn't." He said it almost with vehemence.

"You said it was a stormy winter's day," I reminded him.

He gritted his teeth. "There must be something that forced them to fly despite the weather. Or else, they wouldn't have flown."

I tried to analyse it. "What do you mean? Like they were blackmailed or something?"

He shook his head. "I don't know. That's what I want to know."

I moved my head from left to right. "You can be mistaken, Maks. Maybe they just didn't know there was a storm, and they were caught in it."

"You never knew my father, Zenovia. He was the most cautious person I knew."

Well, that was something. He could be right or maybe not. So far, nothing had turned up from the investigation, so Maksimillian could be wrong after all this time. And maybe what happened to his parents had no connection with those people who now wanted him dead.

Bringing Home A Man

Zenovia

Maksimillian started kissing me. His arms went around my waist while we were entering my apartment.

It was already around nine in the evening, after we had dinner out. After the flight, we went straight to my apartment to deposit our luggage. He wanted to stay with me instead of checking in to a hotel, where he could be more comfortable—in my opinion.

But there was no stopping him. He said it'd be better, and he preferred to be with me, since that was the essence of his stay in Iași. I just rolled my eyes then.

I moaned softly as I kissed him back. He nibbled my lower lip and...

"Zenovia!"

I tore my lips away from Maksimillian, eyes widening. "*Mămică!*" I was surprised to see my own mother in my apartment.

And she was not alone. *Căcat!*

I was totally betrayed by Antonia. She grinned and ogled Maksimillian, who was also caught off guard. We didn't expect there was someone else, or rather elses, in my apartment. There was absolutely no other soul when we left earlier this afternoon to watch a movie first before having dinner.

Heat readily crept up to my cheeks. I was absolutely caught red handed!

My mother's oval face lit up, with such a teasing look that I had never seen in her. I thought she lost weight but in a good way. I heard she did a healthy lifestyle routine, like jog everyday and eat a healthy diet. She probably lost a good amount of ten kilograms from her one hundred something. She also cut her hair shorter, up to her shoulders, which was always way past down her back.

I started to wonder when was the last time I saw her that it was truly noticeable the way she looked.

"Antonia here told me we should drop by to have dinner with you. We even prepared the food for you... two." My mother's eyes also settled on Maksimillian, who was actually blushing up to his ears.

I suppressed a giggle, thinking he was so adorable right now. It was the first time I saw him like this. But I just hid my lips and regarded my mother with round eyes.

"What? But it's so late already! Hadn't you even taken the hint and just... left instead of waiting for me, or us? What if I didn't come home?"

My mother and Antonia exchanged glances and beamed at each other. Okay, what I said was kind of suggestive, but it was too late now. The words came out of my mouth.

I barely took notice of my friend's sleeveless reddish brown sundress and high heels and my mother's plain jeans and blouse paired with black flat shoes.

"You see? She's got a man now, *Mămică*," Antonia teased, calling my mother playfully like her own.

"I'm Maksimillian Usmanov. Nice to meet you," he introduced himself. It made my mother and friend turn to look at him again. He stepped forward and extended a hand to shake their hands like a gentleman he was.

"That's my mum and Antonia," I said even though it was a no-brainer who was who, and he shook their hands each, smiling charmingly.

"We are so delighted to meet you at last!" Antonia spoke eagerly, shaking Maksimillian's hand.

"Antonia, can I talk to you for a bit?" But I almost dragged her to my room, leaving Maksimillian to face my mother alone. He was a big man, so I needed not have to worry. He could handle himself, could he not?

"Hey! You brought him home!" Antonia exclaimed excitedly when I closed the door and turned the LED lights on. These lights were round ones, and there were four of them on the white ceiling.

"It wasn't my plan, but…" I let it trail off, letting my eyes slip to the built-in mirror of my cabinet that was to my right. For some reason, I found myself like a stranger in a blue dress and white shoes that Maksimillian bought for me. "But hey! How did you know I was with him?" I squinted my eyes at my friend.

"I was going to surprise you when you told me you're coming back home! But then, I thought it'd be better to have a chat with your mum, the three of us. So, I kind of opened the curtain for you. She has your apartment key, so I knew there's no problem with it. And then, she started to explore your apartment and guess what? She saw an unfamiliar luggage, which she opened, thinking it was your present for us. And guess what again? She found out a guy's essentials instead!" She wore a huge smile while narrating it.

My mouth gaped open. "She what? She opened Maks' luggage?" My eyes almost bulged even.

She laughed, thinking it was hilarious. "Hey, she didn't mean it. She was just curious since it's your apartment."

I blew my face, averting my eyes. "Well… He's just staying for… a few days."

"Hmm."

"Really. He's going back to Russia!" I hissed.

She quirked an eyebrow. "And you'll just let him slip away?"

I didn't answer her. Instead, I just cleared my throat, noting that I needed to change the light yellow bedsheet of my bed that was pushed to the light green wall on one side. The floral curtains that were drawn at the window to my left would need the same fate. Crap! I had to clean up my apartment after being absent here for two weeks.

"Zen, I think he's head over heels in love with you!"

My eyebrows rose to my hairline, and I laughed. "Antonia, that's not possible. He likes me, yes. But love? We just know each other two weeks! Or less than that, since he went to Finland."

She rolled her eyes. "And you know you're into him, too. Otherwise, you won't be bringing home a man for goodness' sake!" she added.

I scowled upon hearing her words. "No, of course not! I'm not into him!" I denied strongly, heart beating fast and heat crawling on my face.

She looked at me intently. "Okay, if you say so. But I can clearly see that you just won't admit it. At least, you're not ready to face it, and I totally understand," she spoke gently with a gesture of her hands in the air. "It's your first time, and you want to end it before it becomes deeper. But, Zen, I think he's really perfect for you."

I shook my head. "No. No, Antonia. Definitely not this guy. We just... you know..." I shrugged.

"Make a baby?" she supplied in a whisper.

I took a deep breath and let it out heavily. "Just don't tell *Mămică* about my plan. You owe me!" I gave her a warning stare.

She grimaced. "What's wrong with bringing your mum here?"

I rolled my eyes. "I have to rescue Maksimillian. She must be grilling him by now."

She chortled. "Leave her be," she suggested, holding me by the arm. "You still owe me a little bit of details about your making up with your dad."

I didn't need to ask how she knew. She was friends with Mihai on social media, and my brother must have posted something about it already.

"Oh! T-that's because of... Maksimillian. He deliberately set me up with *Tati*, and we talked. I'm not going to tell you it was kind of... intense," I told her.

"Aww..." She gave me a praising look and hugged me. "I'm so proud of you. You finally forgave your dad! It must be so good to feel that you don't hate him anymore. But I do and did understand what you've been through. Believe me, Zen."

I nodded and smiled at her. "Yes… It's a good feeling that we're okay now, thanks to Maks."

"You see? He's a keeper!"

I just scrunched up my nose, making her eyes grow bigger in frustration.

A Break

Zenovia

The same time as I got my period, which was quite disappointing, Maksimillian received a call. He looked at me with pity. He eyed the heat bag he placed on my abdomen before he took the call. He held my hand while talking to Rurik. He was sitting on the edge of the bed, while I was lying on my back and wearing only a flimsy white nightshirt. He, on the other hand, wore a blue shirt and black jeans. Whatever he wore, God! He just looked effortlessly smashing!

"How is it? Feeling better?" He gently caressed my cheek and jaw with his knuckle.

"So-so," I answered, giving him a forced smile. I really hated it when it was the *time of the month*. Even though it was less painful after the surgery, I still had dysmenorrhea. It was awful! This whole thing was my own personal calvary. I really prayed hard it'd give me a nice breathing space in the future.

"Why don't you take a pill?" he suggested.

I shook my head. "I don't want to get addicted to it. Remember I already took some when we... you know... to be sure it'd be painless."

He sighed, bearing my burden, too. "I'm so sorry." He cupped my cheek, caressing my lips with his thumb.

I stared at him for a full minute before saying, "No, don't be. I'm the one who's sorry for binding you to me with that deal."

"Zenovia..." His tone was of protest. The slight scowl he had told me everything that he disagreed with me.

"It's the truth. I was really selfish for doing it, Maksimillian. Whether it was with you or someone else."

I noticed how the jaw muscles of his work when he ground his teeth. "Zenovia, I'm grateful it was me you chose to approach then. I can't imagine you with another guy, okay? So, don't tell me that again and again!"

"But I could've been with anyone, Maks," I countered. "That's the reality!"

"Alternate reality, but it's not!"

I just closed my eyes, didn't want to see the rage in his eyes. He was ticked off by this subject just as before. He was just too sensitive about it. Was it because he really cared?

"Why did Rurik call?" I changed the subject, opening my eyes at last to see his reaction.

Now, he looked away and sighed. "I need to be at the scheduled board meeting in Moscow."

"Then? What's the problem?"

"I can't leave you like this. I want to be here for you, to be with you."

My heart jumped at his being so thoughtful and caring. "I'm fine, so you can just go. What happens to me is not new to me. It's every month, if you want to know. Besides, I think you need to do a lot of catching up in your office. I don't think Rurik is handling everything for you. Not that he's not competent or whatever because I don't know. I believe he's great, 'cause he's your cousin. However, I think you have to do your share of the work, too. Right? I suppose it's time for you to go back to Russia. We both know you must do that, don't you?"

"Zenovia—"

I turned my face away. "Just leave, Maks."

"I can just have a video conference with them while I'm here, Zenovia," he insisted.

I turned my head to look at him again. "I can't get used to this, Maks. I can't let you start to care for me like this. Don't you understand? We just have a deal to make a baby! The agreement didn't bind you for you to take care of me! I can handle this. I was able to endure this in the past, so there's no reason why I can't do that now. Besides, you'll be useless around here while I have my period. I certainly wouldn't want to have sex with you!"

I knew it was sort of harsh, pushing him away like that, but I thought it was necessary, so that he could function the way he should before he met me. I did not want him to just leave his every responsibility to his cousin.

Well, what did I know about their arrangement? Nothing.

Still, I could not just be in the way of his work. As per Marisha, Maksimillian loved his job so much, and he cared about the company a lot. I guessed it was because he inherited the company from his beloved parents and uncle. So, when he went to Finland, that was when I understood very well.

***

Maksimillian

I did not want to go home. But here I was in the conference room, where the board meeting was being held. There were at least a dozen of board of directors (BOD), with me at the head of the light brown-coloured executive conference table. It was a large oval table made of wood with a set of metal legs. It was the same for the twenty seats, which had cushions for butt and back comfort.

I was half listening to what they were saying while I checked on Zenovia, emailing her.

"Hey. How are you?"

"I'll be fine, Maks. Stop worrying! Just concentrate there, will you?"

"How can I when you're in pain?"

"Well, it'll go away eventually. It'll be a lot better tomorrow, I assure you."

"And then what? I'm not there. You shooed me away. Just you wait and I'll come back for you, all right? We're not done making that baby!" I smirked.

Thinking about driving in and out of her body got me a boner right now.

I was in the middle of a board meeting for heaven's sake! But all I could do was to let my mind drift away towards Zenovia.

It was really against my will to go home, but she threatened me to not see me again if I remained stubborn. Well, she did know how to threaten me. My ass was back in Moscow within that day. Yesterday.

Now, I missed her terribly. I wanted to see her face, hear her voice, see how her eyes blink, how she breathes peacefully when asleep, and most especially the way she moans when I romp her hard.

I even played the recorded hot moans of hers before I went to bed last night. It did make me feel aroused, so I called her and had phone sex with her in spite of her period. Oh, how I wished I was there with her instead of being away from her over a thousand and hundreds of kilometers away from her.

Aunt Marisha, being part of this meeting, eyed me. "Maksimillian?" She brought me to where I should be.

"Huh?" I realized just then that they were all staring at me and at the cell phone that was in my hand.

Rurik, who was seated opposite me, slightly grinned. He looked at me with admonishing eyes the next moment, though.

"We're talking about the next real estate project to be planned by early next year," he informed me.

I smiled at him and nodded. "Why not?"

"Instead of late this year?" Rurik stressed.

Everyone was still looking at me.

I cleared my throat before speaking slowly, "Well, if we can't help it, then there's nothing we can do about it, is there?" My eyes went back to my gadget again, to see Zenovia's reply.

"Looking forward to it. ;-)"

My lips were torn into a huge smile that weirded the BOD.

Pregnant

Zenovia

Maksimillian was sweet and true to his word.

I was also thankful that nothing happened like the incident at Dracula's Castle for the past three months we had been together. It even slipped from my mind, since Maksimillian was so attentive to me. That meant he always pleasured me and was always considerate of my pain and discomfort, which he did his best to soothe.

Regardless of my firm protests that would always end up into fights, he still showered me with gifts. In addition to that, even the littlest thing that I *might* need, he did not want to miss and provided for me, especially the non-material things. For that, it made me fall for him deeper and deeper. And yet, I was afraid. Still afraid to make any commitment with him when I knew he was ready for it. Not that he said it plainly and straightforwardly in words but through his actions. Nevertheless, I acted blind to it. I did not want to have that kind of hope, which blossomed in my heart and in my soul, as he might disappoint me in the future. After all, I believed I did not belong in his world.

"I can see that Maksimillian is serious about you, so what's your drama, Zenovia?" my best friend questioned.

We were eating out one Saturday night, her treat. Thus, it was the reason why I ditched *Mămică*'s invitation to have dinner with her at her house. But I did tell my mum I would have it instead with her by Sunday night, which she was happy about. I just knew she would just want to have news, if not gossip, about Maksimillian and fish out some details about my *real* relationship with him.

He was in and out of the country to attend important meetings in Moscow now and then. While there, he would not forget to video call me, which was truly sweet, because I knew how busy he was.

I now regarded Antonia with a pout. "How can you not understand why I'm reluctant about… about this whole thing?"

"You have already reconciled with your dad, so what's wrong?"

I sighed and shook my head. "I-it's different… I… I'm just afraid, Antonia."

"Nothing will happen if are you going to let that fear lord over your life, Zen. Trust me. To be able to overcome your fear, you must face it. You already know this. How will you know what the end point is if you don't move forward? You're stuck, you know?"

Well, that got me thinking. At least, for a little while more. But I guessed, I was too stubborn and maybe a coward to even try.

***

"Stop calling me!" I admonished Maksimillian laughingly.

He was in Moscow to do his business thing, while I was back home. Time zone was no problem, since we had the same time in Iași.

"I just want to know if you already had dinner," he reasoned, smiling.

"What do you think? It's almost ten in the evening. I'm already in bed. What about you?" I raised an eyebrow, smile fading.

I could see that he was still wearing his navy blue three-piece suit. Meaning, he was still at work. I also got a glimpse of his masculine and clean office, which had light blue walls.

He sat back in his black swivel chair, leaning his head on its back. "I miss you!" he murmured instead of answering my question.

"It's just been a couple days since we last see each other in person, Maks."

"Hmm. For me, it's like a couple years."

I laughed at his cheesiness. "Seriously?"

He nodded with those puppy eyes, which made me chuckle.

"Tell me what you and Antonia talked about. Wait, let me guess."

My mouth was a little ajar, trying to supress a smile. "Fine. Then, guess."

"Me." He grinned, wiggling his eyebrows.

I could not hide my smile then, but I bit my lower lip and looked away. It was not only him, but there was also another important topic.

"Hey, I did guess right, didn't I?" he pressed on.

"Just have dinner if you haven't yet. Goodnight, Maks!" I dismissed him in spite of his protests.

I sighed when I turned off my phone. I lay down on my side and stared at the place where he would always lie down next to me. I touched the pillow that he always used.

'I miss you, too, Maks. You just don't know how much.'

I closed my eyes and let my tears roll down the side of my face.

***

The next morning, I stared at the white stick with two red lines. My eyes began to water.

It was positive!

My lips and chin quivered with excitement. I could not almost contain it. My eyes heated up.

I thought I must tell Antonia about this. She had been nagging me about it since last night when we were at dinner, telling me that I could now be carrying a child when I mentioned that I hadn't had my monthly cycle for the second month in a row.

"What? And you're just telling me this now?" There was surprise and disapproval reflected on her face. Of course, she should have known during the first month, as she was my doctor. "Get that test done right away, Zen! Call me at once when you're done, all right?"

So now, I dumped the test kit in the trash bin and went out of the bathroom in a hurry. I was sniffling as I dialled her phone. However, she would not pick up.

I checked the time and cursed. It was eight past eight in the morning. Maybe she turned off her phone or it was still in Do Not Disturb mode since last night. She would usually do that, as she was not a morning person.

I paced around my room, chewing my inner cheek. I could almost taste my own blood.

'Should I tell Maks first?'

A hand flew on my forehead, as I continued to pace around unconsciously.

'Yes, I should. He has the right to know. It's implied in the contract!' the other part of me pointed out.

More fear added up to my previous one. What if I did not want to be with Maksimillian? What if because of it, he would turn back on his word, snatch my baby, and bring it to Moscow? After all, he was filthy rich and powerful. He may not have trouble turning this situation around in spite of the contract we signed. Yes. Yes. What if he could find a loophole, and I would be left with nothing and no one? Especially my baby?

My other free hand instinctively held my still flat stomach. I thought I was going to be in a panic mode. I could not let anyone take my baby away from me. Not even Maks! I would protect it with my life no matter what.

Doamne fereşte!

What should I do now? I could not let it happen, if things would come to that.

Confirmation

Zenovia

"Oh, my God, Zenovia! You really are pregnant!" Antonia squealed happily and almost jumped. She squeezed me in her tight embrace. She was obviously thrilled for me.

Even on a Sunday, we were at her clinic, which had a lab. She drew a sample of my blood and called a health care personnel to measure my hCG (human chorionic gonadotropin). We waited for a few hours, and the result was out. She read it and gave me such an epic look.

My heart was beating so fast as I took in this very reality. My reality from now on.

I was eight weeks pregnant! I thanked God in my head and in my heart. Tears streamed down my face.

Antonia cupped my face as she looked at me. "You should tell Maks! I know he'd just fly here and sweep you off your feet, literally!" she suggested excitedly.

I snorted and laughed, pushing her hands away from my face. Then, I wiped my tears with the back of my hand.

"No! No."

She frowned instantly. "What? Why? Isn't it in your contract? It is done, Zen. You must tell him the truth. Or, do you want to keep him by your side that's why you won't tell him? I mean, you can still do that even though he learns about the news, because I know he cares about you so much! I just know he'll be more than willing to stay by your side."

I swallowed hard and sniffled, shaking my head. "I-I'm not ready."

She gave me a look that was filled with doubt and dissatisfaction. "Then, what about your family? Are you going to tell them about this?"

Her words made me still.

Right. I had my family to tell the news. But... would they be happy that I conceived out of wedlock?

***

"Hey, why do you seem edgy and worried?" *Mămică* asked me when we finished dinner. There was concern on her face as she gazed at me. We were still at the table, sitting across from each other. "Is something bothering you this much?"

I fidgeted on the rose-coloured table napkin. I weighed inside my head whether I should really tell her about my pregnancy or not, without telling Maksimillian first.

"*Mămică*, I..."

She reached for my hand and smiled at me encouragingly. "You can tell me anything, *dragă mea* (my darling)," she spoke gently.

I took a deep breath and let it go slowly. "I... I'm pregnant, *Mămică*." My eyes were intently on her face, gauging her reaction.

Her mouth opened and closed while her eyes went round. "Y-you're pregnant?" Then, she burst into tears with a laughing face. She got up from her seat, went around the table, and hugged me from behind, where I was seated. "Oh, *dragă mea*! I'm so happy for you!"

"Y-you're really happy that I am pregnant?" I squeaked, eyes wavering with tears. I turned to see her.

"Of course, I am, *dragă mea*!" She cupped my face with a teary, smiling face. There was an understanding and motherly love in her eyes. I could see it clearly.

"Oh, *Mămică*!" My fat tears continued to roll down my cheeks.

"I know what you've been through, Zenovia. Having a child is a gift! It's Maksimillian's, isn't it?"

I nodded to her and cried.

"Does he know?" she asked, wiping away my tears.

I shook my head. Hence, confusion was on her face.

"Why? Aren't you going to tell him?"

I told her about the contract and everything between me and Maksimillian, which made her gasp in disbelief. "Zenovia!" Her tone was enough a life-long scold. "You shouldn't have done that! How could you stoop so low and—and—"

"I'm so sorry, *Mămică*... but despite all that's happened or how it all started... I-I've fallen in love with Maks!"

Her eyes softened, and she touched my cheek gently. "Oh, *săraca mea fiică* (my poor daughter)! You can just tell Maksimillian the truth. Don't shy away from it."

"*Nu, Mămică, nu!*" I disagreed almost vehemently.

She looked at me with confusion. "Why not? Not to mention about your contract, he has the right to know, Zenovia. He's the father of your child!"

"I know! But what if he's going to take away my baby? I can't let him do that, *Mămică!*"

She took another seat that was beside mine. She rested an elbow on the rectangular table, which was made of glass and stood on steel legs.

"Remember I spoke with him when I first met him at your apartment? I knew the moment I set my eyes on him that he has feelings for you, Zenovia. I could tell he's serious about you. If he isn't, why is he still coming and going just to see and stay with you? If you think about it, he's a rich man, and he has everything. If he doesn't care about you, he's not going to see you again after what has transpired between you two, contract or not! You have no money to go after him if he breached the contract, do you?"

I sighed. My mother had a point.

"I'd rather that you be honest with him. Hear him out if he has something to tell you, Zenovia. I know that you have that fear in your heart," she added, lightly touching my chest. "But you have to let it go. Don't be afraid to face what's making you frightened. Fear is normal, *dragă mea*. But one way or another, whether you like it or not, time will come that you must face it. It's up to you whether you'll let yourself be crushed by it or not. It's entirely up to you. If you choose to be happy, there should be no more fear in your heart, in your life.

"Because me? I was past that. Take it from me. At first, I was afraid, lonely, and devastated when your father left me for another woman and child. I kept asking myself then, *Can I raise Zenovia all by myself without her father? Can I give her a good future now that Daniel is gone? Will I be enough a parent to her? Does she hate me too, as she hates her father, because I chose to divorce him? How can I make it up to her? Or how can I assure her that I will always be here for her even without her father? How can I tell her not to hate her father that much?*"

"Oh, *Mămică*!" I cried, also watching her tears race down her face. I didn't know this was all that was going on in her head these past years since the divorce.

"Zenovia, your father did fail as a husband and as a father, but it's fine. No one's perfect. Every failure is part of our life, so is every joy that we choose to have. Happiness is a choice, remember that. If you learn to let yourself go, then you'll be free of the sadness, of all the negativities. Just... give everything its own time. A chance. And maybe, you can also give Maksimillian a chance to show you whether or not he's true to you, if you still doubt him, which I don't. I trust the man, if you ask me." She looked at me knowingly.

'I wish I'd stop worrying and just really trust him, Mămică...'

His Arrival

Zenovia

I had just opened the door when someone rapped it one evening, and I gasped when I saw Maksimillian. He did not even had a luggage with him. Anyway, he still had his clothes and underwear in my closet, as well as his toothbrush and whatnots in my washroom.

He stepped inside unceremoniously and took me into his warm and tight embrace, kissing me full on the lips. He kicked the door close and locked it, without letting me go, and I put my arms around his neck.

"Hi." We both greeted each other simultaneously after the passionate kiss, with a smile, looking into each other's eyes. His scent and warmth was more than welcome to my senses, which made all the little fairies in my stomach flutter.

"I didn't know you're coming tonight," I added. It was a nice surprise, because he did not tell me he was coming back. However, I was afraid to tell him about the news of my pregnancy now that he was here, a week after I learned about it.

He grinned at me. "I know. Your gift is late, though. I planned to have it here before I arrived. I'm supposed to come here tomorrow afternoon, but I can't wait any longer. I'm forgiven though, aren't I?"

I laughed at him. "Hmm. A gift? Again?"

He nodded.

I shook my head. "I told you a million times I don't need gifts, Maks."

"And it's the only way I can show you you're so special to me, even without my presence."

I was speechless.

He shrugged and kissed me. "Besides, I'm still courting you, aren't I?"

I giggled at that. "Really? I thought we're past that."

His eyes twinkled. "You mean… we're a thing now?"

"Didn't you know we were, since we started this whole thing?" I returned coyly, batting my lashes as I lowered my eyes, trying to hide a naughty smile.

Doamne! He smelled so good that I wanted to sniff his naked skin. Before I even thought what to do next, my hands were already working to shed all his clothes off.

"Now I know. You've missed me that much, huh?" he mocked, pulling off my cottony night shirt. His eyes zeroed in on my naked breasts, as though it was the first time he saw them. His hot mouth rapidly captured one peak while he pushed my panties down.

I stepped out of them and threw my head back. He sucked my pebbled tip hard. A sexy groan escaped from my throat.

"Where's your lube, *moye solntse?*" he asked in a ragged whisper. "In the room?"

In spite of my wetness, as I was excited, he did not want to take it for granted. I barely nodded to him, and he carried me there. He laid me down on the bed, near the edge. Then, he took the lube from the nightstand and knelt in front of me. He stared at my flushed face when he entered his fingers with lube into me.

I moaned, and my hips bucked. I reached for his hair, grabbing a handful. He withdrew his fingers and anchored himself on the bed with one knee while holding my parted legs. He sank into me with a steady push, all the while looking down into my eyes.

He grunted and called out my name when he was buried deep into me. Without wasting his time, he moved in and out of my body, eyes still holding mine.

My hands were already fisting the sheets. It was so good to feel him inside me, again. It was marvelous to feel him drive in and out, massaging and caressing my feminine walls and filling me wholly.

"I've got something to tell you after this, Maks," I spoke, groaning as he hit the pleasurable spot.

"What is it, *moye solntse?*" he asked, smiling at me.

I smiled back and moaned again. "Ohh… *Doamne*! Yes!"

"I suppose it's really after this, huh?" He plunged in hard and deep, making me mewl again.

"Yes, later! Ahh! Maks!" I almost shrieked. He did not stop pumping me hard. It was so splendid that I could barely breathe and was ready to burst any second now.

He paused, which stopped me from exploding around his manhood. We were both gasping for air when he pulled away from my body to flip me, so I lay on my stomach. He then positioned on top of me, for a modified doggy style. His lips touched my shoulder while he gathered me with his one arm. He spread my legs apart, so that he was positioned between my thighs, and he entered from behind.

Simultaneous groans made their way out of our throats when our bodies became one again, and he was way deeper than usual. I closed my eyes, basking in this beautiful new experience with him. It was more intimate than ever.

He began to move in and out, asking me if it did not hurt me at all.

"Just make love to me, Maks!" I answered him.

I heard his low curse, and he kissed me hard when I turned my face for his kiss. I moved my lips against his while he sank deep into me, burying to the hilt. I could feel his balls against my inner thighs, pressing against them. The sound of our union filled the room; so did our heavy breaths, grunts, and moans.

He continued to slide in and out of my body, increasing the pressure and speed, with varying depths. I tried to meet his every thrust, moving underneath him.

"Ohh…" I moaned again. "*Te iubesc* (I love you), Maks!" It just came out of my mouth. Perhaps my hidden feelings were bared, as I missed him and loved him so much!

He paused for a moment, and I felt his smile on my skin when he kissed me. "I'll pretend I didn't hear it from you. I've always wanted to tell you first that I love you, Zenovia! Why did you have to beat me to it?" So, he did understand what I just said.

"Because you're a slow poke?" I laughed at him, and it was cut off with a groan when he moved his hips in circles to bury deeper into me.

"A slow poke, huh?" He thrust faster and deeper.

"Ohh... Maks, I just love you so much!" I expressed once more, moaning again and again.

"*Ya tozhe tyebya lyublyu, moye solntse* (I love you, too, my sunshine)!" he replied breathlessly. He rammed my body with his hot rod. It was perfect and heavenly.

I could not hold it any longer. I buried my face on the mattress and screamed my sweet release. My body spasmed in the aftermath, but Maksimillian continued to pound me until he, too, groaned when he climaxed. He ejected his load deep into me, making me feel warm and loved more than ever.

I smiled to myself, feeling blissful. I thought this was the greatest union we had, as we expressed our real feelings for each other.

But then, I froze when he asked, "What is it that you want to talk with me, *moye solntse?*"

Her Plan To Keep The Baby?

Maksimillian

My heart skipped a beat when I heard Zenovia confess her feelings for me in the middle of our lovemaking. Yes, I knew from the start that we did not only have sex. It was more than that. The moment I agreed to her to make that baby, it was more than merely a contract or an earthly desire to romp. If I'd think about it, I could say I've already fallen for her the moment we held eyes in The Black Church.

I kissed Zenovia's shoulder when I asked her what she wanted to tell me. It sounded serious, so I slowly lay us down sideways. I did not pull away from her body, letting our united bodies remain as one. I did not want to miss her warmth and her slickness that wrapped around me. I wanted to bask in it for as long as I could.

I pushed my hips to remain inside her when we lay sideways. One hand was on the V of her body, loving the feel of it. She was soft and all woman. My other arm was wrapped around her safely to be nestled well against my hard bulk.

"Maks... I'm so sorry I didn't tell you right away, but... I'm afraid," she began in a small voice.

I frowned upon hearing her words. There was an alarming ring to her tone.

"What is it? What are you afraid of, Zenovia?"

If it was her not being able to conceive, it did not matter to me. As long as she was not in pain or unhappy... And yet, the baby was her happiness. So, this also brought a cloud over my head.

"If you're telling me we're not pregnant, again, I assure you, it's okay. We can still try and try until we have that baby, all right?" I assured her gently, giving her small kisses on her neck and ear.

Bog! Ya tak lyublyu etu zhenshchinu! (God! I love this woman so much!)

She slowly moved, making my semi-flaccid cock slip out of her body. She turned to look at me in the eye. "Maks, we... we already did it."

I blinked fast, trying to process what she was telling me. "W-what?"

She smiled up at me, kissing me on the lips softly. "Thank you, Maks. We're pregnant!"

My heart leapt when I heard that specific word. I was totally stunned that my brain seemed to stop function for a moment or two before I could react.

"What? No reaction from you?" she teased me.

I cursed and held her closer and tighter to me. "I love you so much, Zenovia! It's all right to tell it to my face, not on the phone, because I really, really want to hold you in my arms just as I do now." I kissed the top of her head, forehead, and nose, until I stopped on her lips.

Zenovia giggled and kissed me back. *Chert poberi!* I really loved her taste. It was addictive. And I loved her news, to boot! I could not describe how happy this made me.

"How far are we?" I managed to ask her at last, as she did not fill me in on the details yet. "And are you fine? You feel good?"

She smiled up at me, looking me in the eye. "We're nine weeks, and yeah, so far... I'm good. Nothing to worry about. Just that... I do feel horny."

I laughed when I heard it. "That's good news, isn't it?"

She slapped my chest, cackling softly. Her beautiful grey eyes shone, as I examined them through the lampshade that was left on.

"Must I do it myself everytime you're not around?" She raised an eyebrow.

I gave her a deep kiss before answering, "I prefer you'd do it with me."

She grinned at that. "Well, I agree with you."

"So, let's live together, in Moscow, and marry there. You can leave your job here and be with me, can't you?"

She looked at me with a shocked face. "W-wait... Leave my job?"

"I can support you and the child, Zenovia, if that's what's worrying you," I quickly added. "You know this."

"Maks... Are you... Are you seriously asking me to marry you?" She blinked fast, looking at me with such intensity.

"Yes, I am! I want to be the father of our child. I want to be there for her or for him. I want to be there for you and never leave you alone!"

She swallowed hard, eyes dropping low, as she processed my words in her head. I wished I could read what was on her mind. Sometimes, it was good to know what she was thinking, and I could counter it if she so drifts away from me.

"Hey, look at me," I gently instructed her.

Zenovia raised her gaze to meet my eyes. However, I could see something in her eyes that was not good at all.

"Maks, I don't think I can marry you. Ever."

Something akin to shattering of glasses sounded in my ears. It was my heart breaking, and I immediately felt the pain. It was too much that I could not even describe how hurt I was. I could just stare at her for a full minute.

"W-what did you say?" I croaked. The heat in the back of my eyes bothered me.

"You heard me, Maks. Thank you for this baby, but I can't marry you."

"What do you mean you can't? You mean you won't!" My tone of voice was higher as I snapped at her. I supposed it was because of the hurt I felt inside. I was not disappointed, because I knew what we had agreed and what I signed in that damned contract! But still, I was hoping. I was hoping deep inside that she would change her view and that she would accept my feelings and have a relationship with me, eventually. "What about what you said earlier? We're a thing, right?"

She gave me a confused look. "Well... I..." she stuttered. "I just said, we're past the courting level. I thought you understood what I meant. We don't need it. We have agreed that we'll end the contract once I'm pregnant, haven't we? You did sign it, Maks."

I sat up on the bed, feeling hurt and angry. "I know what I signed up for, Zenovia! Don't tell me as if I'm stupid!"

"I know you aren't. I'm just rem—"

"I don't need a reminder, either!" I cut her off and snapped, eyes flashing at her. "Besides, why are we in this position now when just a little while ago, you told me you love me, and I said I feel the same about you, huh? What was that about? You just said it in the heat of the moment? Was it all because I rammed you so good that it just slipped from your sweet lying mouth?" I mocked.

Her palm suddenly connected with my face. I felt it stung, and the heat of it stayed for some moments. I ground my teeth as I looked at her.

Right. Maybe it was out of line. I deserved it.

"Get out! I don't want to see you again!" Her eyes flashed as she pointed to the door.

"Zenovia!" I raised my voice, but it cracked from intense emotion. I did not want to lose her or the baby. I knelt on the floor, facing her. "Please! I'm sorry I said that. Let's talk about this, okay?" I begged.

She turned her face. "Just go away, Maks. I don't want to speak with you or see you again. This is over. You hear me?"

I cursed and stood up. I crawled back on the bed to embrace her, but she pushed me away.

Now, I knew how it felt to be rejected. Was it my karma for pushing away all those women I had sex before? Was this what they felt when they wanted intimacy, not only sex, with me, but I cast them all away? I wondered for a moment.

"Just leave, Maks. I don't think I can do this anymore."

"Because you already have what you want, the baby," I spoke bitterly.

She put her hands on her face, covering it as she cried. My heart broke into a million more pieces, again. I had no idea if it was tears of joy or if she was also hurt for pushing me away. Why was she crying?

I inhaled deeply, realizing that the tears also slipped from my own eyes.

Maybe I should just give her some time. Maybe she was just being emotional right now, and I should understand her because she was carrying our baby. Perhaps that was the best to do for now. I should leave her, give her space and time, and then, we could talk again when her head is clear.

I turned around to leave her alone in her room. I gathered my clothes, put them back on, and tightened my jaw as I left her apartment.

Moldova

Zenovia

I was in my last week of pregnancy. I already had a doctor that would help me deliver the baby when the time comes. Living in Bender (Tighina), Moldova, for almost seven months was not easy, especially that I had to cope with my morning sickness all alone, without help, in my second trimester. But I did it, and now, it was another ordeal to come. The most crucial one.

My family nor my best friend neither had any clue where I was. It was so that none of them could tell Maksimillian where I was. I rarely even send them news or a picture of me, so that they would not have to worry if I was still alive or not. It was just to assure them that I was fine.

I was careful not to show any landmark, though. The pictures I was in were always inside an establishment or in the little house I rented. I had little savings that I withdrew in cash, so that I needed not use my card. Maksimillian might use his connections to find me using that one. I even ditched my phone and did not use one, so that I would not be tracked.

I was also back to painting and was happy about it. I sold the pieces for a cheap price just to get me by.

But why and how I ended up in Moldova after that night I confessed my feelings for Maksimillian during our lovemaking? It was because of something terrible that happened.

I recalled that Maksimillian phoned me the next morning, apologizing profusely for what he had done the previous night and telling me he shouldn't have left. He clearly regretted it, and my heart went out to him. I wanted to thank him for the expensive hamper and flowers that were delivered at my doorstep that morning, but I could not.

"Come on, moye solntse. *Let's talk, okay? I'll come to your apartment now,"* he said in a beseeching tone that I wanted to give in.

"No! Don't come over, all right?" I stopped him, trying to keep my voice and hands from shaking. My heart though wanted to get out of my rib cage any second now.

I had no clue who the man was, standing in front of me with his gun pointed to my head. I did not even know how he got into my apartment without me noticing it until he was already in. I should've screamed, but I suddenly froze. My brain was still processing why there was a man with a gun inside my apartment.

That was when Maksimillian called me. I reluctantly answered his call, since the big man with a covered face motioned for me to answer. But with it, a silent warning was relayed.

Why did he let me answer it? Maybe he knew I would not risk my life. Did he know I was pregnant? I hoped not. Or perhaps, he just thought it would be better for that someone to hear my voice, for now.

"But why not? Isn't it enough time that I left you all alone?" Maksimillian pursued. *"You have no idea how I'm feeling right now, Zenovia."*

'I know, Maks, but I'm sorry!'

After that, I hung up, and the man instructed me to drop my phone, which I did. Otherwise, he could have shot me, as I believed.

I began to cry, quivering from fear that I might die in that very moment with my unborn baby. I was so afraid that I wouldn't be able to see my baby's face. Or Maksimillian's before I'd die. I regretted why I shooed him away after making love with him. I knew my emotions were all over the place. I should've blamed my pregnancy for it, but I didn't want to. Maybe it was out of my fear that I couldn't handle Maksimillian loving me. The fear of his love that might fade away with time was still there, like a persistent evil that was still shadowing me.

"W-what do you want?" I asked the man in a stutter. He guided me to sit in the living room.

He gave me a white envelop. It was a letter. My shaking hands opened it, and my eyes blurred as I read the words that were printed crisply.

A loud knock on the door disturbed my thoughts. It also made my heart jump. Who could have rapped on my door at mid-afternoon?

Holding my big round belly, I stepped back, holding the back of the long sofa. My heart pumped fast and strong. My breathing began to hitch. I calculated if I could go around the back, as I glanced at the door with fright.

"Zenovia! Open this damn door! I know you're in there!"

My heart leapt when I heard that familiar voice. "M-Maks?" I whispered, clutching tighter on to the back of the old long sofa where I was now seated. "I-it's you, right? This is not a dream, is it?"

I screamed when someone kicked the door real hard. Out of fear, my vision darkened. I couldn't see who approached me after breaking the door.

"Oh, *Doamne*! Please... please save my ba..."

***

Maksimillian

I kicked the door open, and I cursed when Zenovia shrieked. Her unfocused eyes were on me, and she murmured, "Oh, *Doamne*! Please... please save my ba..."

Oh, God. What happened to her?

I could see she was wearing a floral maternity dress. Her big belly was round, clearly suggesting her pregnancy and was ready to give birth anytime soon. My heart swelled at the sight of her. I had been looking for her all over Romania, but I couldn't find her. Turned out, she was hiding in Moldova all this time, a place where none of her family and friend had even guessed or thought about.

I caught her before she fell sideways to the floor. My heart jumpstarted, afraid that she would get hurt if she had fallen. I roared for my bodyguard, Sacha, to get us to the nearest hospital while carrying her in my arms.

'Chert poberi! *Why did she faint?*'

As soon as we were in the car, with her head on my lap, my bodyguard drove like a maniac. Another car followed us. These days, I didn't go anywhere without more security, as I almost died before reaching Zenovia's apartment almost seven months ago. A bullet pierced through my shoulder, almost got me in the heart. I was just lucky.

The shooter was apprehended, but he killed himself while he was being questioned. So, the police could not get more out of him. He did not spill anything in the first place, which was truly frustrating.

I was in the hospital for many days. I tried to contact Zenovia, but I couldn't reach her. I had her searched everywhere. There was no indication that she left the country, unless she used a fake identity, which she probably did given the circumstances. I even talked to every member of her family, as well as Antonia. But none of them had any idea where she was. They just knew she was fine.

Now that I'd found her, I wouldn't let her go.

Right after my driver slash bodyguard stopped in front of the hospital, I almost jumped right out and carried Zenovia towards the interior of the edifice. I shouted for medical attention. I had no idea why my beloved fainted.

"*Ea este insarcinata* (She's pregnant)!" I said in Romanian, as if her state was not that obvious. Moldovans spoke the same language as Romanians, with some slight differences from what I'd learned. "*Va rog să ai grijă de ea* (Please take care of her)!" I beseeched the medical personnel.

One led me out of the ER to give them more space and to let them do whatever it was necessary. I paced outside the ER, peering at the glass door now and then.

My heart jumped again when I saw Zenovia move and try to get up. However, a nurse stopped her.

I rushed inside and shoved the people to get to her, and I embraced her carefully. "Oh, thank God you're safe, my love!" I cried with relief.

Why She Ran Away

Maksimillian

The doctor, speaking in English, thankfully, informed us it was shock and stress that was the reason why Zenovia fainted. He assured us that the babies were fine, though.

"The babies?" My eyes were round. "Y-you mean, we have twins?" I turned to Zenovia, who was still half lying on the bed while I was sitting on the side edge of it. No wonder her belly was so huge. I could see how my love must have suffered living all alone in this condition. My hands balled into fists.

"I-it's a boy and a girl, Maks," she told me with teary eyes.

I held her hand and took it to my lips before I caressed it. "I'm so proud and happy to have twins with you, *moye solntse*."

"We can keep her under observation for the night if you need to be sure of her condition or you can go and come back if something happens. She's due anytime soon, though," the doctor added.

My heart danced at the sound of it. Zenovia would finally deliver our babies soon! I was ecstatic and thrilled! I couldn't wait to see our children!

I looked at her again, grateful that I had found her finally, after such a long search. It was purely coincidental.

"I-I think I'm fine. I want to go home for now, doctor," Zenovia told him.

The doctor nodded and instructed her once she started to feel the contractions and her water break.

I carried her to the car regardless of her protests that she could walk.

"I'm heavier than before, Maks."

"Nonsense! Besides, I missed carrying you in my arms, *moye solntse*," I told her and deposited her carefully inside the rented car, in the backseat.

"How did you know I'm here?" she asked when the car moved towards her rented house, as she instructed my bodyguard.

I wanted to bring her to the hotel I booked, but I did not want to start a fight with her right now. So, I let her.

"It was pure chance," I replied. "As you know, the city once belonged to the Russian empire in the second half of 18th century to 1917, so some Russian journalist did a report on it. One of my people who's tasked to find you happened to see you in the picture at Freedom Square. It was not that clear, but I would recognize you even the tip of your hair, *moye solntse*." I touched her hair and ran the back of my knuckles on her soft cheek.

She blinked and looked away. "You shouldn't be here, Maks. If he knows you found me, and he learns that I'm pregnant—"

I frowned, losing her. "What do you mean? Who's *he*?"

She swallowed. "I shouldn't have said that... I shouldn't have," she mumbled, pressing her lips together. I could see the anxiety starting to set in like a thin blanket all over her.

I held her by the arm. "Zenovia, look at me!" I ordered her.

She hesitated for a moment or two, but she did turn her head and look at me. Her eyes were watery. I could see fear in them. But for what? Why?

"Who is *he*? Why aren't you supposed to see me and be with me?"

"I-I don't know, Maks. I don't know who he is! I-I was just told not to see you again. I-if I did, h-he would kill everyone that I care about... my mum, my dad, my brother, Antonia... you..." Her tears began to race downwards to her chin. Her lips trembled as she spoke. "Y-you have t-to go, Maks... before he'll know that you're here. I d-don't want him to know I-I'm about to deliver our children! I must keep them safe! You have to understand, Maks!" Her voice cracked. She then turned her face away from me, looking out of the window and behind us, afraid that someone might be following us.

I had no idea someone blackmailed her, that was why she was in hiding.

"I thought you just ran away to keep the baby all to yourself, Zenovia. I couldn't let it happen. I want to share our baby. Turns out, we have two. For that, all the more that I can't and I won't leave you alone. Do you understand?"

"But you agreed!" she pointed out.

"Well, I changed my mind."

"You can't just change your mind, Maks! Especially now. Just think about our safety, all right? And I don't want my family and you to die, so just leave me alone!"

I ground my teeth, trying to hold my temper. "As I've said, I will not, Zenovia. Whoever it is that blackmailed you, I'll find out who he is!"

I dialled a number on my phone to reach one of my people in Romania. He was instructed to send people to protect every family member of Zenovia's, including her best friend Antonia. If something happened to them, I'd have their heads next.

After I spoke with him, I turned to her. She was looking at me with wide eyes.

"W-what were you doing?" she queried.

"If I need to send a private army just to protect your family and best friend, I'll do it. So, trust me. I won't let anyone harm them, Zenovia."

"Maks!"

"I can't lose you again, *moye solntse*." I cupped her cheek and kissed away her tears. "You have no clue how I suffered when I couldn't find you! Now that you're here with me, I won't lose you again. No matter what you'll tell me, I'll stay by your side. I won't leave you again. Not now, not ever! Do you hear me?"

She cried hard, and I wrapped my arms around her trembling body.

"I promise, I will protect you, okay?" I whispered in her ear, coaxing and soothing her at the same time.

I caught my breath when she hugged me back. I sniffed her scent, which I missed so much! I buried my nose in her now longer hair and squeezed my eyes shut. Her soft floral scent filled my olfactory sense.

"I love you, *moye solntse*! Please, let me stay with you, will you?"

"Maks…"

"I can't live without you, Zenovia. All those months that I couldn't see you, hear your voice, or make love to you was driving me nuts! I couldn't function well without you. Most of the time, it was my cousin who ran and made decisions for the company. He's also getting crazy because of me." I chuckled.

"Does it mean he wants you to find me then?" She wriggled free from my embrace to look at my face. She held one cheek and caressed it, making me close my eyes to feel her touch.

"No, he told me to move on, but I couldn't," I answered her truthfully.

"So, how are we going to do this, Maks?"

Make It Work

Maksimillian

"I don't want to marry you, Maks," Zenovia added, giving me a pleading look. Pleading me to understand her.

I tapped my fingers on my thigh, trying to think how I'd convince her to let me stay with her and for us to live together. I certainly did not want to let go of her, with our children, to boot!

The car stopped, and I was grateful for the intermission to help me think. I ushered her back to her house that was now with a door.

"You kicked it earlier, didn't you?" she asked.

"I had no choice," was my reply. "I'm sorry. I will take care of the expenses."

"I think the owner saw what you did. She's just living across from me," she informed me.

Zenovia's rented house was not close to any neighbours, but the house that was right across the small street some couple hundred meters away. The rented house was like a cottage, which had a small terrace with hanging plants. The structure was made of concrete foundation and half of the walls in a horizontal line. The upper parts were made of wood, painted uniformly with golden brown. The gable roof was typically made of rust-coloured tiles, with a couple of small dormer windows.

In front of the rented house, there was a front garden. It was filled with June flowers of white, pink, red, and orange colours. At the back was a line of small trees, bushes, and other flowering plants.

I could say it was a nice, quiet place. It could be the reason why Zenovia chose such a place. I knew she hated crowded places.

We went inside her rented abode. The floor had wall-to-wall maroon carpet, which muffled our steps. My bodyguards stayed outside, while

I assisted my very pregnant Zenovia to the small kitchen, which was to the left side of the house.

"Should I give you anything?"

"No, we need to talk," she answered. She settled on a chair.

I took the seat in front of her, giving her a serious look. "All right. I have a solution to what we can do. How about we draw a contract?"

Her mouth was ajar, but she did not say anything. Instead, she just listened, letting me continue to speak.

"We can live together, and we can marry later. That is if you changed your mind, and if it's what you want," I added quickly.

"Maks…"

"Look, Zenovia, I just wish you'd try to have a solid relationship with me and live with me, even for just a while. If you find it like what you've experienced with your parents, then I promise to let go of you for good. I'll not even ask for our children's custody, if that's your wish. I'll leave you alone and never bother you for as long as I breathe. But please, just give us a chance. Let's try to build a family, where our children can grow up normally, with two parents. Because right now, and I just know it's forever, I don't want anything else but you and our children. I don't want to live without any of you."

She stared at me with glistening eyes, filled with unshed tears, which were ready to fall. "Maks! Are you sure this is what you want?"

I nodded to her. "Yes. Anything that makes you happy, Zenovia, I'll do it for you. I won't pressure you about marriage. That's what I can promise you, because I love you so much, *moye solntse*!"

She opened her arms, and I got up to embrace her. Her soft sobs made my heart want to reach out for her.

"I missed you so much, and I do love you, too, Maks!" she cried.

I bent to kiss her and was over the moon when she kissed me back. Oh, how I missed her sweet and soft lips! My gentle kiss became fiery as seconds ticked by. I could feel her hunger, too, when her kisses matched my passionate ones.

My hand went to cup her breast. It was bigger than I could remember. It was clearly due to her pregnancy, as her body prepared to be able to feed our babies. I was careful not to squeeze her boob. It might hurt her. I merely caressed it gently, feeling the tautness of its peak.

I thought I'd lost it when I heard her sweet and gentle throaty moan, begging me to do something more with her body. I could feel it with every fibre of my being.

She turned around to bend a little, leaning her hands on the edge of the table. I lifted her maternity dress and pushed her panties down. Next was my zipper, pants, and underwear. They were halfway my thighs, and I immediately aligned myself behind her. I rubbed the head of my throbbing cock on her already wet center. She moaned and was breathless, moving her hips to urge me to bury myself into her waiting love canal.

An oath left my mouth when I finally sank into her warm and wet depths. She was tight as ever, and it felt so damn good!

She called out my name numerous times, as I drove in and out of her slick body. My hands where on her waist, and I caressed her full belly now and then, loving her even more. Thinking that she carried our twins all this time made my heart swell with pride, love, and care.

Zenovia tried to meet my thrusts, which were gentle and not so deep. I was afraid she might be hurt or it would make her uncomfortable. Nonetheless, I heard her delicious moans that I missed to hear so much.

I did listen to the recording that I still had on my phone when I was without her. But still, it was way different in person. In fact, I missed her even more whenever I listened to it. It was driving me insane.

But now, she was here with me, and I was inside of her. I could not wish for anything more.

I increased my pace as her body suggested. I could read it by the way she moved in front of me. When she turned her face, I leaned closer to her and took her mouth for a sweet and deep kiss. The need to release was too much that I moved faster and deeper.

"Are you okay, *moye solntse*?" I whispered in her ear.

"*Da* (Yes)! Oh, *Doamne*, Maks!" Her moan became louder. And then, a prolonged groan from her told me she was cumming. I could feel her walls squeezing me tighter, more than ever, soaking my cock deliciously.

I was not far behind. Just as soon as she exploded around my hard shaft, I buried deep into her, as though I was trying to reach the deepest part of her and unloaded my hot milk. We were both breathless, but I bent my head again to give her a loving kiss.

"*Slava ne mogut apisat' mayu lyubof' k tebe, moye solntse*," I whispered on her lips, filled with emotion.

She smiled and whispered back, "Can you translate it for me?"

I rubbed my nose against hers and said, "Words can't describe my love for you, my sunshine."

She suddenly gasped just after I said it. Was she shocked. "Oh, *Doamne fereşte!* Maks?"

I felt something warm flooding my cock, and I knew it was neither her love juice nor urine. I cursed under my breath.

"I think *you* broke my water!" she told me, panicking.

The Birthing

Maksimillian

"*Chert poberi!*" I swore and was flustered, too.

I quickly stepped back from her and reached for the kitchen towel to at least wipe my cock before putting my underwear and pants on again. I scooped her up and ran out of the house. But then, bullets wheezed past us to my great shock!

I ducked with Zenovia in my arms, hearing the splintering of the glass windows behind us. Nonetheless, I did not stop running towards the bulletproofed car. She was screaming and groaning, as her contractions began.

Oleg and some of my bodyguards were already shooting back at the gunmen in a speeding car, covering us, and they chased it.

'Who the hell were they?'

"Are you okay?" I asked Zenovia, worried that she might be grazed by some bullets. I looked her over to be sure she was not bleeding anywhere. "To the hospital, Sacha!" I quickly instructed my bodyguard.

He was quick to drive us away. Another car followed us, which was another set of bodyguards. Unfortunately, it stopped as my men were taken down by another wave of enemies.

I cursed at myself. It looked like I led them to where Zenovia was. I wouldn't forgive myself if she'd get hurt because of me.

"Floor it, Sacha!" I commanded with urgency.

"Yes, sir!" He increased the speed of the car, going back to the hospital, which we left not long ago.

I looked back and saw that the enemy car was on fire, just like my bodyguards'. I cursed again. Losing my loyal men made me want to kill whoever it was behind this.

"Maks!" Zenovia took my attention, groaning in pain and breathing hard and fast.

"Yes, I'm here, *moye solntse*. We'll be at the hospital in no time, okay? We can make it. *You* can do this, all right?" I kissed her already sweaty face.

Thankfully, there were no more surprises on the road. It looked like Oleg had taken care of our enemies earlier. I'd get the report sooner or later. But it wasn't my priority right now. It was Zenovia and our babies.

She was immediately taken to the delivery room, when we told the ER people that her water broke. By me? Sure it wasn't! My twins just chose that certain bad time, didn't they?

Oh, *chert poberi!* How could they do this to their father who had just found their mother and reunited with her? Was it their way of welcoming me or did I piss them off for not being there for them for almost seven months?

I paced in front of the delivery room. Zenovia didn't want me inside. I did protest, but she just wouldn't let me in.

What was her problem? I knew other women would want their man to be by their side, holding his hand as they delivered their offspring. But no, not Zenovia. She was different.

I sat down on a bench, tapping my fingers on the surface of it or on my thighs. I had been waiting there for hours. It was already past midnight.

Chert poberi! I thought I was waiting for forever, and I could hear Zenovia's cries inside. I tried to peek, and I could see the medical personnel were all busy trying to help her deliver our twins safely.

Some minutes later, I heard the first cry of our first baby.

"It's a boy!" One of the personnel exclaimed in Romanian.

I saw one pass my son to another personnel to clean up his bloody body and wrap him with a soft baby blue cloth.

Zenovia groaned again while the nurses encouraged her to push one more time. She grunted and our little girl came out crying. I breathed in relief, as the excited personnel did their job well.

I couldn't wait anymore at the door. I rushed to Zenovia's side and kissed her sweaty face and forehead. She gave me a weak smile, still heaving from her great efforts in giving birth to our twins.

"I do think twins are more than enough. I only asked for one, but you gave me two, Maksimillian! Thank you!" she whispered tearfully.

I chuckled. It must have been just a coincidence she had two eggs to fertilize when we did it, but I did forget to mention to her that twins run in the family, on my mother's side. In fact, I had a twin brother, but he died when we were just five months old, due to the so-called crib death or sudden infant death syndrome (SIDS). I heard my parents were devastated by it, but Aunt Marisha helped them cope with it.

***

Zenovia

Maksimillian was an ideal father. Although I insisted that we stay at my rented house, he wouldn't want to hear any of it. We were brought to his hotel suite after getting out of the hospital. I only talked to the owner of the cottage on the phone, and I heard that Maksimillian had already paid her for the damages because of the shooting.

I was truly afraid I'd die at the time, and I was afraid for my unborn babies. But thank God it was all in the past now, and we were safe.

I watched Maksimillian put our babies to sleep. He wouldn't want to leave them all alone and just watched them sleep. He told me he was afraid our babies might suffer the same fate as his twin brother.

"No, it won't happen," I assured him. "Our babies are stronger than you think." I put my arms around him.

"We've been here for seven weeks now. Are you ready to go to Moscow? Your family and Antonia will wait for you there. I've already invited them to come."

"Can't we stay a week more at least?" I begged, putting my arms around him.

The truth was that, I still wanted to be with him, away from his home or from mine, even without the contract he mentioned initially just to make me live with him.

Just us and our babies.

I knew everyone would fuss over us and the babies once we are there. It would be chaotic, that was for sure. They were all excited about the twins, as none had predicted it at first, even Antonia. She had just wondered why my hCG was higher than normal, thinking she must have done some miscalculations on how many weeks I was. She was thrilled when I told her I'd be having twins, after I did my ultrasound examination at one of the OB-GYN clinics in Bender. I just sent her the picture, hiding the name of the doctor and the place where I had my ultrasound taken.

"Okay, if you say so." Maksimillian wrapped his arms around me while we stood in front of the the two cribs that were placed side by side. Our little girl was on the left, while our boy was on the right. They were sound asleep, with a lullaby playing low in the background. Maksimillian bought them a smart lullaby player with lighting options. He chose the starlight projection with light yellow and blue colours.

"I think we should get some sleep even though just a little bit. I'll breastfeed them again in a few hours, and that means little sleep," I told him.

He turned to look at me. "But you'll feed me first, right?" he teased.

Heat rushed to my cheeks, and I couldn't help but gently slap his hard chest. I suppressed a shriek when he scooped me into his arms and carried me to the bed. There, he took my nightie and his own pajamas off, leaving nothing on our bodies.

"Ah, *moye solntse*! I can't get enough of your beauty!" he uttered, staring at my bigger breasts. He dipped his head to imprison one sensitive bud into his hot mouth, making me moan in ecstasy.

"Ohh... Maks!" I moaned, feeling his other hand cup my center.

He spread my legs wider, caressing my femininity. I was getting aroused by it, but he did not forget to reach for the lube just to be sure. I mewled when he dipped his fingers into me, and my hips moved of their own accord in response to his touch.

Not long after, Maksimillian's hard staff already filled my whole being. Oh, *Doamne*! He was truly perfect for me. I felt so happy and whole whenever he was with me.

I moaned now and again when he drove in and out of my body. It was sensual and hot at the same time. I cupped his butt, urging him to go deeper and deeper, making us both mewl in so much pleasure.

"Maybe we can have another baby, *moye solntse*," he teased me, making me cackle.

Domovoy

Maksimillian

A day before Zenovia, the twins, and I had arrived in Moscow with our bodyguards through my private plane, Zenovia's brother, father, mother, and friend had already been waiting for us at my luxurious home.

The huge estate was in a T-shape. It had four stories, twelve bedrooms, fourteen bathrooms, four sitting rooms, an entertainment room, a pool room, a sauna, and an olympic-size indoor pool. It had a detached building for the security and household employees on the left side. The canine houses were near there, too. On the other hand, the garage for a dozen cars and vehicles was on the right side. Behind it was a lawn tennis court and a driving range, where I or some of my employees would use as a pastime or recreational area to practice golf.

The premises also boasted nature, with varying sizes of trees and well-manicured lawns and well-cared gardens. A fountain was in the middle of the lawn, which had a statue of Domovoy.

"What's that statue? It looks creepy," Zenovia whispered, asking me while our babies were each carried by her parents. We were at the huge porch, looking at the vast lawn. A table was in front of us, where we were seated at. Food and drinks were served by a couple of maids that afternoon.

I chuckled at her. "In Russian folklore, Domovoy is known as the household spirit of a given kin. It is a deified progenitor—the fountainhead ancestor of the kin. You see? Domovoy is depicted as an old grey-haired man in a cape, wearing a winter cap, and has flashing eyes. You should see the lights at night. His eyes are creepier," I answered her, still laughing.

"Why do you have that there in the middle of the fountain?" She could not seem to let go of it.

"That Domovoy is believed to protect our well-being. It's been there since my mother married my father."

"Oh."

Overall, the reunion was heartfelt, dramatic, and joyous, if I must say. Tears of delight were spilled, and I was touched that everyone loved our two little bundles of joy.

Aunt Marisha and Rurik were also there. They could not help but also admire my two offspring, who mainly got their looks from me. The twins got their eyes from Zenovia, as well as her beautiful mouth and hair.

I watched as Zenovia surveyed the estate with her eyes. The tall iron gate could not be seen from where we were. CCTVs were all over the place for protection. Armed security guards with their respective Caucasian Shepherd roamed the grounds now and then.

***

It was around midnight when I suddenly felt a jolt, heart pounding fast and hard. I thought I heard something like a thud, but it was all fine. Zenovia was sleeping peacefully beside me, wearing only her thin beige nightie. Nonetheless, I got up, and out of my new habit these past several perilous months, I took my gun with me. It was always hidden under my pillow.

I recalled Zenovia was stunned when she first saw me keeping the gun close by. When I explained to her why, she was horrified, especially when I showed her my scar from the bullet wound I suffered the day she went away to Moldova. From then on, she had not spoken anything about the gun in our room.

Right now, I just needed to check our two babies in the adjoining room. I left the door ajar to go there easily. Although there were bodyguards outside our babies' room, I was still overprotective of them, because I had no idea who was after me and Zenovia until now. My PIs were not able to trace who had hired those gunmen yet. I knew they were even embarrassed to give me reports that were negative. I must say that the person behind all these was very careful and smart. He kept his tracks clean and untraceable.

When I reached my babies' room, I froze. Someone in all black hovered over my son. With my heart pummeling my chest, I pointed my gun at the seemingly familiar person. She turned sideways to let me see her face in the dim-lit room.

"What are you doing here at this hour, Aunt Marisha?" I questioned her with a frown, putting my gunhand down to my side.

"I just want to see them, Maksimillian," she answered in a whisper, smiling up at me. "They remind me of you and your late brother when you were still babies."

I stepped towards her to check my babies, relieved that they were still fast asleep. I could see their small chest rising and falling as they breathed.

Turning my head to my aunt, I wondered why she was wearing an overall black suit, which was quite alarming, if I didn't know her. It was as if she was a criminal sneaking into someone's house at night.

"What are you wearing?" I questioned her, though it was not the first time I saw her in something like that. "Have you been practicing archery again, in that overall suit?"

Aunt Marisha chortled softly. "I can't help it."

"Just go and rest, Aunt Marisha."

"Can I stay here and watch the babies?" she asked.

I shook my head. "No. You have to go and rest," I repeated.

I held her by the shoulder and began to push her gently out of the room. However, she pushed my hand away. With one swift move, she already had my gun in her hand, sniggering at me maliciously. So were her eyes.

My heart bounced in my chest. "W-what are you doing, Aunt Marisha?" I demanded in an angry but low tone.

She snorted. "What do you think, Maksimillian?"

"I have no idea." I gritted my teeth, seeing her smile.

"Maks? Where are you?"

I heard Zenovia shuffle inside our bedroom. At the sound of it, she was clearly coming to the nursery room fast.

"Zenovia, stay there!" I warned her, but I saw her already entering the room.

Zenovia froze upon seeing Aunt Marisha pointing the gun at me. I moved to cover her, protecting her from my aunt, if ever the latter would squeeze the trigger. I couldn't let her shoot Zenovia, if she was indeed going to kill us.

"Don't you move, Maksimillian!" Aunt Marisha ordered me. Her eyes flashed.

"W-what is this, Marisha? Why are you doing this?" Zenovia asked in confusion. Her alert and alarmed eyes darted to our babies.

The One

Zenovia

'*Oh*, Doamne... *Mother Mary, all saints... Domovoy... Please protect us!*' I entreated in my mind upon seeing Marisha holding a gun—Maks' gun, as I recognized it immediately. I glanced at our babies, and I could tell they were still undisturbed despite our presence here.

Maksimillian moved between me and his aunt. I knew what he was doing. He was trying to cover me with his bulk against the gun, if his aunt chose to shoot me. My heart was already beating so hard and fast, and I was filled with fear. I could feel the cold slithering down my spine that my body started to shake.

"Don't you move too, Zenovia!" Marisha warned me when I tried to step towards the two cribs.

I must protect Oksana and Matvey from her! I couldn't let her harm any of my children.

"Zenovia, don't move!" Maksimillian ordered me as well.

Marisha got a clear angle of me that she pulled the trigger. I must say she was threatened by my movement. The next thing that I heard was a loud crack. Perhaps, if Maksimillian wasn't able to grab his aunt's hand, I would've been shot in the chest or in the head. But I could feel like I'd been punched so hard in the arm. It was like a shock. The pain registered in my brain next.

I held my bleeding arm while watching Maksimillian wrestle with his aunt until he got the gun back. He was leaning forward, with his aunt lying on the floor. However, another loud crack sounded. My jaw hung open.

"Maks!" I screamed.

But then, I saw him slowly move, with Marisha lying still on the floor. My eyes were round, almost not hearing the hurried steps and voices from the hallway. It was then that the babies started to cry.

The door to the nursery burst open. I saw a couple of guards were lying on the floor. They were the ones who were on duty. Marisha must have done something to them before she entered our babies' room without us knowing.

More guards came in, including Rurik. His agitated eyes directly went to his mother's lying, bloody figure on the carpeted marble floor. The wound in her stomach continued to bleed, and Maksimillian rushed to my side to check my wound. He immediately bound it with his shirt to stop the bleeding. Thankfully, it was just a graze. Still, it hurt so much.

"*Matushka* (Mother)!" Rurik exclaimed, kneeling at her mother's side. "What have you done?" he added, crying.

Meanwhile, I went to pacify my children, rubbing them by the chest to stop crying. It was to silently tell them that everything was okay. I was relieved that they stopped crying.

Marisha laughed without mirth, groaning as the wound pained her. "My son, Rurik…"

"Why did you do this, *Matushka*? I told you not to do this!" Rurik spoke again.

Maksimillian and I turned to look at him.

"You knew she was going to do this?" Maksimillian roared. He went to his cousin and held him by the collar.

One guard already called for emergency. They were ready if ever Rurik was going to do something to Maksimillian.

"Yes, b-but it isn't h-his fault, M-Maksimillian. I j-just want t-the best f-for Rurik," Marisha said through gasps.

I slowly approached them, even though it made me wince when I moved. *Căcat!* So, this was how it felt to be shot.

"I tried to stop her. I even tried to save Zenovia. I sent a man to make her stay away from you, so that *Matushka* wouldn't go after her, that's why I helped her get a new identity, and she could go to another country without being traced. *Matushka* wants to strip you of everything just as your father stripped her of everything, Maksimillian! She was sold to my father instead. She suffered a lot from my sadistic father just so you know."

"W-what?" Maksimillian looked taken aback. Obviously, he did not know this was happening to his very own aunt.

"I-I thought t-taking away o-one of his sons w-was enough. But no," Marisha spoke haltingly, looking at Maksimillian, who now dropped his hand to his side, while the gun was still gripped tightly by the other. "I-I wanted y-your father g-gone, too. U-unfortunately, y-your m-mother was w-with him."

"You caused their accident?" Maksimillian was enraged at that revelation.

Marisha laughed like crazy. Or was there an inside joke in her head?

"I p-put a fake b-bomb on board t-the helicopter. When it e-exploded with smoke and fire, t-the pilot p-panicked, which c-caused the crash." She coughed and groaned again.

I swallowed hard, glancing at Maksimillian's angry look that was directed to his aunt.

All this time, I knew that he respected and loved her. But knowing all this, I knew it was hard to accept it, and it must have pained him.

"M-Maks, I think she needs medical attention." I touched his arm.

"I-I don't t-think I'll m-make it, Z-Zenovia… but t-thank you f-for being n-nice to me, a-and I-I'm sorry… y-you're caught u-up in a-all this…" Marisha forced herself to say.

Maksimillian sniffled and yelled in frustration. I signalled his security guards to bring Marisha to the hospital. Rurik then turned to us.

"Thank you and I'm so sorry for what *Matushka* did to you both."

"You think sorry can make up for it, Rurik? Look what she's done to Zenovia! I almost lost her if I hadn't stopped your mother!" Maksimillian bellowed at his cousin.

Rurik stepped back, afraid of Maksimillian's wrath. "I-I can understand your outrage, cousin. My mother did a lot of bad things. She poisoned my father and caused your parents' accident, as well as your brother's and our grandparents' deaths. She… she hated them for letting your father sell her to the Frolov family, just so the two companies merge. True, she hates you, too, but I tried to make her see sense. She can't make me the sole heir to the company. It belongs to the both of us."

Maksimillian ground his teeth while he listened to his cousin speak. Nevertheless, I knew that he was hurt and far more dismayed and got betrayed by all that had happened tonight. They were his only family he's got left, but they betrayed him.

"I want you to give up all your stocks and leave the company first thing tomorrow, Rurik."

"Maks!" I uttered in surprise.

"But, cousin—"

"I don't think you're my cousin anymore, Rurik. After what you've done to me, to Zenovia? You betrayed me!"

Rurik's eyes were filled with tears as he stared at his cousin. My heart went out to him.

I knew Rurik only wanted to protect us, and he was torn by his loyalty and love for his mother and his cousin. But hiding the truth from Maksimillian, it was just not right. I could not blame Maksimillian for feeling like this and for deciding such a thing.

Rurik hung his head, sniffling. "I'm so sorry, Zenovia, Maksimillian. I'll try to do what's right." With that, he turned away and followed his mother to the hospital.

"What's going on here?" my parents asked. They were followed by Mihai and Antonia. They must have woken up by the ruckus.

"Is everything all right, Zen?" my brother asked. His eyes zeroed in on my bleeding arm. "You're hurt!"

All were horrified by the blood they saw on the floor, especially on me. Maksimillian had to explain what had happened, which shocked them all.

Antonia immediately checked the wound. "You're lucky this doesn't need a stitch."

A maid arrived with a first aid kit after being called by Maksimillian through the intercom.

Antonia fixed me up right away. The twins chose to cry at that moment once again. They must have sensed that life-threatening scene.

I had to breastfeed them, so Antonia and *Mămică* helped me. We then moved to the master bedroom.

"Are you sure you're okay?" *Mămică* asked while shushing Matvey, who was in her arms.

I was feeding Oksana first. She was fast to finish anyway, compared to her brother.

"I'm not sure yet. I still have to process all these, *Mămică*."

"Do you want to go back to Romania, Zen?" asked Antonia.

Days Of Wine And Roses

Zenovia

About five years later, after that fateful night in the nursery room of our twin babies, I was now walking on the aisle with my parents, who would give me away to Maksimillian. The aisle was matted with white and yellow rose petals that Oksana spread. She looked so cute in her white dress, holding the yellow basket that was filled with rose petals.

The entire Black Church was decorated with white and gold colours. Aside from the standing displays, the pews had accents and bows of the same theme colours.

The wedding march was played as I walked and looked at my brother and best friend standing on one side, at the front pew. Rurik was also there, on the opposite side. I was happy that he and Maksimillian had reconciled two years ago, after what late Marisha did to us. Because of what she had done, my partner in life did not even attend his aunt's burial, although I sent our condolences through flowers and a card, without Maksimillian's knowledge. I only told him later on, but I was surprised he did not make a fight over it, which was a good sign. I even told him Rurik appreciated it.

I was just glad it did not take a lifetime for Maksimillian to forgive his one and only cousin. Rurik was back at the company, after living outside Russia to heal. Upon his reinstatement to his old job, he assisted my husband-to-be with all the works, whereas I worked as a full-time painter and a mother to our twins.

Endometriosis was still part of my life and womanhood. But to me, the pain was manageable after I paired my medicines with acupuncture, which Antonia agreed that I should try. So, I did. Maksimillian empathized whenever I had my painful monthly cycle. He would stick by my side to help me soothe it, which I was always grateful. Sometimes, even my kids would stay with me when it was the time of the month. They would caress my abdomen or my back, depending on how I positioned myself on the bed. They imitated their father, and this would make up as our bonding time, too. It was kind of ironic, though.

Despite the pain, I was happy that my loved ones were there for me. And I was grateful to The One above for giving me such precious gifts in this lifetime. And today, on my wedding day, I felt truly fortunate to have them.

Only a few were invited to our solemn wedding in a Catholic church in Romania. I wanted to do it here, rather in Moscow. Thus, here we were on the twins' birthday. We specifically chose this special date, so that it could be merged together with our wedding day. And then, we could celebrate it in just a day. It symbolized a lot for me and Maksimillian.

He proposed to me last year, during our twins' fourth birthday. It was so sweet and a surprise, with all the balloons, cakes, flowers, and the most expensive diamond ring I had ever seen.

"What? It's a long way to go if we'll hold our wedding on the twins' birthday," Maksimillian protested after I agreed to marry him—and after telling him my preferred date. He was all sweaty and nervous, because he was afraid I might turn him down, knowing that I hate marriage.

He was very surprised, however, that I agreed without any protest. The truth was that, after living with him for four years, I secretly hoped he would bring up the marriage topic. And, it happened. I was like transported to the heavens when he proposed to me last year, together with Matvey and Oksana. Who could turn him down then? The man was quite good at that kind of strategic plan. But I didn't mind. As I had mentioned, I secretly prayed he would finally bring up the marriage topic once again, and as usual, Maksimillian had never disappointed me. It was like he was waiting for the right time, and he read my mind.

And my heart.

My attention was now on my waiting groom at the altar, beside the priest who was holding a Bible and a microphone. On the far side was the choir we hired, as well as the photographer and videographer to capture every moment of our special day.

Maksimillian's short hair perfectly matched his three-day stubble, as usual. He certainly looked gorgeous, wearing a white three-piece suit that matched my snow-white wedding garment. It was a stunning fit and flare, simple crepe gown with sequined embroidered lace paired with a semblance plunge to adorn the bodice. Meanwhile, the back constituted a breathtaking cathedral length spectered train with an open back and thin straps.

My hair was kept in a simple but elegant updo, with curls at the side of my face. There were glittering hairpins of diamonds to keep my hair up. A pair of dangling earrings, a diamond-and-white gold choker, and a bracelet adorned me as well. These were all my husband-to-be's gifts for our wedding day. Plus, he had no idea he had a separate one aside from these. The most precious one, in fact.

He.

Maksimillian held my hand when I reached him at the altar. My parents murmured things to him, kissed us on both cheeks, and left for the ceremony to begin.

During the ceremony, Maks and I kept looking at each other, listening to the priest. Our kids would sometimes come to us, and Mihai and Antonia would always take them away to not disturb the priest. Maksimillian, the guests, and I would laugh whenever this happens.

We had our photos taken after the ceremony, after the priest blessed our marriage. We were ecstatic that we were finally one in a holy bondage. I hoped this would never break for as long as we breathed.

I knew it would remain to be seen. Nonetheless, I would just place my trust on Maksimillian and on his love for me.

***

We were on our private jet, going to Maldives for our honeymoon.

With our kids.

We could not just leave them behind, even though my brother wanted to look out for them. He was so sweet to offer it, but Maksimillian and I thought it would not be fun without our kids. So, he just tagged along with us anyway, just in case we needed help, especially on our sexy time. We had to be sure that the twins were safe by the time then. The twins loved their uncle very dearly, so it was truly a good thing to be together on this honeymoon.

Now, Maksimillian, on his back, with me on top of him, grunted upon climaxing. Our eyes held each other, while our breaths came in gasps. I leaned forward to kiss him.

"*Te iubesc atât de mult* (I love you so much), Maks!" I whispered to him.

"*I ya tebya tozhe lyublyu, moye solntse* (And I love you, too, my sunshine)!" he whispered back, with a loving smile on his lips. He tenderly kissed me again and cuddled me. "I'm so lucky to have you, Zenovia. My life is now complete."

I smiled at him sweetly upon hearing it, heart swelling with happiness and love.

"You took the words right out of my mouth, Maks, my love."

"I'm glad I did, because you always make the first move and say the words, instead of me."

I giggled, remembering our first meeting and how I told him the first time that I loved him. "If I hadn't talked to you at The Black Church, would you have done it instead?" I wondered aloud, brows raised.

He grinned at me charmingly. "Of course, I would have, and we'll still end up here and now."

I chuckled at that. "Really? You're that sure and confident, huh?"

He caressed my cheek with his knuckle tenderly, looking deep into my eyes. "I just knew the moment our eyes held in The Black Church that you'd give eternal sunshine to my bleak life, Zenovia, *luybov' moya, dushen'ka* (my love, my soul)…"

The end

About the Author

Darla Tverdohleb officially joined the writing industry in 2011. Her first ever accepted manuscript was published in the same year. Then, a couple years ago, she started writing on different online platforms and passively earning from them. Recently, however, she's studying IT/Programming and is writing whenever she has the time to. She tries to squeeze it in, as writing is in her soul.

www.ingramcontent.com/pod-product-compliance
Lightning Source LLC
LaVergne TN
LVHW041917070526
838199LV00051BA/2647